The Wind Will Catch You

Also available by Michelle Theall

Teaching the Cat to Sit: A Memoir

The Wind Will Catch You

♦ *A NOVEL* ♦

MICHELLE THEALL

alcove press

This is a work of fiction. All of the names, characters, organizations, places, and events portrayed in this novel are either products of the author's imagination or are used fictitiously. Any resemblance to real or actual events, locales, or persons, living or dead, is entirely coincidental.

Published in the United States by Alcove Press, an imprint of The Quick Brown Fox & Company LLC.

Alcove Press and its logo are trademarks of The Quick Brown Fox & Company LLC.

Library of Congress Catalog-in-Publication data available upon request.

ISBN (paperback): 978-1-63910-465-9
ISBN (ebook): 978-1-63910-466-6

Cover design by Sarah Brody

Printed in the United States.

www.alcovepress.com

Alcove Press
34 West 27th St., 10th Floor
New York, NY 10001

First Edition: September 2023

10 9 8 7 6 5 4 3 2 1

For Dad

"We owe our children, the most vulnerable citizens in our society, a life free of violence and fear."

—Nelson Mandela

♦ 1 ♦

2019

Austin, Texas

I SKID TO A stop in front of the door to Voodoo Doughnuts and check my hair and clothes twice, before deciding there's no use trying to put this shitshow back together. Laura, my caseworker, will see right through me. I glance at my iPhone. I'll make this quick, give her ten minutes—tops. I throw open the door.

Laura's face beams when she sees me, and even though I'm a soggy mess from the rain, she hugs me full force—enveloping my slight and bony frame into her tall, athletic one. At twenty-three, she's a few years old than me, and only a couple years into her job with social services. We've met twice before, and as far as caseworkers go, she's the most likable one I've had. Laura keeps her hair cropped short and bleached and wears a skort with a tank top, her muscular arms and shoulders lean with sinew. She's pretty, even though she doesn't try to be, confident and positive, tough in a way I'd like to be, but capable of being soft enough when it matters.

After we hug, she adjusts her canvas messenger bag, which overflows with paperwork, pamphlets, and an inordinate number of tissues, as if she's ready for all her clients to burst into tears. But no one cries at Voodoo Doughnuts. Whether it's the smell of icing, the bright yellow windows, or being embraced by another human being who is warm and smiling, I feel less sleepy and anxious than I have for the last twenty-four hours. I order two donuts, intending to eat one quickly and keep the other one for later: the Oh, Captain, My Captain, which is topped with vanilla icing and Captain Crunch cereal, and an Old Dirty Bastard, laced with chocolate frosting, Oreo cookies, and peanut butter. Laura turns to me at the counter and confesses, "I love the names they have, even though sometimes I get embarrassed ordering them." She scans the pastries in the glass case and turns to the cashier. "One Voodoo Doll, please."

The employee hands her a donut that's shaped like a person with a pretzel stick poking out of its heart. Crimson icing pours from the wound. Chocolate sprinkles form Xs over the eyes. "Poor fella never had a chance," she says, removing the pretzel and eating it quickly. "There. Curse removed."

I get the feeling she purchased the stricken donut because she felt sorry for it.

After she pays, we sit down at one of the multicolored tables. "So, Biscuit, how you holding up?" Laura asks. I suspect she uses nicknames to put her clients at ease, to make them trust her. It works too, in that easy southern way that disarms people. I wonder what it would be like if we were just two normal girls, dishing about classes and crushes over lattes. But I remember what's real: she gets paid to meet with me.

"Long night," I say, then realize what she's really asking. "Oh, right, midterm exams. Yes, good. Totally ready."

"Looks like you're limping. You hurt yourself?"

"Oh, that," I say. "I was at a party, totally hammered, and I fell off—"

Laura puts her hands over her ears. "La la la. Can't hear you. I'm begging you. Please do not tell me any details. You're twenty—underage. I'd have to include it in my report."

"But you wouldn't, right?"

"Just don't put me in that position." She looks serious.

"Hey, if it makes you feel any better, I'm just doing what every kid my age is right now. Hanging out with friends. Going to parties." I like the way it sounds. Normal.

"Yeah, I'm not sure about that. I mean, I never did," she says. "I worry about you." She shakes her head. "Well, you didn't have to meet with me today. You could've made an excuse." She takes a big bite of her donut, wipes the frosting off her cheek with the back of her hand, and leans back in her chair.

"Sure, because ditching meetings with social services at the last minute would somehow work in my favor."

She ignores my sarcasm. "If you hurt your ankle, you have a good excuse."

"Whatever. The last time I did that *your predecessor*, my old caseworker, panicked and sent police to my room for a wellness check. When I opened the door, I found three sweaty men staring at me. You should've seen their faces crumple. It was like they were disappointed to find me alive and drinking coffee in my pajamas."

"'Course they were surprised. At Manor House, they're used to finding piles of newspapers and feral cats nibbling on human remains," Laura says.

"Nice," I say. I take three quick swallows of coffee, burning my tongue. I remind her, "Y'all are the ones who put me there." I shove the donut into my mouth and check my watch. "So, you mentioned some forms I'm supposed to fill out?" My iPhone vibrates on the table in front of me. "Mind if I get this? Whoever it is won't stop calling." She nods. "Hello, yes?" I say.

There's a long pause, and just when I'm certain that an automated voice will fill the other end telling me the warranty on a car I don't own is about to expire—a woman says, "I'm looking for Sky Rayner." No one has called me by that last name in years. "Ms. Rayner?"

"My last name is Fielder now." My finger hovers over the red "end" button, but I can't seem to touch it. The sound of my old name is a shock of cold water. Laura's eyebrows arch as she listens to my end of the conversation.

The woman continues, sounding slightly panicked. "Wait—please. My name is Dr. Kaya Nez. I'm calling from Banner University Medical Center in Tucson."

"Tucson? I don't know anyone in Arizona." I try to sound polite, instead of confused. I heard her clearly. She called me Sky Rayner—still . . . "I'm sure you didn't mean to reach me," I say. "And I don't have any money to donate."

"Sky Rayner from Eden Park, Texas. You have a brother named Ben."

It's the first time I've heard Ben's name in years. All I can think of is dirt, miles of it, and stained clothes, but then I see wild hair and tan skin. I smell sage. I'm as afraid to end the call as I am to continue it.

"Ms. Rayner? I mean Fielder." Papers rustle. "Sky?"

I picture the road we lived on, Ben leaping from a tree into the arroyo, our hikes into Skeleton Canyon. It takes me a minute to find my voice again. When I do, it's small with sadness. "Where did you get my number?"

"The police helped me track you down. I need you to make some medical decisions for him—for Ben—your brother."

"That's impossible." I force myself to speak, the bitter coffee at the back of my throat. "My brother died when I was eight." My mind flashes to the rusted truck with its crumpled hood. My stuffed bunny on the floorboard. Blinding rain. Ben slumped over the wheel. "Who is this again?"

"If you'll just let me explain—you're the only family member I've been able to find."

Her words ring in my ears, become hollow and fade. Before I hang up, I whisper into the receiver, my voice trailing and uncertain—a question and an answer: "I don't have a family."

⋆ ⋆ ⋆

I place my phone on the table like it's a loaded gun. Laura stares at me, and I stare at my phone.

"You look as white as America's one percenters," she says. "What's going on?"

"So, that was . . . I don't know what that was," I stammer.

College students move around us as the line forming at Voodoo circles the block. There are backslaps and hugs. A video is passed around of someone crowd-surfing at Maggie Maes. A group takes a selfie in front of the donut selection. I think for a moment about jumping up to join them. I wait it out. The hum becomes white noise. I debate whether to tell Laura the details of the call. I don't know how much information she already has about me tucked away in her files, but I'm not about to volunteer more.

"Nothing," I say.

There's a flash of hurt behind her eyes. "Okay, well." And suddenly we're back to business. "Focus on exams. It's twenty-one and done on the tuition waiver. You can't afford to fail."

I don't tell her that my grades this semester are sliding faster than a Texan driving on ice. She stands to leave, and I realize I don't want her to—that I've made a mistake. "Hey, would you mind giving me a ride back?" I point to my hurt ankle, knowing she won't say no.

⋆ ⋆ ⋆

The entire way home, I think about the call and Ben. Laura hums to the radio, an old track of the Black Pumas. I try to concentrate on the music, but I can't do it. My stomach twists. My head throbs. I fear organ failure if I stay silent one minute longer.

"So, that was super random," I say, louder than intended. "This *doctor*"—I add air quotes—"in Arizona said my brother Ben is in her hospital."

Laura looks at me and back at the road again. "But you said your brother was dead."

"He is. It's a scam."

"Definitely."

We wait at a red light. I scrutinize the faces passing by at the intersection. A man on a skateboard. A businessman in a tailored suit. Could I have passed my brother on the street over the last twelve years and not even known it? No. Impossible. I chew on my lower lip. "The thing is, now, I can't really think of anything else. I mean, she didn't ask for money or my social security number or anything. So what's her angle?"

"You remember her name? Google her."

I use my phone and type in Doctor Nez and Tucson. A woman, mid-sixties, with kind eyes and a stethoscope around her neck appears, along with a bio. "She's real."

"Well, *she* is, but that doesn't mean the person on the other end was her. Call that number back and see who answers."

I dial the phone number attached to the "unknown" caller ID, and I put the speaker on so Laura can hear. An automated message answers: "You have reached Banner University Medical Center. If this is an emergency, please hang up the phone and dial 911." I hit the end button. We stare at each other. Goose bumps rise along my arms. Laura parks in front of Manor House.

"When's your class?"

"I've got an hour."

"Hmmm." Laura runs her hand across the top of her hair. "No, you need to study."

"It's a review day. No exams. Plus, it's a blow-off class." There are no blow-off classes.

Her fingers drum atop the wheel. "Start from the beginning then. Maybe I can fill in some gaps, make sense of this. How did you guys end up in care?"

"You've got my file."

"Biscuit, I work for the government. I have the *last* file, the one started in this county after you turned eighteen, with very little information before that. Reconstituted facts, you know, thrown up and digested again and again. Like we're baby birds. That's it. You think records get passed along? Hell, half of them aren't even accurate."

"Right," I say. "Well, you've already figured out I'm a human disaster, so what does it matter?" I stare at a small tear in the fabric of my shirt and touch my tongue to the roof of my mouth, which is dry as Texas cotton from a hangover. I unravel my memories, a tangled ball of yarn for her to sort through—starting with the truth. "I was the reason that Ben and I were separated. It was all my fault."

♦ 2 ♦

2007

Sky

I WAITED FOR THE bus next to Ben, both of us shivering, and the hunger rats—as Ben called them—gnawing at my empty stomach. Ben blocked the wind, using his flannel-lined hoodie like a shield around us. I leaned against him. "Take extra," he reminded me. "Don't get into trouble or draw any attention to yourself. Just be a normal kid."

The bus pulled around the corner and much as I didn't want to, I slid away from the warmth of my brother and up the steps. Once I was seated, my brother jutted his chin into the air, before nodding. *Keep your head up, don't let the idiots get to you.* He sagged as the bus pulled away—worry etched his forehead.

I adjusted my jacket, a pink puffy donation from the Salvation Army, which had holes along the sleeves. The girl next to me, a second grader from my class, held her nose. "You make my eyes water," she said. The boy behind us leaned up and over the seat back and pulled at the collar of my jacket. "That's my sister's old coat! Mom threw that out last year! Her name's right here in ink." I ignored him. I dipped my chin to my chest and tried to make myself small. I hated school. Hated my ratty clothes. I tucked my hair behind my ears, the way the other girls wore theirs, but my fingers caught in a tangle, and I stifled a yelp. The day only got worse from there.

At lunch, I stood in line and caught snippets of conversation from the girls behind me, who talked about some movie they were going to see over the weekend. I wanted them to ask me to go with them—even if I had to say no. Listening to them felt like being held under water. I took my time picking out my food, desperate to stay near them a little longer—to make them consider me.

When I got to the granola bars and packets of jelly and honey, I hesitated. Ben had told me to take extras. The girl behind me snapped her fingers. "Hurry up. God, she's slow," she said. And another, "Sheesh. Leave some for the rest of us." A trail of laughter chased me as I pulled back my empty hand and hurried toward the cashier, who stamped my lunch voucher while the girls sneered.

I picked a table and sat a few seats away from the other kids. I ate in silence. When the bell rang, I waited until the cafeteria had all but emptied out and made quick work of any of the trays that hadn't been bused, stuffing half-eaten Rice Krispies treats, apples, and juice boxes into my pockets and school backpack. When I finished, I hurried into the hall, where Miss Dunbar, the school counselor, stood waiting. Her brows arched with concern, maybe pity too. "I'm late for class," I said trying to inch by her.

She placed a hand atop my head and lifted my backpack off my shoulder. "I'll write you a pass," she said. "You're not in trouble, but I do need to talk to you for a minute, okay?" She ushered me toward her office, motioned for me to sit. I did as I was told, swinging my legs back and forth beneath the plastic chair. I picked at a snag in the leggings I wore. She cleared her throat, a motor starting.

"Honey, I've tried to reach your parents a few times, but the number on file isn't working. Hasn't been for a while, apparently."

I stared at the floor.

"Your teachers and I are worried about you—that maybe you're not getting enough food at home, that you might not be safe out there. You live next to the Ramseys' farm, right?"

My heart pounded like a rabbit caught in a trapline. "We're fine. I'm not hungry. I took that food because it was going to go to waste, and it's a sin to waste it. It's for our dog."

"Sweetheart," she pulled out a piece of paper with a few sentences and a signature scrawled on it. "Who's been signing your permission slips?"

"My mama." I jutted my chin. Stuffed back tears. "There's no crime in being poor. We have all we need. People should mind their own business." I'd heard that line from Papa more times than I could count.

"Mmm. Well. I might have the county out to check on you, just to make sure everything's okay. We want to help." The heat clicked on above our heads. I was sweating but wouldn't take off my jacket. I couldn't afford to lose it or get it stolen.

"I'll have Mama call you or come by the school." Panic rose, stinging bees inside my chest. "Papa doesn't like visitors. He has a shotgun. More than one," I added, in case she didn't get my meaning.

⋆ ⋆ ⋆

When I got home later, I walked from the bus stop, past the No Trespassing sign tacked to the oak at the beginning of the dirt path leading toward our trailer. Samson, our old coon dog, met me as I came up the drive. I loved all over him. Scrawny as he was, he kept us safe, guarded the two chickens we had left. The second I got into the trailer, I started the wood stove, making sure the flue was open, that smoke was rising, and that I kept my hands away from the iron door.

I waited for Ben to get home from middle school. Would Miss Dunbar send the county? I had no idea, but I wasn't about to say anything. We'd have to move again. Cold as that old drafty trailer was, I liked where we lived, next to Skeleton Canyon, miles of open space that Ben and I used as our playground. Plus, there was Mama and Papa to consider.

After Ben got home, I crept alongside him, inching through the tall grass, our bodies hidden inside the brush. He smelled like wood smoke and pine sap and something musky, like bear or fox. Ben raised the rifle to his eye, flipped the safety off, took a deep breath and squeezed the trigger. The buck dropped and Ben clapped a hand across my shoulder.

"Goddamn right!" he yelled. I followed my brother, his lanky forearms dangling at his sides, long dark hair hanging like a curtain in front of his eyes. He spat to the side, and I did the same, drooling onto my shoe. Samson barked at our heels, happy with the hope of being fed. The sun hung low in the sky. "Gotta be fast," Ben said. He strode over to the deer, which lay against the mesquite like he was waiting for us. I stared into the dull eyes of the animal. The clean shot that stopped his heart. "That'll last six months," Ben said. "And we can sell those antlers."

Hungry as I was, I felt sorry for the buck. His life for ours. Always seemed like there should be some other way.

"Why can't we just go to the grocery store like everybody else?" I asked.

"C'mon, you ask that question every single time. We're losing light. We need to hurry." He grabbed the antlers and inched the buck away from the tree. When he looked back at me, his face softened. "I know it's hard, but where do you think grocery store meat comes from? Burgers and hot dogs, they were once cows and pigs. At least we aren't cowards, letting other people do the killing for us. At least this guy lived his life wild and free up until now, right?"

He looked from me and into the eyes of the deer. He stepped toward me and extended his hand, rough with calluses. "You're right, though, Skylark. Let's give him a good send-off, okay?" I bowed my head with my brother, and he took my hand and held it. We said a few words of thanks, a prayer for the animal's soul. The last of the golden leaves fell around us.

Afterward, I followed Ben to Papa's survival cache where he slid the branches from the top and lifted the plywood. He descended the steps quickly and handed up the tarp, saw, knives, newspapers, and buckets one by one for me to set aside. We gutted the deer where he lay before Ben wrestled him onto the tarp, and I helped him drag it to the picnic table. Ben did most of the hard work, while I used a knife to trim the fat and silver skin the way he showed me, the way I'd been doing since I was five, without so much as a scratch. I separated the meat into piles and wrapped each portion like a present we could open later and stacked them in the freezer.

The work was an exhausting, nonstop race against the light. When we were done, I could barely lift my arms, which were speckled with blood and bits of animal flesh. Ben let me sit while he grabbed kindling and cooked.

Over the fire, we ate backstrap and watched the sun crack the notch of Arapahoe Peak, splintering it into rays before disappearing. With full bellies, relief flooded us. It was like a fever breaking. We leaned into each other like books on a shelf, sated, tired, and happy.

Once we got inside the trailer, Ben had me settle in for the night. He sat next to me, reading me a story he'd written in his journal. He wanted to be a writer, and Papa made fun of him for it, but it never stopped him. He always had his head in a book or his journal. If you asked him what his favorite book was, he'd tell you it was the dictionary, because every story ever written was inside it. I was almost asleep when it started hailing, and thunder rocked the walls of the trailer. I jolted and curled against Ben. "I'm right here," he said.

"Is it a tornado?"

"Nah, just a run-of-the-mill Texas storm."

Still, I yanked the covers over my head. I felt Ben rise from our mattress, heard him shuffling around. When he ducked in next to me, he held a flashlight. "Hold this," he said. "Point it at my hands."

He linked his thumbs and fluttered his fingers, creating the shadow of a bird flying across our tented universe. He followed this with a dog barking. A pirate ship in a storm. He did voices and sounds, creating a whole world for us to get lost in. And before I even knew it, I was asleep.

⋆ ⋆ ⋆

The next morning, Samson growled and gave his "warning" bark. Tires crunched gravel and dry grass. Ben flew off the mattress where we slept and staggered for the gun. "What the hell?"

Out the window, I could see two cars; one was the sheriff. Guilt all but swallowed me whole. "We could hide," I said.

Ben ducked down. "Too late to make it to the cache like we practiced. Even crawling out the window, they'd see you." He rubbed his hand against the barrel of the gun. "Alright, so maybe it's nothing. Let me do the talking. It'll be fine." He set the gun down. I heard footsteps on the porch, then the knock. Always, that knock. Except this time, the county was done with our excuses.

⋆ ⋆ ⋆

Ben held my hand in the back seat of a car that smelled like oily rags. "This is bullshit," he said. The woman driving ignored his use of language and told us she was taking us somewhere safe. We'd been to the safe places before, and they weren't, not always. Ben squeezed my hand like a pulsing heart. I wiped my eyes with my sleeves and stared out the back window. Houses passed and streets blended into one another. I lost track of turns and stop signs. Everything unfamiliar.

"It's okay, Sky," Ben said. "Just think of this like one of our adventures. As long as we're together, it's going to be just fine." I sank back in the seat, relieved, knowing Ben would take care of me.

The lady with the crepe paper hands and brown spots like a leopard said, "God knows this has been hard for you kids." I watched the woman's eyes in the mirror. She winced like it hurt to speak.

Trees blurred past the window, the kind I had climbed a million times around Skeleton Canyon. Low, thick branches spread out like arms. Then one by one, mile by mile, the trees disappeared. The car turned down a dirt road, ruts from last spring's floods jarring the tires. Rows of trailer homes sat next to one another. Two men drank beer on a step in front of their trailer, hunched against the wind. Kids bounced on a trampoline in back of another. We pulled up to a double-wide, laundry pinned to a line whipping in the wind, and the lady cut the engine. "So, I'm afraid social services couldn't find an emergency intake that had room for both of you today. We have to separate you for tonight, three days at most, until we can find something more permanent," the lady said. "Sky," she said. "This is where you'll be tonight. Miss Cindy will take good care of you."

I wrapped my arms and legs around Ben, realizing what was happening. My guts twisted, and I moaned like Samson did in the thick of winter. I would not let go.

A bony woman appeared at the front door of the house with a toddler held against her hip and a cigarette in her right hand. The deep, sunken circles around the woman's eyes made her look like a goblin. "I hate it here," I said. I buried my face into Ben's jacket. The fabric smelled like a warm fire, like home. "I won't go."

The car door opened. Hands reached toward me. "C'mon, baby," a voice said. "Don't make this harder than it already is."

I screamed, high-pitched, from the back of my throat, and when I ran out of air, I pulled a deep breath and let it go again. The social worker pried my fingers from my brother's arm. But Ben clasped his hand over the woman's. "I won't take up any room," Ben said. "I can sleep on the floor." His voice cracked at the edges. "She's never really been without me. She doesn't know these people."

Hands encircled my waist, tugged at my middle, lifting me from my center until I was bent like a horseshoe with my arms and legs holding on to any part of the car or my brother I could reach. Once I was clear of the car, I used my limbs to kick and punch and scratch—anything to break free and be with Ben where I belonged. Wild with fear, it took me a while to notice that Ben was the one holding me now. Out of the car. Hugging me to him. Loving the fight out of me.

"Hey." Ben knelt. He leaned into the car, rifled around in his backpack, and pulled out Bunny. "Look at me, Sky.

It's not forever. Two or three days, right? Nothing's going to separate us, okay? I won't be far. Count on it."

He gripped me hard with arms full of promises I believed he would keep. I held Bunny against my throat, moved my lips against the soft fur. The lady with the cigarette put her arm across my back. I glanced at my brother in the back seat of the car as it pulled away, part of me weak and shaky, the rest holding on.

♦ 3 ♦

2019

Laura and I sit side by side on the twin bed in my room at Manor House. "That wasn't your fault," Laura says. "You were, what, eight years old? Where were your parents?"

The pipes clank and then rattle like bones. "Buried next to our trailer."

Laura shakes her head like she's got water in her ears. "Come again?"

I heave a sigh. "They were sick, and they died, and Ben buried them on the land." I picture the mounds of dirt, the makeshift markers we made.

"They got sick—at the exact same time?" She presses her lips together in a straight line. "From what?"

I shrug. "I don't remember." It isn't a lie. Flickering images of my parents were about all I had left. Mama measuring me and Ben on every birthday, notching our heights onto a plank of wood. Papa hoisting me on his shoulders and running with me through the grass while I giggled and held onto the sides of his beard. Papa taking medicine, stored in a cigar box next to the tin where we kept our cash. Mama disappearing for weeks at a time.

"So you two were on your own that year. Unbelievable."

"Not just that year. Three years. We lived there *three years* before the county figured it out." A woman down the hall yells into her phone, "I only missed one meeting. I don't give a rat's ass what the courts say."

"That's insane. You realize that, right?" Laura says. "He was, what, fourteen?"

I nod. "Eleven when they died. I was five."

"Oh, Sky. I'm so sorry. I can't imagine how hard that must have been."

Thoughts and prayers. Sorry for your loss. But when Laura puts her hand on my shoulder and squeezes it, I allow the possibility that she might mean it.

"We hunted. Stole electricity from the neighbor's place. Went to school." I tilt my head and shrug. "It wasn't so bad, really. I was with my brother. It was home. I didn't want to go anyplace else, certainly not anywhere without him. We were okay."

Laura picks up the 4×6 frame from the cardboard box I use as a nightstand. "Is this him, Ben?"

I panic. Before she can examine it too closely, I grab the photo and set it back on the stand. "No, not him," I say. I shift my body to hide it from her view. I don't tell her that the image she's looking at is the one that came with the frame—that I never changed it. I was going to, but then I noticed that the little girl in the photo was tow-headed like me. She's standing with her family in Paris, with the Eiffel

Tower behind her. *Oh, yes*, I can pretend. *There we are. On vacation. My parents, brother, myself. They live in California now. I visit them on holidays.* All bullshit, but still. No one except Laura knows I'm attending UT on a tuition waiver and getting by with subsidized housing and SNAP benefits—and I aim to keep it that way. At times, I almost believe the lies myself.

Laura juts her chin toward the frame. Her eyes widen. "What about a photo? If this guy in the hospital is your brother, maybe the doctor could send you a photo of him. Do you think you'd recognize him?"

I consider this. I know there's no way in hell that my brother is still alive, and I'm not interested in going further down the rabbit hole of my past—but there's something about Laura . . . her intensity, maybe. And for now, that's enough. What will it hurt to play along? "Maybe. Worth a try."

I dial the hospital, and eventually get patched over to a voice mail for Dr. Nez, where I leave a message asking her to text me a photo of her patient. Laura drops me off for my class, where instead of listening to the TA, I keep looking at my phone. I don't expect a photo of Ben to show up—but I can't help myself.

★ ★ ★

After class, I walk toward the parking garage where I work. In between cars arriving at my window, I try to study, but my ADHD makes it all but impossible. There's no response from Dr. Nez yet, and until there is, I will check my phone every five seconds. A woman alone in a minivan hands me her ticket, along with a credit card. Her makeup is slightly smeared; her hair mussed. Affair, I think. Definitely. She's got one of those stickers on the back window of a family of four, stick figures, holding hands, along with another saying that her child is an honor student at Clearview Middle School. "Go Rams," I say. She smiles at me but angles her chin away as if I might recognize her. I imagine her lover met her at the Hilton nearby. That he rented a room on the top floor and had champagne delivered before her arrival. I build on the story, my mind whirling as I process her payment. I imagine he's a teacher but has told her he works in the tech industry and that he created an app for monitoring heart patients. It's specific enough for her not to question its validity. The woman in the minivan clears her throat, and I startle. I hand her a receipt and her Visa. She scowls and returns them to her purse in the passenger seat.

After she leaves, I read five sentences about digital content creation before the next car appears. Another woman, this one young, with a very bohemian, hippie vibe drives up in an old, oil-belching VW bug. Her piercing green eyes are as clear as sea glass, and she wears several loose bracelets around her wrists. I bet she reads tarot cards and guides people on psychedelic mushroom trips toward enlightenment. When I hand her the receipt, she holds my gaze a beat too long, and I look away quickly. That's all I need: some groovy Wiccan chick putting a hex on me.

A line of vehicles forms. I settle into the work, grateful it's Friday night and busy enough to keep my thoughts off Ben or studying. I hope I'm too tired to do anything but sleep when I get home. But if not, there's always a party on campus where I can lose myself and add to my mounting list of regrets.

* * *

That night, I fall into a blissful haze of dreamless sleep at Manor House. When I wake, there's still no text from Dr. Nez. However, there are two others: one from Laura, asking me if I've heard anything and want to meet her for coffee, and another from a guy I know named Keegan inviting me to a tailgate party. I choose Keegan—because he's the least complicated choice. I text Laura a thumbs-down emoji along with a thank you, hands-in-prayer, gratitude one.

I meet Keegan in the parking lot of the stadium, at his Ford F-150 that's surrounded by a mass of people wearing burnt orange, Longhorn jerseys, and face paint. Shirtless dudes bounce to 21 Savage; the truck rocks with bass from the open cab. "Fuck yeah," Keegan says, and hands me an overflowing cup of beer still foaming from the keg. I chug my drink. Keegan hands me a molly with a heart etched into it, and I swallow it down. Twenty minutes later, everything is alive with color. I taste sweat in the air flung from jostling bodies, beautiful and glistening beneath a Texas sun. Keegan touches my thigh, my neck. I watch sparks of light arc from his fingertips against my skin, like static electricity. I close my eyes and spin in circles, one hand reaching toward the clouds, my face turned to the sky, warm with happiness. I love everyone here, and everyone loves me. I loll my arms across Keegan's neck, and he kisses me on the lips. Another person wraps their arms around me from behind, sandwiching us together. The natural mingling of our bodies melting into one another makes it hard for me to discern any separation. We are one.

Before kickoff, Keegan leads me into the stadium, where we find our seats. I disappear into the collective roar as the team enters the field. The marching band plays the fight song, and I mouth the words as if I know them. Notes hang in the air, take shape, fly like butterflies. Six cheerleaders face the stands from the sidelines. One of the guys lifts a girl straight up in the air, holding her shoe in his palm, raising her like a trophy above his head. It's almost more than I can bear. I never want it to end. I pull out my iPhone and take a few selfies and a quick video.

Everyone around me does the "Hook 'em Horns" gesture with their hands, pointing a pinky and forefinger into the air. I upload the post to SnapChat, and a text comes through. It's from Dr. Nez. From her private cell number, apparently. At a glance, I can see she's sent me two images. Two tiny boxes. That's all they are unless I click on them. I want to look and don't. I'm terrified to see my brother's face and equally frightened I won't. I put the phone back in my pocket. The molly is wearing off. I turn to Keegan. I ask him for a bump. I swallow the tablet with a slug from his flask.

The Longhorns fumble the ball in the end zone, but it doesn't matter to me if they lose or not. I fade to that place inside my head where I no longer care. I am just another happy, drunk coed swaying with the crowd.

⋆ ⋆ ⋆

The first thing I notice is that I am fully clothed—a relief. The second is that there are two men passed out on the bed next to me. The three of us slept in a pile. I move an arm from around my torso and let it flop onto the mattress. I sit up and look at the faces of both guys. Neither of them is Keegan. I can only find one shoe. I point the flashlight of my iPhone around the room and get down on my hands and knees. Under the bed, I discover a pair of panties, not mine. A red Solo cup and a baggie with a handful of Oxy sit on a plastic milk crate serving as a nightstand. I pocket several of the pills. I won't take them unless I need to, but it's comforting to know I have them. The room stinks: it's a cocktail of sweat, sex, and an air conditioner struggling to keep up with the Texas heat.

I stagger into the living room, which sags with hungover bodies in various stages of undress. I stuff my single shoe into my backpack. My clothes reek like a forgotten burrito beneath a car seat. I have no idea where I am or how I got here, but I do know I'm incredibly thirsty. I shuffle toward the kitchen and grab the first glass I see on the counter. Without bothering to rinse it, I pour tap water into my mouth as quick as I can swallow. I'm like a golden retriever, sloppy and noisy, slurping and dousing myself in my haste. It's as if my organs have turned dusty and brittle. I still haven't looked at the images that Dr. Nez sent, or if I have, I have no recollection of them. One of my classmates stirs from her place on the floor. She takes out her vape pen and flashes me a peace sign. I nod and stumble out the door into a blinding, headache-inducing light.

I try to catch the bus to get back to Manor House, but the driver takes one look at my bare feet and points to a sign requiring shoes to board. I tell her I have one shoe and that

I'm willing to hop on that foot, but she closes the door. I slog past the bars and boutiques of downtown Austin, only half paying attention as I cross against a red light and get honked at by a truck. Last night's storm has left ankle-deep water in places, and I try not to think about my exposed skin as I splash through runoff that smells like stale beer, cigarette butts, and mold. Worst-case scenario, I get a hypodermic needle between the toes—a thought that should bother me more than it does.

Turning on 6th Avenue, I pass Carl, huddled in a doorway with his hands tucked beneath his armpits. A wedge of cardboard at his feet reads *27 Days Sober. Need Bus Fare.* He's been 27 Days Sober for a year now. When I have extra food, I give him some. In all fairness, I have no idea if his name is really Carl because I've never asked. But he looks like a Carl, and when I pass him in the evenings, the food I leave for him is gone. Every now and then, he offers me a word or two of wisdom. But today he is silent. I wave and keep moving.

⋆ ⋆ ⋆

Back at Manor House, I go to the bathroom in the hall. It's early still, but no matter what time it is, there's never hot water. I brush my teeth. Toothpaste clings to the edges of the sink from whoever used it last. It's too quiet here. My thoughts race. It's enough to make me want to get high again. But I don't because it's seven AM and that would mean I've crossed a line, and part of me knows that once I do, there's no coming back from it.

I take my phone out. In addition to the text from Dr. Nez, Laura has tried to reach me three times. "Did she send u it yet?" "Is it him?" "Where r u?" My gut reaction to seeing her name is one of excitement and possibility. I tamp it down. She is doing her job. I am a client, a curiosity at most. I warn myself, *don't confuse obligation with friendship.* Still. My palms sweat.

I sit on the bed in my room. I take two deep, cleansing breaths. I can't remember the name of the therapist who taught me to do that. Sometimes it works. I read the text from Dr. Nez. "I have to warn you that your brother may not look the same as you remember, and not just because you last saw him when you were young. I work in the trauma unit at the medical center. The police believe the man was a transient in the area—they couldn't find any identification—no license or credit cards. We tracked you down from something written in the man's notebook. This is my cell."

The trauma unit. I prepare myself. This guy, whoever he is, is seriously injured. Even if he's not my brother, I'm not sure I want to look at something that might give me more PTSD than I already have. My hands shake, but I click on the first image. A stranger's face, with disheveled hair, a beard, and hollowed-out, sharp features lies on a hospital bed. He looks more like Carl on the street corner than my brother. It's a close-up shot. He's got a mask and a tube over his mouth and gauze wrapped around his head. The man's eyes are closed. Peaceful. My brother was never peaceful. He was always in motion. There's a second image of a tattoo, a stallion with a flowing mane. My brother didn't have any tattoos when he was fourteen, and even though he liked horses, and we snuck over to ride them at the neighbor's farm, I can't imagine he'd grow up to get this one. I zoom in on the image of the man's face again. It's not him. Of course it isn't.

My hands shake and I text Dr. Nez. "No. Sorry. It's not him. Maybe fingerprinting or dental records could help? I hope you find his family." I toss the phone onto the sheets. I listen to footsteps down the hall. Laughter. The beep of the microwave. A new day beginning. The emptiness of the room suffocates me. I don't want to be alone—it's unbearable. I wish I hadn't left the party. Now I have no place else to be and nowhere to go. Except . . .

It was Laura's idea to ask for the photo, so in a way it's her fault that I feel like this. Social services is supposed to help people. So, fine. She can help me. Even though it's early, she picks up on the first ring.

Laura explains she's got a commitment, but that I'm welcome to hang out with her. I tell her, "I don't care where we go. I just need to be around people."

Laura picks me up. I slide into the passenger seat of her Prius. The minute I see her, it's like jumping into a cool lake on a hundred-degree day—all that positive energy—a rare and surprising relief.

"Wanna talk about it yet?" she asks.

"Not yet. Still processing," I say.

"But Dr. Nez sent you something?"

I nod and change the subject. "Where are we headed?"

Laura's dressed in long mesh shorts, athletic shoes, and a New Orleans Pelicans jersey. "Got a pickup game. We play early to beat the heat," she says. "Every Sunday morning, sort of like church." She pulls into a parking lot. A few girls are already there, warming up. "You want to play?" she asks.

I laugh. I'm five foot three and stagger in a breeze. "Alright then," she says. She grabs a duffel bag from the back seat, and I sit on the metal risers and watch her stride onto the court. Her teammates greet her with fist bumps and hugs. "Yo, Ra!" they yell to her, short for Laura, I'm guessing—and I instantly regret never having tried out for team sports.

Instead of shirts and skins, one side strips down to sports bras. I watch Laura peel off her jersey, revealing a lean, ripped torso, a chest flatter than my own. These days, I prefer to hide my body, wearing oversized clothes whenever possible. Laura stands at the top of the key, calls a play, passes off the ball, runs around the side of her own player, who has picked off a defender, and sets up outside the three-point line. She gets the ball, all alone on the perimeter, and nothing follows but the sound of the basketball swooshing through the net. Watching her play is truly a thing of beauty, like watching a dancer moving to music the rest of us can't hear. I envy her, and not just for her athletic ability, which is impressive—but for how easy it is for her to fit in and be so well liked. She's not much older than I am, and she really has her shit together.

When they finish playing, Laura stands next to one of her teammates. She swigs some Gatorade, wipes the sweat off her forehead, laughs at something the other girl says. The laugh is a surprise to me: full-throated and unbridled—the kind of laugh that makes other people who hear it smile too, even though they aren't in on the joke.

I realize I like Laura, and more important, that I can't afford to. She's with social services, which means I can't trust her.

I ease my way down the risers and around the chain-link fence surrounding the court. I'm about to round the block and head toward the bus stop when I hear feet behind me. "Hey!" Laura shouts. "Wait up!"

I don't turn around or slow. She catches me by the elbow. "I've got a thing I forgot about," I lie. I keep my back turned to her.

"I call bullshit," Laura says. "What thing?"

"I could have a thing."

"You could, but you don't." She walks around me until she blocks my path. I bristle and take a step backward. "Come on. I'm trying to help. Clearly whatever that doctor sent you has shaken you up."

Her worry softens me. "I love that my messed-up life gives you a sense of purpose."

"Absolutely, Biscuit. You're my entire reason for being."

I plop down onto the curb, and she sits next to me, resting her duffel bag on the sidewalk. "Hit me with it," she says.

What are my choices, I think. I can't talk to anyone else about this. I hold out my phone. "So Dr. Nez sent these photos. I don't recognize the patient or the tattoo. I really don't. And I truly didn't expect it to be him. I *know* he's dead. I think I asked for it because you wanted me to." Heat flares to my face.

"Okay. I'll own that if you need me to," she says. "But you don't strike me as someone who just does what other people ask, no questions."

Behind us basketball shoes slide across blacktop. Someone yells, "Defense, Jesus!"

"So how'd they get your number?"

"The doc said something about my name in his notebook."

"Maybe you don't recognize him because he's older now, and his face is cut up and bruised."

"No. I told her it wasn't him and suggested she try dental records or fingerprints to identify him. They do that, right?"

She shakes her head. "If he was dead or under arrest maybe, but not unconscious. He's still got rights."

I stare at the photo of the patient and look at Laura, an old soul, creases of caring around her eyes. I want it to be Ben, but it's not. She places a hand on my shoulder, and I want it to stay there. Would it be so wrong to offer her the possibility that Ben's alive? Laura stares up into the sun, her face still glistening with salt and sweat.

"I looked in your file last night," she says. "The only mention of Ben is indirect: 'brother deceased.' I know this is hard, and you don't have to tell me if you don't want to, but how did he die?"

Her eyebrows arc with interest and concern, and before I can stop myself, I answer her. "Trying to keep us together," I say. "And instead of helping him, I only made things more difficult."

♦ 4 ♦

2008

Sky

Months had passed since the day the county knocked on our door in Eden Park and separated me and Ben. It might has well have been years. Fall turned to winter, winter to spring, and spring to summer. As it was, I scarcely remembered Mama and Papa—what they looked like, how they sounded, smelled, or moved. I had been so little when they died.

Sometimes I lay awake at night, curled up next to Jasmine, my foster sister, trying to remember a particular detail, like Papa's snore or the lilt in Mama's voice, which seemed impossible, like trying to hold water in my hands. Worse, my memories of my brother were fading too. I hardly ever saw him, since he lived in Sweetwater at a boys' home and I was at Miss Cindy's in Wingate, about thirty miles away. The few times I spoke to him on the phone, his voice had gotten deeper, though it still cracked every now and then, which I found reassuring. My whole world without him was radio static, but then the voice I remembered would come in clear, like a song I suddenly recognized—reminding me who we were to each other and where we'd been.

At first I hated Miss Cindy's. I thought I needed to—that if I didn't, I was making a choice between my family and a new life. Miss Cindy's double-wide had warped wood veneer paneling, a black vinyl couch with rips in the upholstery where the sofa spit foam chunks onto the linoleum, and a television set to cartoons for most of the afternoon, until Miss Cindy switched over to a televangelist. Plastic ashtrays filled with lipstick-stained butts littered the table in front of the couch, and toys lay abandoned in the middle of the hallway, creating a path to the two bedrooms that housed three girls and two boys. Just like a few other places I had stayed in the past, the trailer had an indoor bathroom, which was only slightly better than the outhouse we had at Eden Park. With six of us in the trailer, most of the time there was a wait for the bathroom, so we ended up doing our business outside anyway.

Truth was, Miss Cindy's was just fine—and yet, any time I admitted that to myself—while eating a full bowl of oatmeal or drying my sweat in front of the air conditioning unit—guilt gnawed at me. The room I shared with Jasmine and an older girl named Hailey had one bed and two smaller mattresses, a dresser with a half-filled fish tank on top, and a closet missing a door. The two mattresses lay side by side on the right side of the room. The real bed sat against the opposite wall, as if it were trying to run away. I found out later that Hailey, a girl who still wet the bed and believed in Santa Claus, had been adopted by Miss Cindy—that for some reason, Miss Cindy decided she was the one to keep. Hailey's corner of the room had posters of Leonardo DiCaprio and NSYNC tacked to the walls, a boom box beneath the bed, open CD cases strewn next to it. Jasmine warned me not to touch Hailey's things on her side of the room or Hailey would knock me sideways.

Jasmine had been living at Miss Cindy's for eight months. She had dark, curly hair and black, flaky skin, and one of her eyes wandered off to the left in such a way that even though I tried not to stare, I found myself looking at it. Mostly, as Jasmine spoke, I wondered if she could see two different things at the same time, like security cameras I had seen at the correctional facility in Eden Park when we went to visit Papa once in jail. I didn't ask, though. Jasmine sat with her elbow on her knee, chin resting into her palm, the eye hidden by her fingertips.

Shortly after I arrived, she told me that ten other kids had come and gone while she'd been living there. She said that some went back to their families, others to group homes, and some got adopted. Jasmine said, "I never knew my dad, and my mom is in prison. They'll never give me back to her. My brothers got placed in two different group homes, one in Oklahoma, I think, the other in New Mexico. And this . . ." She waved her arms around the room. "It's nice. But it's not forever, not until you get adopted. They can just keep moving you around." I thought about Ben and how long we'd already been separated, even though social services had said it was temporary. Jasmine picked at a scab along her forearm. "And no one wants to adopt older kids.

The babies go first—then toddlers. White kids. Everyone wants those too."

At night sometimes I cried. I couldn't fall asleep without Ben and his stories. My sniffles would wake Jasmine. Each time, Jasmine took my hand and whispered to me, "Don't worry. It'll be okay." Part of me knew she was telling herself too. I pretended to fall asleep. My body shuddered beneath the sheet, where I clutched Bunny in my arms. Shadows crossed the walls, taking the shape of monsters. But every night, without fail, Jasmine would hold my hand. Eventually, we got into a routine, whispering stories and secrets, shoulders touching, the warmth of a bath still on our skin. We fell asleep that way and woke curled up like kittens, nestled into one another for comfort.

★ ★ ★

The day Ben came to get me, I was jumping on the trampoline with Jasmine and three other kids from the neighborhood, enjoying myself despite the heat. As we played, the sun beat down on the thick, black tarp, searing our exposed skin. I wore socks to keep my feet from blistering, leaving a trail of small, sweaty footprints across the canvas behind me. Bouncing with the others, I rose and fell with Bunny held out to my sides, loving the freedom of flying. Time froze in that split second between up and down, and all my worries held in that space in between.

Earlier that day, Miss Cindy had left for a double shift, trusting the old lady two trailers down to watch out for us. It wasn't the first time Miss Cindy had left us alone, but on that day she seemed more worried than usual. Jacob, my foster brother, was just getting over a cold and sore throat, and I had woken up with a stuffy nose. Miss Cindy had felt my forehead, never saying if I had a fever. Either way, it didn't stop her from leaving.

After Jasmine and I set a new record for thirty-three successful bounces in a row, I crawled off the trampoline to get a drink from the hose, which was draped next to the chalk drawings on the sidewalk we'd made earlier. The tall weeds swayed, and I paid attention. The day before, I had found the skin of a rattler near that hose, so when I heard a hissing sound, the hairs on my neck stood on end.

The hissing continued until it turned into words. "Psst. Sky. Over here." I wheeled around and there was Ben, peeking out from the grass, one finger in front of his lips to shush me. I threw myself at him, chest first, arms wide. He held onto me for a good while before breaking away.

After I got over the shock and thrill of seeing him, I wondered why he was there and why he was hiding. I started to ask when he whispered, "I need you to do something." He jutted his chin toward the trailer. "Act like you're going back to Miss Cindy's to get something, but then meet me in front of the parakeet house. You know the one, two rows back?"

"With the cage in front of the window and the two green birds? Why, what are we doing?"

"Don't ask questions, Skylark. Just do it for me. Quick like. I'll be sitting in a white truck."

I kept my questions to myself, did what Ben asked, grabbing Bunny and my shoes from the grass next to the trampoline. I snuck around the back side of Miss Cindy's trailer without going in and headed toward the trailer with the parakeets. When I rounded the corner two rows back, I found Ben sitting in the driver's seat of a white truck, motioning for me to climb into the passenger side. I hopped in, dropped Bunny on the floorboard, and used both hands to slam the heavy door of the truck. The birds in the window of the trailer squawked and beat their wings against their cage. Ben gripped the wheel with both hands. "Whose truck is this?" I asked. It looked familiar to me, but I couldn't place it—old and rusted—with busted headlights.

Ben put the truck into gear and pressed the gas pedal. The truck jerked forward. Ben knew how to drive, had driven tractors at a livestock auction, and had even taken the wheel from Papa when we had a car that ran. Still, the way Ben leaned forward to see over the steering wheel made me giggle. The harder I tried to hold it in, the more I snorted and coughed. Ben shot me a warning look, but it eased into a grin. A few seconds passed before we burst into full-on, hold your sides, can't breathe laughing. One of us would try to stop, which only made the other one get going again. When we settled down, Ben wiped at the corners of his eyes, and said, "Damn, that felt good." I waited a beat to ask him where we were going.

"On an adventure," Ben said.

I looked out the window. Dirt roads. Cotton fields. Barbed wire. Miles of nothing. "For how long?" I thought about Jasmine, the air conditioner unit in the trailer, Miss Cindy's meat loaf.

Ben hammered his fingertips on top of the wheel. "Does it matter? You're with me." Irritation tore at the edges of his words.

"We should tell Miss Cindy where I'm going," I said. "She'll be worried."

"You're kidding, right?" He clicked on the radio. Country music played from the front speakers. Some guy singing about losing his house and his wife but not caring, because he still had his truck, a case of beer, and his dog.

Ben kept driving and I fell asleep with my head against the window, a fog of breath encircling my face. When I woke, it took me a moment to remember where I was. The old truck. The smell of gasoline and grease. Ben noticed me stirring and spoke. "Because of the busted headlights, we can't drive at night. We'll get pulled over. So we'll camp until sunup. Just like old times, right?" Ben pulled off in an area with a sign that had a stick-figure hiker, a fish on a pole, and a tent. He circled the area and picked a spot away from the few other vehicles that were already there, got out, and unhooked a tarp covering the bed of the truck. I followed him, a nagging doubt tugging at me. Ben stood on the running board. He pulled out canned beans, an opener, a pot, and some matches. Papa's guns stuck out from the corners of a blanket. I shivered, but Ben puffed up his chest and moved with energy. "Don't just stand there. Help me collect some wood. It's just beans tonight. I can't use the rifle to hunt until we get a little farther away. Too much noise. New Mexico maybe." His words burst like rapid fire.

I stood there. "You went home?" I pictured the house, Samson, the chickens and tire swing. "You went without me." I kicked my foot in the dirt. "Why can't we go there?"

"Sorry, Sky, that's the first place they'd look for us."

"Who's they?" I asked, but Ben didn't answer.

Ben took a pocket hatchet to some larger branches, laid them on top of dry pine needles in the firepit, pulled a grate over the top. I sneezed a few times and wiped my nose on my forearm. "You cold?" Ben asked. "Still feels warm out here to me, but that's alright." He ran over to the truck and unfurled a sleeping bag with the flick of his wrists. He unzipped it, draped it around my shoulders. I sat on the log next to my brother while he stoked the fire and heated up our dinner.

When the beans bubbled, he used the sleeve of his jacket to grab the handle of the pot, scooped out a spoonful, blew on it, and held it out to me. I took the spoon and swallowed a bite, but for once I wasn't hungry. Ben stared at me. "What? You don't like my gourmet cooking anymore?" Ben nudged me with his elbow. "When'd you become a picky eater?" He smiled when he said it, but there was disappointment underneath. "More for me, then." He offered me the pot again, but I turned it down, and he finished off the rest.

That night, we slept under the stars, our bags touching each other. Ben lay on top of his with his hands behind his head, a handgun at his side. I curled inside of mine, aching, cold, and miserable. I begged Ben to tell me "The Legend of Skeleton Canyon," a story he'd written about lost treasure and bandits in the canyon. It was one of my favorites. One he swore was based on a true story. There was something comforting about the tale taking place in the canyon that ran from our trailer through two other states and all the way to another country. It made me feel like we could always follow it and find our way back home.

He cleared his throat and started at the beginning. "So, back in the 1800s, Mexican bandits robbed a bunch of banks near Juárez, Mexico, hauling off millions in gold and silver bars, boxes of diamonds, and rare coins. But this American dude named John Banks, not a good guy either, found out about the robbery and that the Mexicans were planning on smuggling the loot across the Mexican border through Skeleton Canyon."

"How did he find out?"

"How else, he got them drunk on tequila," he said. "He tricked them into thinking that they were all good friends, drinking buddies."

"Do the voices," I begged, my throat feeling like I'd swallowed gravel.

He continued in a gruff drawl. "Alright then. So Banks rode back and told his gang, 'Grab your horses and say goodbye to your women. We've got work to do!' The outlaws waited at the top of the canyon and ambushed the Juárez gang as they rode along the narrow ravine. They killed every single one of the Mexicans." He sat up, grabbed the handgun, and pretended to have the bandits in his sights. "Pow, pow, pshew, pop!" I rolled my eyes. He set the gun back down. "Okay, the mules that were carrying the loot through the canyon started running away. To save the treasure—"

"The outlaws killed the mules too." I said, filling in the rest. "But they were stupid."

"Right, they were stupid. Because without the mules, they had no way of hauling out all the stolen booty. So they stuffed their pockets with as much as they could and then left the rest in the canyon. Two of the men stayed behind to guard it."

"Get to the double cross," Sky said.

"Man, you sure are bossy," he shoved me playfully in the shoulder. "So, while the other men were spending their new-found money on women and liquor in town, the two friends left behind to guard it, a couple of outlaws named Swing and Zane, decided to double-cross the gang by moving the treasure and keeping it for themselves. Swing said to Zane, 'Why shouldn't we keep it all? Ain't it our God-given right?' And Zane agreed, thinking about all the whores and tequila they could buy."

"What's a whore?" I asked.

Red heat crept up Ben's neck. "A woman who gets paid to be nice to men."

"You mean, like a waitress?"

He laughed a little. "Nah, more romantic like. Stop asking questions and let me get on with it." He paused, and when it was clear I was going to let him finish, he continued. "So they took their time moving the treasure into a nearby cave. But their gang came back sooner than they thought, and Swing and Zane heard horses coming and hid out with the treasure, waiting for Banks and his men to give up looking for them or the loot. Four months passed, and during that time, Zane wrote letters to his sister in San Antonio, giving her directions to the location of the treasure, including maps."

"I like that you put a sister in it," I said. "Would you have sent me a map?"

"Of course, Sky."

I sneezed twice. "So how'd he mail the letters to her without a post office?"

"Good question. He'd hike out three miles to flag down the stagecoach to get the letters out, wait until the horses disappeared, and then squirrel back away in the treasure cave. He knew as well as anyone that either his own gang would find them and kill them for stealing from them, or a bounty hunter would. He was afraid he might not get out alive and wanted her to know how to find the treasure. Of course, he never knew whether she got them. It wasn't like she could write him back. Still, four months is a long time to have all that money and no place to spend it, and the men got tired of waiting. Swing said, 'What good is being rich if you can't buy nothin' with it?' So he convinced Zane that they should ride into town one night and buy whatever they wanted."

"And they got caught."

"Red-handed, drinking at a saloon. Banks threatened them and beat them, but neither of them would tell where they'd hidden the treasure. Finally, Banks gave up and hung them from a tree on top of their horses. His men fired a shot in the air to scare the animals. The mustangs took off and the men dangled there, necks broken. Supposedly, Zane's sister went to find the treasure and never came back. Maybe she found it, maybe not. After that, some say an earthquake collapsed the entrance to the cave. Others say the ghosts of people slaughtered on that land haunt the cave. Every now and then, hikers find a gold coin or a human skull. But no one really knows what happened to it. You know what I think? I think the treasure, worth over eight million dollars now—"

"Is still out there waiting to be found." We finished in unison.

I rolled a blade of grass between my fingertips. "Why does Zane have to die? Why can't you have him and his sister end up with the treasure?"

He flung a rock, sidearm, into the dark. "I don't know, Sky. I just don't like a tidy ending is all. That's not how life is. You can write the story however you want to. You don't need me to do it." He turned on his side with his back toward me. "Get some sleep."

I enjoyed the story, but not as much as I usually did. I rolled over in my bag. I couldn't get comfortable. Tiny rocks dug into my side. My arms fell asleep and then tingled back to life. I noticed every sound: coyote yips, sparks crackling from the fire, brush rustling in the wind. My ears pulsed with a dull ache, and I shivered.

The next morning, Ben nudged me awake. I wiped the crust from my eyes and when I yawned, my ears exploded with pain, and sandpaper scraped at the back of my throat. My eyes stung. "I don't feel good," I whined to Ben. I stayed in my bag on the ground. Thunder echoed in the distance. A bruise of clouds formed on the horizon. Ben scribbled a few things inside a notebook before putting it in his pocket.

"Storm's coming. We best get moving." Ben cleaned up the campsite and poured water from a jug on what was left of the fire. He tucked the handgun into his waistband like an outlaw from one of his stories.

I groaned and squirmed deeper inside the bag. "I don't want to go."

Ben knelt beside me and peeled the covering from my face. He sighed with frustration and placed the back of his hand against my forehead and cheeks. His palms and fingertips were rough, blackened with dirt and ash. "You're fine, Sky. Must be all the smoke from the fire getting to you. Time to cowboy up, alright?" He smiled but worry creased the corners of his eyes before he turned away. I stayed in my bag. "Please, Sky," he said. "Do your business and then get in the truck, okay? There's a lot of miles ahead of us, and I don't want to have to stop every five minutes."

I wriggled out of my bag and went to pee behind the bushes. A crack of lightning lit up the trees in the distance. Thunder rumbled the ground beneath me.

♦ 5 ♦

THE TRUCK LACKED AIR conditioning, or one that worked. I hand-cranked the window down as far as it would go, but I could still taste heat at the back of my throat. Every time Ben stopped at a railroad crossing, the cross breeze died, and it felt like we were being roasted on a spit. My ears pulsed with pain. Sweat ran down my face, arms, and chest, soaking me. Ben kept talking, but my head felt like it was stuffed full of cotton, and I had trouble understanding him anymore. I was floating, then fading. After more hours than I could count and a few dead-end roads that Ben explained away as "just exploring," I started coughing, a ragged and dull saw inside my throat. I couldn't stop or catch my breath, and then something changed inside of me.

My skull vibrated, an earthquake inside of me. I called out to Ben, but it was like trying to scream inside of a dream. Buzzing and ticking, rhythmic jolts came next. My body had a mind of its own, was doing what it wanted.

When I came to again, I was slumped in the passenger seat, my shorts drenched with urine. The truck sat in the middle of a dirt road. My door was open, and Ben stared down at me, his eyes wide and relieved. "Christ," he said.

"What happened?" I asked. I tasted metal, and when I wiped my mouth, a streak of blood trailed across my palm.

"You had a seizure," Ben said. "Like you used to when you were little and got those high fevers." He tilted my head back and held the water jug for me to drink from. He wiped the blood from my mouth. "You bit your tongue a little, that's all. Not a big deal."

I stared at the blood, the shock of red. "What if it happens again?"

"I'm not going to let it happen again," Ben said.

His mouth twitched, and we both knew he'd made a promise he couldn't keep. "I want to go home." Tears fell in rivers down my cheeks, and I let them. I didn't have the strength to wipe them away. My fear, anger, and sadness tangled into choking sobs, and I coughed until I gagged and then puked onto my shirt and shorts, which made me cry more. I expected Ben to reach out to me and tell me it would be okay, but he was glaring at me instead.

"Yeah, and where exactly is home?" Ben said. His words hit me hard, like a wall I'd slammed into. "I'm your home, Sky." His eyes softened for a moment. He handed me Bunny, grabbed a rag, and wiped me off. From the bed of the truck, he retrieved a clean blanket and tucked it around me. My ears buzzed, thick with pounding and tears.

Ben started the engine and turned onto the main road. Rain spat against the windshield and lightning burst like a loose wire. Ben set his jaw and gripped the wheel. The truck shuddered with speed. I tried to sit up, but my body seemed too heavy for me to carry. It was as disconnected from me as the fence posts out the window.

We drove a few more minutes. I could barely see the road through the sheets of rain. "Where are we going?"

"Skeleton Canyon across the border on the Mexico side. We'll go through New Mexico and Arizona before dropping down."

"I don't want to go to Mexico."

"Goddammit, Sky. You don't know what you want, do you?" Ben yelled at me. "I'm trying to help you. No one else sure as hell is. You see that, right? No one gives a shit about us. No one gives a shit about you but me. And no one ever will. Got it?"

I clutched Bunny against my chest and leaned far away from my brother and his words, but they followed me anyway. "I hate you. I want to go live with Miss Cindy."

"Really? Miss Cindy? Is that right?" He let out a huge laugh. "There's no Miss Cindy's anymore. She gets paid to take care of you. You know that, right? The government pays her, like she's a babysitter. She's not your family. She doesn't love you."

"I miss Jasmine. She's my best friend."

"You can make friends anywhere, Sky. You've only got one brother."

My mouth quivered and tears caught at the corners. Ben shook his head at me. Anger and hurt played a game of tug of war across his face. He tightened his lips to a thin line.

In the side mirror, a police car shimmered. Two more appeared. I thought about warning my brother, but I was mad at him. I wanted to get caught, to be back at Miss

Cindy's—in a warm bed with food and water and Jasmine next to me. Ben pressed the gas pedal, clutched the wheel, and mumbled, "Hold on. Just hold on."

My body ricocheted from side to side, banging against the center console and the door. The truck shimmied. The road ahead washed out beneath pounding rain. Water pooled in the low spots, causing the truck to float and skid. Ben punched the wheel and let loose a string of curses.

In the rearview, the cops gained ground. The truck fish-tailed sideways, its tires unable to hold the road, and Ben turned with it, righting it at the very last minute. I tried to grip the door handle and the edges of my seat, but it was impossible. Bunny lay on the floorboard beneath me. "I'm just trying to do the right thing," Ben said, wiping his forehead with the back of his hand. His eyes widened with panic.

The truck spun out over the ruts in the road, gained traction, then skimmed over standing water. It didn't seem to matter which way he turned the wheel—the truck had a mind of its own, and the road was getting worse by the second. The cops gained on us until they were close to the truck's bumper. Ben wiped the fog off the inside of the windshield with his palm. Through the driving rain, I saw a bright yellow sign: *Welcome to New Mexico.* But in front of the sign, still on the Texas side, lights flashed red and blue. No way forward and no way back.

"Goddammit!" Ben yelled. His eyes darted right and left. "There," he pointed. "Short cut." To our right, a bar-ren patch of ground ran through a field and out the other side across the state line. But a deep ditch ran parallel to the road, overflowing with water and bordered with barbed wire on the other side.

"Stop!" I cried out. "No . . . no . . ."

He ignored me, spun the wheel right, and took the nose of the truck down the embankment. The front wheels gripped the mounds of grass up the other side and propelled us through barbed wire, which caught and dragged, banging the sides of the vehicle, scraping the metal in high-pitched shrieks.

A cop behind us bottomed out, and Ben laughed. We jackhammered through the rough field over rocks and ruts. The truck moaned like a wounded thing. I glanced in the rearview; the police were falling behind, losing ground on us. I wanted them to catch us. I didn't want us to make it past the state line.

The moment I thought it—maybe even willed it into being—a boulder the size of a steer rose from the tall grass in front of us. The truck slammed into the rock. The force of it threw me forward. My head cracked against the dashboard. My body curved like a dishrag around Ben's outstretched arm, which twisted with the impact, and when he tried to rotate it back, it hung loose by the gear shift. Blood poured from my forehead, and my leg angled beneath me, bent in places other than my knee. I faded in and out. I caught pieces of what was happening. Sound bites. Still images.

The cops moved their cruisers nose to nose behind us. Officers crouched behind the vehicles. Lights pulsed red and blue.

The engine of the truck ticked down in the heat. A drumroll of raindrops beat against the crumpled hood.

My eyelashes stuck together, matted with blood. My brother slumped against the wheel. His ribs poked through his white T-shirt, blood soaking through like spilled ink on paper. He wheezed twice, then nothing. I screamed, tried to scoot toward him. But every inch felt like trying to run under water.

After that, I woke up in a hospital in Abilene.

⋆ ⋆ ⋆

2019

Cars and trucks whir by as Laura listens to my story. She kneads her hands together, taking it in. A loose basketball crashes into the chain-link fence behind us, followed by feet and someone yelling, "Out on me." When I look at Laura, tears fill her eyes. "That might be the saddest thing I've ever heard," she says. "And I've heard some things."

I don't tell her that I still miss him—that I think about him every single day. "When I woke up in the hospital, I kept asking about him. A few days later, when I guess I was well enough to hear it, a hospital social worker came and told me he made it to the ICU in Lubbock but died from his injuries. Part of me already knew."

"I'm so sorry," Laura says. "That's just a terrible way to lose someone you love."

"It was a long time ago."

Cars pass. A woman holding the hand of a little boy, who grasps the hand of his younger sister, runs across the busy street, testing their bonds against the oncoming traffic.

Laura massages the muscle on her calf. Rubber-soled shoes skid across the blacktop behind us. "This will sound horrible, but how do you know for sure he died? I mean, you didn't see his body or go to a funeral, right?"

I consider this. "No, but he looked bad. And, seriously, I can't imagine anyone lying about something like that."

"Maybe not lying. Maybe misinformation. The more agencies and people involved, the more everything gets lost in translation. Sounds like the accident was in one county, the hospital in another"—she waves her hands—"social workers from all over."

I try to figure out if she's defending or criticizing social services. "I seriously doubt it. Regardless, I wish I could take back the last things I said to him. I was just so sick. And it was the first time I realized that my brother couldn't take care of me. I lost faith in him—which was probably the worst thing I could've done to him."

"You do hear yourself, right? Seizures. Cops. Car crashes and floods. Add some zombies and an asteroid and you guys were in an apocalypse movie." Laura stands and holds out her hand to pull me to my feet. "He knew you loved him." She slings her duffel bag onto her shoulder, checks her watch. "C'mon. I'll give you a ride home."

I've hijacked her day off, and still I want more of it. I know she's got things to do—an actual life outside of her job. On the ride back to Manor House, I try to come up with some reason I need to spend more time with her—a problem only she can solve. As we pull up to the curb, I still haven't thought of anything good when she says, "Look,

I've got some things I have to do, but then I'm free the rest of the day. Do you work tonight?"

She feels sorry for me. And I don't care. I'm happy to jump on the opportunity. I don't tell her that I have a shift tonight at the parking garage. I'll call in sick. "Sure, where do you want me to meet you?" I sound too eager. "I can push a few things around," I add.

"I've got a studio downtown. You could bring the stuff you need to study."

"Good one," I say. "Oh, you're serious."

"Five PM? I'll order pizza and text you the address. It's right off the bus line."

"Done," I say. It occurs to me that she's only trying to help me pass my midterms, but I figure at the very least, I'll get a free meal out of it.

⋆ ⋆ ⋆

I get off at Jay and Main and walk a block over to the address Laura gave to me. There's a Mexican diner, Caballeros, with a bright yellow door, and next to it some stairs leading to the floor above. I take the steps, leading to a hallway with apartments. I find Laura's and hear music thrumming from inside. I knock, gently at first, and then louder. A high-pitched bark and the click of nails across the floor follow. Laura opens the door, a small, curious dog in her arms. I let out a muted squeal and stretch out my hand for the dog to sniff.

"This is Bella," Laura says. She sets Bella on the floor, and I plop down inside the doorway and let the compact, white-with-brown-ears terrier leap all over me. When I stand again, the pup jumps with excitement, over and over, the top of her head reaching my chest.

"It's an impressive vertical, right? Like if she played basketball, I mean, WNBA pro level," Laura says, clearly proud. She holds out her arms and Bella leaps into them. I pet Bella's velvety ears and we rub noses. I realize how much I've missed having a dog in my life, the way they can fill a room with energy—how even the smallest ones have the biggest presences.

Laura's loft is open and inviting, sparsely finished, and no frills, with a futon that pulls out to a bed, an area rug with a sunflower pattern, a wooden table. There's a small kitchen area, a bathroom, a closet, but little else. It's light and optimistic, a bit like Laura.

A row of lights points toward framed photos on the walls, highlighting the rich black and white tones of the prints. I stand in front of each one, taking it in.

In the first one, a Black man, in his seventies maybe, sits with his back to a mural. He wears a tattered poncho with the hood up and partially obscuring his face, the gray of his beard touching his collarbone. A blanket covers his legs, but one of his bare feet sticks out from beneath it. His huddled body takes up the right side of the frame in sharp focus, while people passing by the man are obscured, a blur of motion, their heads cropped out of the frame. It hints at something unyielding: the anonymity of our lives, too busy to take notice. I move to the next one: a young white woman with a baby on her hip pushes a shopping cart overloaded with blankets and with plastic bags tied to every possible surface. The woman stares into the distance. Her eyes are fierce, defiant. I run a finger along the frame, sweeping dust away from the inside edge.

"What is all this?" I ask.

Laura watches me carefully. "It's a collection I've been working on about the homeless population in Austin," she says. "I live here in the studio, but it's mixed use, and I'm going to open it up to the public and have an auction." She moves alongside me and lowers Bella to the floor. "I did something similar for the transgender community. But that one was sponsored by Austin Pride. I'm terrified no one will show up for this one."

"These are stunning. Really, heartbreaking. Arresting, that's the word I'm looking for," I stammer. She took these photos, and they are brilliant. My body and face spike with heat. I don't feel jealous. Jealousy is something you feel when you think you deserve something another person has or has accomplished. I feel inadequate. I want her to see me as her equal, or at the very least as a functional adult with potential.

I stand before the next image, shifting my weight from one foot to the other. It takes me a minute to recognize the man in the photo, but when I do, I gasp. "I know this guy," I say. "I leave him food. Sometimes he talks to me." In the image, Carl leans against a stair railing in his usual place next to his sign, *27 Days Sober.* He smiles at the camera, his lower lip concave from missing teeth. I feel like I am looking at an old friend.

"This guy's name is Wayne. He lost his house and job in the 2008 crash. His wife left him. He started drinking. If he's not sober, they won't allow him into the shelter."

Wayne, I think, reassessing this man and Laura—who had taken the time to learn Wayne's story, his real name, to get involved. "The funds from the auction will go toward expanding the existing homeless shelter through DHHS. The new wing we're trying to build is a 'wet house,' which allows clients to drink. It's a little controversial. Sort of like handing out clean needles to heroin addicts. But if you take away the judgment, these programs save lives."

"Rules were meant to be broken?"

Her eyes widen. "Not at all. I'm a rule girl, Biscuit. But that doesn't mean I can't get creative," she says. "Rules were meant to be challenged, re-created, updated—especially when they get in the way of helping people who need it most." She touches the edge of the frame. "This photo of Wayne reminds me that we all need a little help. Any of us, at any given time, could be Wayne."

I stare into Wayne's eyes, the creases of brokenness that tell me he is weary, but not yet at rock bottom.

Laura orders cheese pizza, and I spread out my class notes on the table. My phone vibrates. It's a reply from Dr. Nez. I'm certain it will merely say "thank you" or "sorry for any confusion." It reads: "I got your message. But I also found this photo tucked into one of the pages of his notebook. It had the names Ben Rayner and Sky Rayner written on the back with the date January 16, 2008."

I click on the image. I cling to the phone. My fingertips pulse red—and heat moves like a wildfire from my feet to my scalp. Two kids. Me. Ben. Definitely us.

My insides cramp. I know this shot. I know it. And yet I'm disoriented. I posed for this. I look at the backdrop, a wall of blue. January 2008, where were we? I scan my brain—the answer at the edges, just out of reach. I stare into my eight-year-old eyes, which are red from crying, and at Ben's face, which is rigid, his jaw thrust forward like it's cut from stone. And then I remember the day we took that photo, and I want to hug both of us—to warn us what's coming. I set the phone down.

"Is the pizza that bad?" Laura asks. "You're turning a shade of green I don't have a name for." She pats my back. "Tell me, Biscuit," Laura says. I nod to the phone. She picks it up, reads the message, and uses two fingers to zoom into the image. "For real, it's you?" she asks. She scans my face for an answer. "It is, isn't it?"

I wrap my arms around my stomach. "I need a minute," I say, and I escape to her bathroom. I feel nauseous and dizzy when all I want to feel is numb. I sit on the lid of the closed toilet and put my head between my knees. Breathe. Ben did have a notebook. He was always writing in a journal. And that photo is real. But he's not alive. And if I let myself consider the possibility . . . well, I can't and I won't. I want to rewind the last twenty-four hours and forget any of this ever happened. I stare at my face in the mirror: sunken eyes from lack of sleep, sharp cheekbones, brittle hair. It's more than I can handle, especially with Laura here. I refuse to let her see me fall apart over what has to be a hoax—even if I can't see the angle yet. I dig in my pocket and hold two Oxy in my hand. I have no idea how many milligrams they are. I weigh the odds of overdosing. I'm not snorting or shooting it. Doctors prescribe it, after all, for pain. I'm in pain. I cup my hands to the faucet and swallow down two pills. I beg them to work quickly.

When I return to the room, Laura looks concerned. "You okay? Sit." She pats the spot next to her on the floor.

I tuck my hair behind my ears and smooth down my shirt. I shrug, try to feign nonchalance. "It was taken way before the accident as part of our file," I tell her. "So I have no idea how anyone else would've gotten ahold of it, including Ben." I clear my throat to continue. "I remember our caseworker had us stand in front of a mural on the back wall painted with blue swirls, waves of an ocean. They fed us animal crackers and gave us juice boxes. There were huge, plastic LEGO blocks strewn across ABC mats interlocking on the floor. It was the first time I had seen my brother since the day they'd separated us, and I had assumed I'd be moving to a new home with him, or that maybe he'd be coming to live with me at Miss Cindy's. It was stupid of me. I had no idea it was just the beginning." I wring my hands. "You know, parents take photos of their kids because they love them. They post things on Facebook like, 'We're so proud of Sue or Joe or little Bobby for riding a bike or losing their first tooth.' Social services does it so they can identify you if you run away or turn up dead." I rub a spot of skin on the back of my hand until it burns. "That day . . . the day they took that photo . . . the state of Texas became our parents. I had no idea what would happen to us after that. It just seemed so lonely and final." I swallow my anger, but I feel eight years old again. "The room had a fish tank with a puffer fish in it, and when they told me I wouldn't be going home with my brother that day—I shook that tank until it teetered on its stand, until the puffer fish blew up like a balloon, it's soapy blue eyes bulging out. And then I threw up the cookies they gave me onto my shoes."

Laura places a hand over my own. "I'm sorry they did that to you. It's just an impossible situation. No easy or quick answers. And so absolutely hard for young children to process."

The room is quiet, and I break it with the hard edge of my voice. "But you are them."

Her face falls. "No, I'm me, Biscuit. And you have no idea the lack of resources available to us—how hard this job really is."

"Yes, you guys have it really tough. Whose side are you on, anyway?"

"There are no sides."

"There are. Trust me."

"How about you trust me?" Laura says. But she has no idea what she's asking.

In unison, we sigh. Our shoulders rise and fall in tandem. Laura slides a little closer to me, hesitant, sensing I'm in fight or flight mode. The soft weight of her chin landing on my shoulder startles, then steadies me. She points at the phone in my hand.

"So the man in the hospital has to be Ben, right? How else could some random guy have your brother's journal and that photo of you two? What would be the point?"

"I don't know. Maybe the patient is our old caseworker, and like, he was super into his job—you know, like serial killers who take a lock of hair from their victims."

She sits back and crosses her arms across her chest. "So now social workers are like serial killers."

"No offense," I say. She looks deflated. "Too far, sorry," I add and mean it. "There's got to be a reasonable explanation.

I just don't know what it is." I feel the Oxy hit. Edges soften. A blissful haze.

Laura cleans up the pizza and I help her. My legs are heavy. She says, "Maybe you should go see him?"

"Dr. Nez sent a photo. It's not him."

"Are you sure? One hundred percent?"

I hesitate. "I can't just up and leave." I hold up fingers one by one, counting. "Midterms. Transportation. Money."

"Sure. Midterms." She rolls her eyes at me, clearly not buying my excuses, but she doesn't press the issue. "What if you asked Dr. Nez to send you his journal?" Her eyes dance with hope. "Maybe you could learn something from it—or at least if it's his, you'd have it, right? Wouldn't you want something of your brother's?"

She places her hand over mine. It covers the chafe marks I've made from rubbing them together. Her belief and her tenderness slay me. Of course I would want something of my brother's. Beyond that, I want to keep Laura engaged. I don't want the evening to be over.

I text Dr. Nez and ask her to send me the notebook. Together, Laura and I wait, with her hand still on mine.

Three dots . . . then, "Sorry, with HIPAA laws, I can't release his personal belongings to someone who isn't family."

Laura grabs the phone out of my hands and starts typing. "Could you release it to someone working for the Department of Health and Human Services?"

Three dots appear, disappear. We wait. Laura's breath warm against the back of my neck. Three dots again. "Yes."

"Great, I'll have Laura Moss get in touch with you directly," Laura types, and smiles using her entire face. The competitor in her . . . victorious. And yet I feel guilty. The man can't possibly be Ben, and yet we're asking to read this stranger's diaries, perhaps what might even be his last words. But I'm selfish. Laura cares about me, and her enthusiasm is infectious.

She pats my shoulder. "That's the way things are done!" she says. Bella barks. "I know!!" I relax into her hope. She bustles around me—capable, on fire with possibility. I hear her contact Dr. Nez with her credentials, arranging for the journal to be shipped overnight FedEx to arrive in the morning. She gets on her laptop. My eyes flutter. I let go. My body liquid. I drift.

⋆ ⋆ ⋆

I wake at dawn, and it takes me a minute to get my bearings—the recurring theme of my life these days. I'm in the loft at Laura's. On her futon. She is curled in a sleeping bag on the floor. I don't remember falling asleep. Bella sees me stirring and leaps onto the futon, licking my face. "Sweet pup," I say. "I'm a mess, yes, I, am." I say it in the baby-talk voice people use on toddlers and pets.

I imagine what it would be like to actually live here, for this to be my life. What would we do today? Take Bella to the dog park maybe? Yes, and then we'd have lunch overlooking the kayaks at Lake Travis. We'd come back here, to our apartment, work together to hang more of Laura's images. I see us holding up a frame, measuring, laughing as we try to stop one of the photos from hanging askew. Laura wakes. "Sorry," I tell her. "Guess I crashed."

She doesn't answer.

"Thanks for letting me stay here."

Still nothing.

Laura goes to the kitchen and grabs two glasses and pours water into them. She comes over to the futon and sits on the edge, hands me the water. "Don't tell me you just fell asleep. You were unconscious."

Her anger surprises me. It fills the room. "I—"

She holds up her hand, stopping me. "I'm not allowed to have clients spend the night, but there wasn't much else I could do with you in the state you were in. Don't confirm or deny any of it. When you finish your water, I need you to go. Please."

I take the glass and without taking a sip, slam it onto the table in front of me. It sloshes onto the table. She flinches. "You think this is easy for me? This is my life we're talking about. I'm just barely hanging on here." I realize the truth of it as the words leave my mouth.

She sets her jaw. "So it's okay if you get me fired? Or if you OD? You don't care about that?" She stares at me, her eyes hard. "What is it with you?"

"I just needed a little help, something to take the edge off."

"Yeah, well, I'm not going to be a part of it. I can't." She looks at her feet, softens for a moment. "I know a good rehab place."

I scoff at the idea. "I don't need rehab," I say. "I dabble. I'm careful."

She won't meet my eyes. And there it is—that line in the sand.

"I don't need this shit," I say, and I brush past her, gathering my things. "And I sure as hell don't need your judgment.

I've had enough of that for a fucking lifetime. You think—" I freeze mid-rant. She's getting the patient's notebook today. FedEx. Damn it. I backpedal. I relax my tone. "What about the journal?" I ask.

Her mouth twists, her eyes flicker. I know what she's thinking. *I care about the journal. I don't care about her.* I let her believe it, because I'm hurting, and I want her to know what that feels like.

She shifts her weight to her heels. "Just go," she says. She folds her arms across her chest. She strides into the bathroom, the only room where she can escape me. I pet Bella's head and shoulder my pack. The door shuts behind me. I grip the rail to steady myself down the stairs. Whatever this is between us, I've blown it.

♦ 6 ♦

WHEN I GET BACK to Manor House, I pace the communal kitchen with a cup of coffee in my hand. I drink it quickly, trying to kick my brain into second gear so I can think clearly. But it doesn't work. I skip my first class. I can't eat or sleep or study knowing that Laura is getting the journal. I have nothing left from my life in Eden Park, not even very many memories. If it is Ben's journal, I deserve to know what my brother wrote. A tsunami of thoughts propels me forward. What if she already has the journal and is reading it? Who the hell does she think she is? I dig my fingers into my arms and wait until the pain is what I'm focused on instead of Laura. It works, but only for a minute.

I text Laura. "That journal is mine. You have no right to it." I was stupid to trust someone working for the county. The message is delivered and read, but she doesn't respond. I want to hurl the phone at the wall, but I hear one of my old therapists' voice inside my head: *Self-sabotage hurts you—no one else. It snowballs until it buries you in an avalanche.* Whatever. It's all I can do to get myself out the door and to my exam—one I can't miss, but desperately want to—as if it will serve Laura right if I fail my classes.

The TA passes out tests. Sheets slide across the rows. I read the first question, but instead of answering it, I think, *What if she sends the journal back?* I tap my pencil against the desk and the girl two seats away glares at me. *Or, what if my brother has written something horrible about me, something I'd never tell anyone?* I read the question again. I stare at the back of the guy's head in front of me, seething at his man-bun. He's the kind of guy who tells girls he's a poet. He plays a mandolin and does yoga and smokes a ton of weed. He cries at the TikTok video of a golden retriever befriending a baby chick. I scribble in the oval next to the letter C. I darken it until the paper almost rips. The lead breaks, but there's an edge remaining. Fuck it. I take my pencil and darken all the letter Cs as the answer to every question on the exam. Who really cares? All I know is that I can't breathe. I have to go. Now.

I scurry down the row to the stairs, take my paper, and drop it on the desk at the front of the room. The TA looks at his phone, at the time, knows I can't possibly be finished. I shrug. There's a basket with granola bars and bananas and a sign: free brain food. I take four bars and two bananas, feeling satisfied, like I've gamed the system—really stuck it to the man.

My smug satisfaction lasts until I open the lecture hall door and slam into a wall of heat outside. Panic, then, of course, regret. Fuck me. Why do I even try? I pass beneath billboards, one selling a gleaming F-150, another announcing the dates for the Texas Livestock Show and Rodeo with a teen leading a steer into an arena. It's a beautiful, well-groomed longhorn with a blue ribbon—which will still end up at the slaughterhouse.

I shuffle along with one foot on the sidewalk and the other off the curb, kicking a rock into the gutter, and listening to the satisfying plunk below. I'm well into a second helping of self-loathing when I spot Wayne huddled in a doorway, close to his typical spot, half asleep. I walk over to him. His eyes open and he moves his hand to block the sun. I hand him two of the granola bars. He takes them and nods. He makes a dramatic, sweeping arc with his arm, like he's clearing a table, and motions for me to sit. I slide my back down the wall. I think about what I know about this man and how he ended up here.

I tear open a granola bar and eat it, and Wayne does the same. He chews on the side of his mouth with teeth, and in between bites, he raises a finger and points it at me. "Always be who you are."

"That's good advice," I tell him.

"Unless you're an asshole. Then you should probably work on that." He laughs until he coughs, and I reach out my hand, tentatively at first, and then commit to patting him on the back until he regains his breath. I smell alcohol, fermented and sweet.

We aren't so different, I know, especially if I fail out of UT. It was stupid of me to blow that exam. There won't be any help coming once I turn twenty-one, and I refuse to ask my adoptive parents for any.

Crumbs fall from Wayne's mouth onto his pants, and he licks a fingertip to pick up each one. "Just remember, you can't control other people. Just your reaction to them."

"You said it." We eat in silence, until we're both done.

I hand him a banana, and he says, "It's the perfect food. It comes in its own wrapper."

Wayne is a wise man. I brush myself off to stand. "Thanks for having breakfast with me," I tell him. Wayne salutes me like I'm a soldier off to war. In some way, I do feel fortified, ready to fight. Because while it's true that I can't control what Laura thinks of me, I'll be damned if I sit back and let her read the journal, or worse, return it. She requested it on my behalf. It's just wrong. I text her again, and when I can see that she's read it and chooses not to reply, I make a decision.

I catch the bus. I climb the stairs above the Mexican diner. I stand in front of Laura's loft. I knock twice. Bella barks. But no one comes to open the door. I make certain no one is watching. I take my school ID from my pocket and slide it across the lock. I've never done anything like this before, and so I'm as surprised as anyone when it works. I slip inside, love all over Bella, whose tail beats like a metronome. I call out to Laura, but no one answers. Satisfied that she's not here, I look around the room. I shuffle through a stack of magazines on the coffee table: *Psychology Today*, O magazine, *Sports Illustrated*, *National Geographic*, *Essence*. Next to the futon on the nightstand, there are a few books. The spines are aligned and facing the same direction. I scan those as well: *The Underground Railroad*, *Between the World and Me*, several mass market John Grisham thrillers, and surprisingly, what looks to be a romance paperback novel. But no journal. The girl is neat, I'll give her that. Tidy without anyone around making her be that way. At least I hope that's the case. I think she lives alone, but maybe she's seeing someone.

I open a drawer on the nightstand. There's a journal with a pen attached, some lip balm, earplugs, and what looks to be a handheld muscle massager, but could easily double as a vibrator. I blush. I want to read her journal, but I know that would be wrong. I came here to find something specific—not to snoop. Still.

I lift the corner of the notebook, just enough to peek at the page where she stopped writing. I tilt my head sideways to peer into it, as if it's somehow less wrong if I don't actively lift it into my hands or touch it too much. "This girl will be my undoing," she writes, "bent on self-destruction as she is." I don't read any more. I inch the drawer closed, feeling caught in the act, like I'm watching someone sleeping. I wander to the bathroom, where I check her medicine cabinet. I find nothing stronger than Advil or Allegra. I try to convince myself that if I *had* found some pain pills or Adderall, that I wouldn't have taken them—but my disappointment tells me I'm a liar. I poke around until I end up in the kitchen. I examine the photos on her fridge, the magnets holding them in place. There's one of a young girl standing between a man and woman who have their arms around her. Laura looks like them. It must be her parents with her when she was a kid. They look like they are in a city with street performers behind them. Not Austin. There's another shot of her with her arms around some friends, taken at Six Flags amusement park according to the logo. A third shot shows her standing with her arms locked together with another man, roughly our age, at the YMCA. Maybe a boyfriend, though they don't look particularly romantic. I resist the impulse to tear the photo into tiny pieces. Beneath the kitchen sink, I find a trash receptacle and recycling bin. Inside, right on top of last night's pizza box, there's an empty FedEx package from Banner University Medical Center. Wherever Laura is, she has Ben's journal with her. In minutes, I'm seething again. I pace her loft until I feel dizzy, with Bella trailing after me. After that, I sit on her futon and wait.

When Laura comes in and sees me, she is furious. Her eyes are focused and defiant. She moves in long strides across the room, shoves her messenger bag into the corner, and hurls her keys onto the table. "This is a complete invasion of privacy. It's breaking and entering. I should call the police." The muscles in her jaw twitch. Her hands squeeze in and out of fists.

I stand and take two quick steps toward her, defying her to yell at me more. "Really, let's talk about an invasion of privacy." My stomach tightens, anger and nerves mixing with my Oxy withdrawal and coffee. "You get to know everything about me, all of my mistakes, embarrassments, things I've done, and things done to me—all the shit I hide from everyone else. Doesn't matter if I trust you or hate you or if you're good at your job or suck at it. How is that fair? You could be a total fuck-up too, and I'd never know it."

"So that gives you the right to break into my apartment?" She straightens the magazines on the table, which I've left fanned out instead of stacked the way she had them. "You went through my things." She folds her arms across her chest like a shield against me. "Where do you get off thinking that's okay? What's wrong with you?"

My face burns. I swipe at my eyes with the back of my hand. "You've read my file. You already know the answer to that."

We stare at each other, both breathing hard. I hate that she can see that she's hurt me. *What's wrong with me?* It's a question I've been asking my whole life, but hearing those words from her cuts deeply. My shoulders sag. I don't have the energy for this fight—and what's more, I realize I don't want to.

She plops down onto the futon, head in her hands, elbows on her knees, looking like a player who's just been benched. Silence stretches between us—long and wide. A void that may become a bridge if one of us takes a step across it.

"I shouldn't have said that. There's nothing wrong with you—just your actions."

"No, there's plenty wrong with me. I deserved that. I shouldn't have broken into your apartment. It was wrong, and I'm sorry," I say. I sit next to her. Rain taps against the roof of the building. It starts slow, then grows steady, rolling in sheets down the windowpane. "We need that," I say. "It'll cool things off."

We watch the rivers of water create new channels down the glass. "I'm sorry too," Laura admits. "You're right, it's not fair. I can't imagine how awful it feels to have your life flayed open to a stranger—to someone you don't like or trust. You aren't allowed to set any boundaries, and I am. I have to. They warned us in training not to get too close to our clients, too attached. It never works out well. Believe it or not, I'm the one who usually ends up getting hurt."

I stare at her doubtfully.

"Really. One of my first cases. I had a single mom who I just loved—we were friends. She was an awesome cook—best green chile enchiladas I've ever had. Funny. Magnetic personality. Good-hearted. She convinced me she needed money to get her kid a birthday present. I saw her using it the same day for drugs. I got put on probation at work. Then when her kid got taken away by the county, she blamed me. Said she hated me. I should've seen it coming, but I didn't. It really hurt me, and lesson learned, I suppose." She takes a deep breath. "I got into this work because I wanted to help people. I try to keep my distance, but it's impossible when you care—and you have to care. And caring means that I get hurt. If I'm successful at my job, it means that my clients will move on with their lives without me. I get invested. I get left behind, which sucks."

"So am I a client or a friend?"

"I care. I'm invested in you. I can help."

It's enough. It has to be.

7

LAURA GETS HER MESSENGER bag and takes out a spiral-bound notebook. She sets it on the table in front of us.

"Ground rules, okay? Because I'm legally responsible for this." I nod. "You don't get to keep it. You can read it, but you have to do it here, because it has to stay in my possession. I'm not allowed to make copies."

"Okay," I say. I take the notebook into my hands. I recognize it. But I also know Ben had another one when we were young, one that was small and square with a deer hide cover and a split in the leather. This one is filled with ruled paper and a bright yellow cover, the kind found in every school supply aisle at Target. I open it slowly.

"Is it okay if I sit next to you and read along?" Laura asks. "It's alright if you don't want me to. I'd totally understand."

My first instinct is to say no, because it's so private. But because I just looked at her diary less than an hour ago, it only seems fair. Plus, I don't want to be alone in all of this—whatever this is. She leans against my shoulder, her head tilted toward mine.

"Breathe with me," she says. And together we take three long, cleansing breaths.

On the first page, there's a sketch of a building, beneath a heading reading: Sweetwater, November 16, 2007. It was the day after the county came and knocked on our door, after I got taken to Miss Cindy's house.

I met our new caseworker today. God. Help. Us. If I could draw people as well as I do birds and bats, I'd draw him, but since I can't I'll use words. One look at him, this is what you'd come away with. Smooth pasty white skin, rumpled dress shirt with a faded food stain, receding hairline with a bald patch—tufts remaining there like an eagle picked on by crows, scuffed dress shoes, belly overlapping his belt. Maybe mid-thirties. No wedding ring. A soft man. An indoor man.

After the social worker dropped off Sky at the lady's trailer in Wingate, she drove me another thirty minutes to a boys' home in Sweetwater—Xavier—where I sat waiting for someone to show up. I was counting backward from one hundred, reading the inspirational posters on the office walls, when a man opened the door, juggling papers, wiping his hands down his slacks, and tossing a wad of foil from something he'd just eaten into the trash bin near the empty office desk. When he reached out to shake my hand, he stifled a burp. Even though he said he was sorry, that he'd gotten a burrito on the drive over, I wasn't sure what the appropriate response should be, so I kept my mouth shut, shook his greasy hand, and watched him land in the folding chair next to me. He said his name was Harrison. From there, it went like this:

Harrison: "I'm really sorry about what you've been through. I'm going to do my best to help you."

Me: "We don't need any help. We just needed to be left alone. We were doing fine."

Harrison: Opening folder, brow creasing—like he's concerned, but more likely he's got heartburn from that burrito, the smell of which wafts from the trash: "I know the sheriff already asked you this, but I have to do it again. Can you think of anyone who might be able to take you in for a while? Grandmother, teacher, neighbor, parents of a friend or classmate?"

Me: Staying quiet but screaming inside my skull: "We have no one. Check the files in your hand. No one cares. No one's left. It's just me and Sky. Why would you make me say it out loud?"

After that, he said that all the licensed foster families and homes were full. That he had to put me here. Here being Xavier, a group home for boys who'd been kicked out of foster families, expelled from school, or sent over from juvee. Scary guys—guys that had done a whole lot of bad shit. Maybe Harrison saw me sweating, because he rushed to tell me that I hadn't done anything wrong, that this was temporary. But here's the thing. Nothing's temporary about social services. Time moves in slow motion. I could be here for the rest of my life.

So I told him, "I'm not staying here. You can't keep me here." He didn't answer. So I'm considering other options. The best one I've come up with so far: Run away and get Sky. But then I hear Papa inside my head, always when I don't want him to be. Running makes you look like prey. Start running, and you best not stop.

★ ★ ★

The "house mom" showed me to my room and gave me a few school supplies, including this notebook, which will have to work as my journal until we get our things back from the trailer. My room's a small, rectangular space with four cots that smell like B.O., dirty socks, and bleach. Momma Blanche runs Xavier. She's a large woman with a poodle of thinning black hair. I get glimpses of her pink scalp through the tight curls. She holds her meaty hands at her sides like they're too heavy to hold up for long, and she walks off-kilter like her hips hurt. She wheezes at the end of each sentence, a frightening hiss, but her eyes crease with kindness at the edges—which is something, I guess.

My roommates are in high school, a head or two taller than me, with deep, low voices and stubble on their chins. They already know I'm different—beyond just keeping to myself and writing constantly—and they haven't even seen my shoulders yet with the birdshit birthmarks that never tan.

Xavier has a communal shower, but the first day I got to use it while the other guys were in class—and OMG is all I can say. First of all, hot water. Second, an honest-to-God almost full bar of soap. While I was in there, taking my sweet time and letting the steam fill my lungs, I checked out my birthmarks. Mama said maybe they'd fade over time, but no. I swear those spots are getting bigger, growing when the rest of me doesn't seem to. Mama used to measure us on every birthday. The year she died, she could tell how disappointed I was that I hadn't gotten taller. "Don't worry. You'll shoot up one day. It'll happen when you least expect it," she said.

I think about that plank of wood now, with our heights and dates and initials etched into it, left behind, like everything else.

December 18, 2007

We got some of our things back today. Harrison dropped by Xavier after I finished classes. He carried a black trash bag—the official suitcase for foster kids—and motioned for me to sit across from him in the kitchen area. He asked how things were going. I told him the other guys picked fights with me, came in after curfew drunk or high. That they had stolen the few things I had. Harrison promised he'd look into it, which was laughable. The man had barbecue sauce clinging to the collar of his shirt and a patch of stubble on his chin he'd missed while shaving. I told him not to bother, that I'd handle it one way or another. Let it go at that. What I didn't say: I can't sleep. I'm terrified most of the time. I want to go home.

At the table, Harrison slid the bag across to me. The top portion of the sack folded in on itself, looking half empty. I didn't open it in front of him, but I told him it seemed light and asked if anything was missing. He got this serious look on his face before telling me that our trailer had meth residue and black mold—that we couldn't get back anything that was "toxic or perishable or could be used as a weapon." Then he opened his file folder and said, "Says here you told the sheriff that your parents died of a meth overdose three years ago in another county."

I stayed still. The lie hung in the air. I waited. He followed that up with, "Are you using?"

I shook my head, hoped he couldn't see the relief on my face. "Drug test me if you want. I don't care."

He didn't press the issue, but I had questions of my own.

"What's going to happen to Samson and our chickens?

He looked away, sputtered out an answer. "Animal Control took possession. Likely Samson will be adopted out by the Humane Society."

"Right. So you guys can just give away our dog to some other family, without even asking?"

I didn't mind putting him on the spot, watching him squirm. Harrison winced. "Look, I know you're mad. I'm mad too," he said. "You shouldn't have been put in that position in the first place." He squinted, like he was trying to read a sign that was too far away. "You know it's not your fault, right? I've been doing this a while, and I can tell you: you mix substance abuse, homelessness—the kind of poverty and isolation you guys were dealing with—well, it ends up this way. It doesn't take much for things to go sideways either, like how a penny on the tracks can derail a train."

That got to me, I admit. My eyes watered, not a good thing in a place like Xavier. I changed the subject. "How do I know Sky's okay? What if some perv is messing with her at that house? I've always been there to protect her."

"She's fine, Ben. Miss Cindy's place is safe. Just the kids and her, no boyfriend or husband or anything."

I picked at a dried splatter of ketchup on the table. "Still, she can't keep an eye on her twenty-four-seven. Shit happens. We both know it." My legs jiggled up and down, rattling the table. "If anything happens to her, I'll kill someone, I swear it."

He ignored my threat. "We'll try to set up visitations between you guys, whenever transportation can be arranged. Weekends maybe. You could call her too, except that it's long distance from the house phone here. But I'll see what I can do about that."

I leaned forward, spoke slowly and deliberately, like he was the kid in the room. "I shouldn't have to call her. I'm her brother, the only family she has. We need to live together in the same house."

"I hear you, Ben. I really do. We're working to get you guys adopted."

"I don't need to be adopted." It sounded ridiculous. "And Sky has me. We don't need a new family."

"You guys are still too young to be on your own. I'm sure you don't feel that way, but it's the law."

The muscle along my jaw spasmed. "Whatever. Fine. As long as we stay together."

"I'm working on it, promise," Harrison said. But I swear, he hesitated.

★ ★ ★

I waited until he left, and I was back in my room alone to open the sack. Inside it, I found a few of our parents' things that I'd stashed away after they died. I'd all but forgotten about them. My parents' wedding rings, two silver bands with a river encircling them, were wrapped inside a bandana. Both pieces of metal were scratched and dented, scarred from their marriage. They never took them off, no matter what they were doing or how bad things got.

I smelled the bandana, but it didn't have any scent left. Papa used to wipe his neck with it after chopping wood. Everything I knew about nature, I learned from him. He wasn't much for books or for learning, but he could identify a bird flying overhead just by the way it rode the wind—which was a kind of poetry of its own. He told me to watch him so I could learn things, and I did. I watched every move, especially his hands. More information in those hands than any other part of him. I knew them at rest, in a fist, working with a knife or gun, rendering a deer, or shaking from withdrawal. I knew the pain they could cause.

I remember the day he found that abandoned trailer in Eden Park, the one that became our home. He stood us in a row facing it and told us to take a good look. He made promises: He'd shore up that porch, reinforce the walls, add bigger windows so we could see all the way through Skeleton Canyon and out the other end thousands of miles away while we ate breakfast. He clapped a hand across the back of my neck. "It'll be a good project for us to do together," he told me. "Hard work gets a man out of his head." I was unclear whether he was talking about his head or mine or both. It didn't matter, though. He never got any further than digging the survival cache and a pit for burying our garbage. The entire time we worked shoveling that dirt, it felt like we were digging our own graves.

I got my journal back, which was a relief, like seeing an old friend. Deer hide. Cracked spine. I still have blank pages left in it, but I'm not going to add to it, because I've already started this one, and then everything would be out of order. My life's confusing enough as it is.

It's night here now, and I'm writing using a penlight while my roommates snore and fart in their sleep. I keep thinking about the stuff in the bag, how little there is left of us. The police or whoever cleaned up our house likely couldn't tell what was important or what was garbage. Things are missing, and I keep remembering them, which makes it hard to sleep. Arrowheads, feathers and quartz, fossils and fool's gold. Deer antlers we kept to sell in town. The water-stained and torn dictionary that was missing sections T–W, the one I read cover to cover, eating up words when nothing else was available. Other things too: the bundles of sage Mama lit, which made the house smell like a clean rain. Some of the stories I wrote on loose sheets of paper. Sky's drawings. And the animals. I can't even go there. And here's the thing: the place where we lived looked like any other bombed-out trailer you'd pass on the highway and not look twice at—weather-beaten and rotted—but we had a life there. Harrison called us homeless. But this was the first time I'd ever truly felt that way.

• 8 •

May 25, 2008

HARRISON IS A LIAR—A fucking, two-faced liar.

A few days ago, he surprised me, showing up unannounced at Xavier to take me to the Rattlesnake Roundup in Sweetwater. I'd always wanted to go, but we never had the money or transportation to make it happen. I should've known Harrison was up to something. Instead, I was a dog after a treat, too distracted to see the cage trapping me.

As soon as we got to the arena, I talked Harrison into buying me a bunch of food, using up all the petty cash he had in a fat envelope stamped Child Protective Services. I got a ½-pound burger and fries, a can of Red Bull, a box of Twizzlers. I convinced him to try the barbecue rattlesnake nachos. I told him they weren't half bad if you breaded and fried them, though they were a little chewy, and then I watched him turn a few shades of green. I made the most of our all-expenses-paid outing, dragging him to every event in the arena, totally confident that I was the one who was working him, instead of the other way around.

We elbowed our way through crowds of Roper boots and Levi's jeans, back pockets faded with circles from Skoal tins, making our way to the exhibits, skipping the cookoff and barn dance, but taking our time at the gun, knife, and coin show. We sat through the crowning of Miss Snake Charmer, a pretty girl from San Angelo who wore a cowboy hat and little else. We watched as competing teams of wranglers hauled in thousands of captured rattlers and dumped them into a holding pit to be sold to the Jaycees and made into belts, boots, and wallets. I made Harrison look over the edge of the pit with me, where below, those hissing, knotted vipers rolled over each other like an oil slick. I wish I'd pushed him in there.

There was a snake-handling demonstration in the main arena. Harrison and I took our seats a few rows up with a good view of the action. This cowboy wearing elbow-length, thick leather work gloves stood in the center of the ring facing a snake coiled up on a table. Then he took an orange balloon and moved it closer and closer to a rattler until the rattler struck at the balloon and popped it. The blast echoed like a gunshot. The cowboy kept doing it over and over, until I found myself rooting for the snake.

While we sat, Harrison asked me casual questions without really paying attention to my answers. Did I like that the weather was changing? What were my plans for the summer? Had I given any thought to the programs social services sponsored for teens—maybe the graphic novel workshop or creative writing? *Then he came out with it.*

"So I've got some good news. There's a family in Dallas that's been approved to adopt Sky."

There it was.

Just Sky.

Without me.

I went crazy, leaped to my feet before he eased me back down in my seat. "Do I have a say? Does she? Because she won't go anywhere without me." Of course, even as I said it, I wasn't sure it was true.

He went on about why Sky getting adopted without me was such a great idea:

He didn't have any families looking to adopt a teenager.
No one was interested in taking on more than one kid.
He was lucky to find a place for Sky.
Sky would have parents to look out for her—a good education, a safe place to grow up.

I started getting tunnel vision. I told Harrison to fuck himself. I gripped the can of Red Bull to give my hands something to do besides punch him. "I'm her family. I'll take care of her," I told him. "It's what I've been doing all my life."

But nothing I said mattered. He rambled on:

You're too young to emancipate.
You don't have a job or housing or money.
No one is going to give you legal guardianship.

I kicked the empty seat in front of me. The force of it shook the entire row. A few people stared. I reminded Harrison what he said when he first met me: that I wasn't in trouble, that I hadn't done anything wrong. Which was bullshit, because it sure as hell felt like I was being punished.

Harrison put both hands in front of him, motioning for me to take it easy, to settle down. But I couldn't anymore. I kicked the chair until I heard the satisfying crack of plastic. Harrison stood, grabbed the back of my hoodie, and dragged me backward down the aisle toward the exit. I yelled at him to get his hands off me and leave me alone. As we struggled down the row, a red-faced man, an asshole in a ball cap, told us to sit down and shut up. I wheeled around and told the dick to fuck himself and mind his own business. The guy in the ball cap took quick steps toward us. I glanced at my hand, which still held the can of Red Bull, and chucked it like a rock at the man's head. The end of the can landed solid on the bridge of his nose. Blood trickled out where the can sliced the thin layer of skin just above his nostrils. The guy jumped toward me, grabbed at my shoulders, trying to wrestle me to the ground. Harrison wedged himself between us, and security came running.

Once we were separated, the three of us glared at each other, panting. The guy pinched the top of his nose, and someone handed him a couple of napkins. Beneath the wad of tissue, the man told security he wanted to press charges—for assault, which I thought was hilarious, until it wasn't.

At the precinct, Harrison sat with me in a holding room, while the officers talked to ball cap-douche bag someplace else and tried to sort things out. I put my head on the table in front of me. "I thought the can was almost empty, and that I'd just get Red Bull all over him. I didn't think it would hurt him." I bounced my forehead against the table in slow repetition, making a dull thud.

"Come on, don't do that." Harrison stuck his hand in between the table and my head to stop me from beating it against the surface. "I should have told you about Sky in the office or something. I just thought maybe it would take some of the sting out of it if you were away from Xavier, and that you know—maybe in public you wouldn't"—he put both hands in the air—"do something like this."

Heavy footsteps and voices passed the door and faded down the hall. "Are they going to put me in jail?" I asked.

"Doubtful. They just want to scare you a little. We're going to be here a while, though, so just sit tight."

I rolled my shoulders to ease the stiffness in my neck. I flicked my fingers against the table. "How far away is Dallas?"

"As the crow flies, maybe 250 miles."

"How long a bus ride is that?"

"Four hours, maybe."

I closed my eyes while Harrison talked on and on, giving me a full court press about how I should be happy that Sky was being adopted, how I was still her brother no matter who her parents were. Could Sky love some other family hundreds of miles away without forgetting about me? I didn't think so. I heard Harrison saying, "People do things out of love all the time, and sometimes that means letting go." I rested my forehead against the wall next to the table. No family had asked about me, which was fine, I didn't need anyone. I chewed on my fingernails, biting at the cuticles until the edges bled. Harrison would take my sister away from me. They all would, and there was no way of stopping it. I shoved my hands deep into my pockets. "If they're in Dallas, how did they even find out about her?"

"There's a website called Texas Heart Gallery where kids who are up for adoption are listed. We posted your photos and bios on there once you were both legally free."

"What photos? The ones you took at social services for our file?" I asked. He nodded. I tried to imagine people scrolling through pictures of children like they were shopping for a used car. How was it that perfect strangers could know everything about us without us having any say in the matter?

"So what does our page on this heart site look like?"

Harrison took out his phone, typed for a moment, and handed it to me. I stared at the screen. I clicked on a link under the heading Meet the Children. Hundreds of faces smiled back from the screen. At random, I clicked on a photo of a Black kid named Devon, 17, who appeared to be around 12 when the image was taken. The site withheld last names, but gave a short profile of each kid, including how they were doing in school and what special needs they might have. Devon, for example, needed a family who understood substance abuse issues and could facilitate his ongoing rehabilitation. Timothy, a white eight-year-old, loved Legos and video games, but needed to be placed into a family without any pets or young children. Most looked like normal happy kids, except I knew better. No kid ended up in the system because of something normal. I kept scrolling until I got to the photo of Sky. My breath caught in my chest. She had one hand on her hip and the other leading out of the frame and her eyes looked red from crying. You could see part of my left arm, but I'd been cropped out of the image.

Cut out. Just. Like. That.

I scrolled quickly to my page. I stared at myself, at my father's eyes, defiant and guarded. It would appear as though I was standing alone, except you could see Sky's fingertips, barely visible, gripping the other side of my stomach, holding on like she meant it. To Harrison's credit, both our bios mentioned the importance of "facilitating the ongoing relationship between the siblings." Still.

"You told this family in Dallas about me, right? Why can't they take me too?" I thought about all the trouble I'd gotten in, about my suspensions from school, about the police station where I sat.

"It's not that simple, Ben. I tried. I really did. I can't force them to adopt two kids." He took out a folder from his briefcase and set it between us. "I wasn't going to show this to you, but I think it might help. It's the home study for the family adopting Sky."

I stared at the file without opening it. My shoulders sagged. Harrison tapped the manila folder. "Seriously, take a look. Even if you can't meet them, you'll learn everything from reading this—more than you would in any conversation with them. Everything I know about them is in here."

I kicked my feet against the wall next to the table. "Does she know about them yet?"

"Not yet. They transferred her case to Dallas County. They'll have the permanency hearing there. I plan on telling her this week."

My chest burned. I couldn't let this happen. "When does she leave?"

"Next Friday. You'll get the chance to say goodbye, though."

Goodbye. Never. My jaw hurt from clenching it, but I bit down harder.

"I'm going to see what's taking so long. Give it a read." Harrison stepped out of the room to speak to the officers.

I waited until I heard Harrison's footsteps recede down the hall before opening the file. The home study was more than 50 pages, heavy in my hands.

The first page gave basic info leading into a summary and recommendation.

Names: Jack and Samantha Fielder

Ages: Jack Fielder, 52 / Samantha Fielder, 38

Address: 652 Highlands, Dallas, Texas

Jack ran some kind of investment company dealing with oil and gas. Samantha's profession: homemaker. Religion: Catholic. There was a detailed section from separate interviews with Jack and Samantha, and one with them together. When asked why they wanted to adopt from foster care, Samantha had answered that her own parents had died in a car accident when she was five, and she was raised by an elderly aunt on the east coast—who was long gone now. Samantha and Jack had tried to get pregnant—all she ever wanted was to be a mom, and her life seemed incomplete without a child. After seven miscarriages, she felt like God was trying to tell her that she was supposed to adopt an older child, maybe close to the same age as she was when she lost her parents. They quoted her on one of the interview transcripts, saying, "God punished me for being ungrateful."

They ruled out foreign adoptions for cultural reasons and had explored private adoptions, only to learn that most of those opportunities were for infants—and Samantha Fielder superstitiously believed that if she adopted a newborn, it would die.

There was a checklist included in the file, which struck me as ridiculous—like you could order up a child with the same amount of thought you'd give to getting takeout at a restaurant. I ripped out the page and kept it. It seemed important—a concrete answer to why no one wanted me.

Characteristics Checklist for Placement Matching Mark "X" for all that apply.				
Maybe = depending on specifics	**Yes**	**Maybe**	**No**	
Gender/Sex of Child				
Male	X			
Female	X			
Race/Ethnicity/Culture of Child				
A child of the same racial/ethnic/ cultural background as that of the family	X			
A child of any racial/ethnic/ cultural background			x	

Characteristics Checklist for Placement Matching Mark "X" for all that apply.				
Maybe = depending on specifics	**Yes**	**Maybe**	**No**	
Number/Type of Children				
One Child	X			
Two Children			x	
Three Children			x	
Four or More Children			x	
Teen Parent with Child			x	
Age of Child				
0–5 Years of Age	X			
6–10 Years of Age	X			
11 or Older			x	
Health of Child				
Legally Deaf			x	
Legally Blind			x	
Dental Problems (May Require Treatment)		x		
Orthopedic Disorder (May Require Treatment)		x		
Seizure Disorder (May Require Treatment)		x		
Traumatic Brain Injury			x	
Education of Child				
Achieving below Grade Level		x		
Needs Emotional Handicapped Education (Self-Contained Classroom)			x	
Has a School Behavior Plan			x	
Has Serious Behavior Problems at School (Multiple Disciplinary Referrals)			x	

Characteristics Checklist for Placement Matching Mark "X" for all that apply.				
Maybe = depending on specifics	**Yes**	**Maybe**	**No**	
Characteristics and Behavior of Child				
Frequently Wets Bed		x		
Frequently Wets during the Day			x	
Has Difficulty Maintaining Personal Hygiene		x		
Frequently Soils Him/Herself			x	
Masturbates Frequently and/or Openly			x	
Has a Problem with Lying		x		
Has a Problem with Stealing			x	
Frequent Physical Altercations with Other Children			x	
Tends to Abuse Animals			x	
Frequently Destroys Personal Property			x	
Frequently Uses Explicit Language		x		
Engages in Self-Harm (Cutting, Head Banging)			x	
Has Difficulty Accepting and Obeying Rules		x		
Has a History of Inappropriate Sexual Behavior			x	
Has Sexual Identity and/or Transgender Issues			x	
Sexually Active Teen			x	
Has a History of Running Away			x	
Has a History of Setting Fires			x	
Substance Misuse History			x	

Characteristics Checklist for Placement Matching Mark "X" for all that apply.				
Maybe = depending on specifics	**Yes**	**Maybe**	**No**	
Has a History of Throwing Urine or Feces			x	
History of Juvenile Delinquency Involvement			x	
Child Mental Health				
Has a Mental Health Diagnosis			x	
Prescribed Psychotropic Medication			x	
Has Emotional Issues Requiring Therapy at Present		x		
Has Emotional Issues Requiring Long-Term Therapy			x	
Has a History of Psychiatric Hospitalization			x	
History of Psychiatric Residential Treatment			x	

Reading the list hurt. If you were in foster care, people assumed you were a psychopath or a criminal, that you'd done something wrong to be taken from your family, instead of the other way around. Kids in the system: we were defective, unlovable, unwanted. We had no rights, and when we acted out because we couldn't take it anymore, it only added another column onto their fucked-up spreadsheet.

A photo was clipped to this part of the home study. In the shot, Jack wore a suit and tie and fancy shoes, shined up and two-toned, white on black. His dark hair, flecked with gray, was thinning. He wore glasses and smiled without showing any teeth, as if he were self-conscious. He looked slightly nerdy—more like a James than a

Jack, and much older than his wife. She was seated in a chair, and he stood behind her, like maybe she was taller than him and he was trying to hide it. I did a double take on the wife. Samantha was smoking hot. She had on a pretty dress with a dangly necklace and earrings to match. She had blonde hair. Fair skin. Crisp blue eyes.

Sky could pass for their kid easily. I could see it: the braces, the straight white teeth, gathering around the Christmas tree, lights strung along the roof, Santa with reindeer in the yard. They'd send out Christmas cards each year with a photo of their family on the front. Carve a big turkey. It was so far away from anything I had experienced that I had trouble believing they were for real. There was a photo of their house, and a page attached listing the details. A mansion, basically—12,000 square feet and next to a large park. Ten bedrooms, eleven baths, with two acres. A live-in housekeeper. Landscapers. A pool with a cabana. A putting green.

I thumbed through to the completed form of all the things this family had to do and provide to get certified to adopt from foster care: fire escape plan, locked box for medicines and chemicals, sixty hours of parenting classes, CPR and First Aid certification, individual and couples interviews, fingerprinting, and background checks.

Any horny asshole could have a baby, but to adopt one you had to get security clearance from the Pentagon.

I thought about our parents. The baggies of crystal meth. The smell of the trailer, mold and mice shit. The scabs on Papa's skin. Mom cowering when Papa got violent. Curling up with Sky on our mattress, waiting out the yelling and shattering glass, as much to comfort myself as her. But we had been safe there, until the second that we hadn't.

I flipped to the income sheet next and blinked hard. The Fielders were worth over 200 million dollars. Two hundred million. I had to read it three times to make sure I had it right. Sky would be rich. I could never give her what these people could, a fact that didn't make me happy like it probably should, which made me feel guilty and angry at the same time. A boxing match raged inside my head. I was both fighters, and still, I was losing.

From the hall, I overheard Harrison, "good kid . . . misunderstanding . . . lots of transition . . ."

Transition, my ass. The word implied movement, and I wasn't going anywhere. But Sky? Harrison had found a family for her worth 200 million.

I read back through every line of the report, wanting to find some awful detail that had been overlooked that would prevent them from getting her. But there was nothing. They were clean, at least on paper. I was just about to close the folder when I got to the last report, a section about how Sky had come into care. Paper-clipped to it was the photo of us together, the one taken that day at social services in Sweetwater—the original, without either one of us cropped out. It about broke me. Why should the county have a photo of us when I didn't even have one? I slid it into my journal.

Harrison came back into the room, picked up the folder in front of me. "Good news. You've been let off with a warning." He smiled like he was proud of himself, but I didn't really care anymore.

Since then, I've been thinking about that file nonstop, trying to make sense of it. And here's what I've come up with.

Sky doesn't know about the Fielders yet.

How can she miss what she's never had?

Why should I trust the Fielders just because they have money? Why should I trust anyone at all to take care of what is my responsibility?

Time's up. By next Friday, this is over.

♦ 9 ♦

May 26, 2008

The Plan, by Ben Rayner

1. *Create a new routine: Go to the library every morning, so people get used to me leaving with my backpack and not getting back until late in the evening.*
2. *Get directions: Swipe a road atlas from the library and plot out a route.*
3. *Money: Take $$ from roommates as payment for the things they've stolen from me.*
4. *Buy time: Leave a few of my things behind to make it look like I'm coming back—like I haven't run away.*
5. *Hitchhike to Eden Park.*
6. *Take the Ramseys' truck.*
7. *Drive home and load up supplies. Canned goods, sleeping bags, lighter, guns, ammo, road atlas, tarps, cookware, water jugs, gas can.*

8. *Pick up Sky: Drive to Wingate. Wait as long as it takes for an opportunity to get Sky.*
9. *Start our lives over again and don't look back.*

* * *

June 1, 2008

No one looked at me twice when I left Xavier. I found a ride easy. When I got to the Ramseys' place, I hopped the fence and made my way through the field. The Ramseys were good people, and I felt guilty borrowing their truck without asking, even if it was an old beat-up Chevy they only used during hay season.

At first, I couldn't find the keys. I looked in the ignition, behind the visor, inside the glove compartment, and came up empty. I was about to give up and hike to the next farm over when I peeled back the moldy floor mat, and bingo—a single key. After the Chevy finally started, I got back on the main road and took the next turn at the No Trespassing sign in front of our old dirt driveway. I remembered painting that sign for Papa, and him nailing it to that oak. Never mind that it wasn't our land and never had been.

I drove the overgrown path toward the pile of brush covering the survival pit. Our trailer leaned toward the earth like a headstone. Seeing it again was a complete soul grinder. The empty chicken coop, broken tire swing, Samson gone. Memories of Mama and Papa—their graves just beyond. The silence, all that nothingness, so heavy it took shape and form all its own.

At the pit, I dragged away the branches, flipped over the plywood covering, and climbed down, collecting things I thought we'd need.

After that, everything went according to plan. I picked up Sky, and we put some miles between us and Wingate before dark. Then we made camp at a recreation area, which is where we are now. Sky's still asleep, which is good. I'm worried she's getting sick, so I'm letting her rest a little longer. We're not safe yet, but I'm optimistic. I have to be. Moving. Taking action. Feels so much better than waiting—putting our lives in someone else's hands. Plus, it's good having Sky with me. We're together, as it should be. I'm her brother. And I don't plan on leaving her.

Sun's coming up. Nothing better than a West Texas sunrise, in my opinion. Heavy clouds on the horizon, though, so rain is on its way. I'd best get us moving. People will be looking for us now.

★ ★ ★

June 4, 2008

The best laid plans. Steinbeck, I think. But what does it matter?

I.

Fucked.

Up.

I hurt Sky. I hurt myself.

I can't get a good breath. My head feels like it's going to explode.

They handcuffed me to the hospital bed. A cop sits outside my door.

They talk as if I'm not here. And most of the time, I'm not. Not really.

Surgery. Concussion. Stitches.

Infection. Pressure. Internal bleeding.

I don't really care what happens to me now.
I deserve the worst of it, which doesn't mean I'd change a thing.
There's right and wrong.
Harrison had told me that sometimes loving someone meant letting them go. But he was full of shit. It's the exact opposite.
If you love someone, you fight like hell for them.

♦ 10 ♦

2019

Laura sits next to me cross-legged on the floor with her back to the futon. Bella is curled up next to me. I turn the page but there are no more entries. For a moment, I've gotten so wrapped up in Ben's story that I've forgotten how it ends. Of course, there are no more entries. My brother died in that hospital, just like they told me.

I put down the journal and bite my lower lip to keep from crying. I look at Laura, and tears roll freely down her cheeks. I almost laugh because her face is a mess. Mascara streaks down to the corners of her mouth. She allows herself to feel so much for others. I reach out my hand to wipe away the black smudges beneath her lower lids, but at the last minute, I draw back. I want to be closer to her, but I can't risk it. This is also an ending I know well.

Laura swipes a hand across her own cheek and takes my shoulder and pulls me to her. Her touch surprises me, but I allow myself to be held. I place my head in the crook of her neck, unsure how long I should stay there. I'm not used to being comforted, but I want to be—especially, I think, by Laura. When she lets go and leans away, I'm as relieved as I am unsettled.

"So, did you know any of this?" Laura asks.

I clear my throat and rub my hands across the thin spiraling wire holding the notebook together. "Only some of it." I count on my fingers the things I just learned. "I don't know how to get a grip on it. I imagine it's sort of like being blind and having everyone tell you what you look like, and then—boom—you get your sight back and find out you've got bad hair and crooked teeth—and everyone was trying to spare you from it." It makes me wonder what else my brother has kept from me.

"Sounds to me like he was desperate to keep the two of you together," Laura says. "And he was just a kid."

"It's weird because I never thought of him like that. But when I look at the photo of the two of us"—I glance at my phone, at the image—"I see a boy."

"Can you see a little girl too?" Laura asks. "One who never asked for any of this? One who needed protection and didn't get it?"

I rub my hand down my jeans, feel the outline of a few more pills left in my pocket. I want to take them—need to. But then I think about what I just found out. My parents died of a meth overdose. They were addicts. I need to be more careful.

As if she's read my mind, Laura unfurls herself and walks to the kitchen. She grabs two sodas from the fridge, and hands one of them to me before sitting back down. It's like a consolation prize at the fair. Instead of winning the life-sized stuffed teddy bear, I get a pencil eraser. I pop the top, which exhales at the same time I do.

"So he never made it out of that hospital?" Laura says.

I sag. "He's been dead for more than a decade; you'd think I'd be over it by now."

"No one ever gets over something like that," she says. "So, back to the million-dollar question: Who's the patient at Banner, and why does he have your brother's things? And don't tell me it's your old caseworker, because the guy in the photo isn't old enough."

I shrug. I tap the journal against her leg. "I know you love a good mystery, John Grisham and all." I point to her end table. "But it doesn't really matter anymore, does it?"

Laura seems unconvinced. She wrinkles her forehead, picks up the journal, and pages through it. She stiffens and yanks my arm. "Whoa," her eyes widen, and she blinks hard. "Hey, some pages were torn out." She runs her finger across a quarter inch of paper still attached to the spiral binding. She flips a few blank pages past the perforation. "There's more writing! Look. Right here!" She holds up the journal, and sure enough, there are a few pages just before the back cover that have scribbles on them.

It's not possible. I shake my head. "Laura, seriously, I can't take any more of this. You realize that every time you come up with some new angle, my brother dies all over again for me."

"I know, and I'm sorry. But look." She shoves the notebook into my hands, and I take it. I stare at the page in front of me. Immediately, I can see that the handwriting is different—almost illegible. I squint. I make out a sentence or two. "It says something about getting picked up by a semitruck in Danville. He talks about disguising himself, growing out his hair and beard, wearing a skullcap—I can't quite read this part—he's worried about someone with the initials ABT finding him. Evidently, he was supposed to meet someone in Houston, but is on the run instead. Oh, and his name is Zane now. Clever." I toss the journal back to the floor between us. "Mystery solved: the patient is a thief named Zane from Danville who stole my brother's shit."

Laura grabs the journal off the floor and puffs air through her tight lips. She opens the journal to the back page again. "No, look, he writes the same way. Listen to this: 'Oil rigs bobbed their heads like they were drinking from a river I couldn't see.' I mean, the dude is seriously flexing. He's a writer, your brother." She hands it back to me. "Finish reading it. There's only one more page."

I close the cover. I don't need to read the last page that some stranger wrote. "Here's what I think. The guy in the hospital is definitely not Ben. Ben says he left a few of his things behind at Xavier to make it seem like he was coming back. Once the guys in the house heard he was dead, one of them probably took his stuff. Those were bad kids, remember? Kids who'd been in trouble."

"Okay, fair enough. But why would one of those kids keep the photo of you guys all this time? It wouldn't mean anything to him."

I think about the framed photo I keep in my room at Manor House, the one of the girl with her family in Paris. Heat fills my cheeks. "People are weird. Who knows why anyone does anything?" I stand and step away from the journal, the couch, Laura. Laura gets up too, walks toward me like I'm a child about to run into traffic.

"Okay, so what about the missing pages?"

I groan and thrust my hands into the air. "I don't know. Maybe the guy used them to throw away his gum or make paper airplanes. It doesn't matter. I can't keep doing this."

"I get it, Biscuit. I do." Laura skims the page in front of her. "But—"

I grab her by the shoulders. "Do you ever listen to yourself? All that optimism and positivity. *Everything's going to turn out right in the end.* But it doesn't. Most of the time, in fact."

"I admit to a cheery disposition," Laura says.

"*It's a different guy!* There aren't any pages after the accident because Ben died, and someone stole his journal. I'm done. All this hope is killing me."

She puts her hands on top of my shoulders, mimicking me. With mine on top of hers, it's like we're at a middle school dance. A shock of warmth fills my stomach. A small, growing ball of fire I need to extinguish.

"Biscuit, hope is the thing with feathers." She manages to keep a straight face.

"If hope had feathers, my family in Eden Park plucked and ate it. That's what happened to hope." I take my hands off her shoulders and create distance between us. Laura walks to the futon and sits. Bella joins her. She pets Bella and stares across the room.

"Can we please do something else? Anything? I'm begging you," I say. But as soon as the words leave my mouth, I realize the assumption I've made. Why would she hang out with me when there's nothing left to solve anymore, no reason for me to be in her apartment? We will go back to regular meetings and social services forms and safety checks. I'm an idiot. She was interested in the mystery of my brother. She was never interested in me.

Laura keeps petting Bella without looking at me. I hurry to gather my things, almost falling as I slip on one shoe and then the other, while hopping in between. I'm about to open the door when she yells, "Hey! Where are you going? You said anything, right?"

I freeze mid-step. "Nowhere, I just didn't think you heard me." I turn back toward the room and face her. I lower my things onto the countertop. She is smiling. For a moment, it's all that there is. I recover.

She chews on a thumb, rubs the top of her head. "I'm not used to asking for help, but I might be in trouble here. Plus, you said you'd do something, anything else." She lifts a piece of paper off a stack on the end table and hands it to me. "So I printed up these flyers and left them in local coffee shops, but now I'm panicking. I don't think anyone is going to come. What if no one shows up?"

I read the flyer. Her fundraiser for the wet shelter is in two days. "Why didn't you tell me?"

"You needed to focus on midterms. And this stuff was going on about your brother. And, as I mentioned, I'm not good at asking for help."

"People showed up to the last one, right? The one you did for the transgender community?"

"Yeah, but that was part of a huge Austin Pride event that they promoted the heck out of. This one's on my own.

DHHS wouldn't commit to sponsoring it. They're using the success of the event to gauge public interest."

"Well, no one ever asks me for help, so I happen to be available," I say. "But you should know, this morning I confused my toothpaste with my sunscreen, so you get what you get." Laura, the optimistic, capable woman I've come to know, looks shaky. I'm excited to reverse roles, to be the one helping her instead of the other way around. And I'm ready for our relationship to be about something other than my brother. "Kidding. Where's your laptop?" I ask. She points to the kitchen counter. I open it. "Lucky for you we just finished a course on social media marketing." She looks over my shoulder.

"So you know what you're doing," Laura says, with the lilt of a question on the end of it. Her voice sounds hopeful.

"I only slept through part of this class. And I passed. Barely, but still." I want to help her, even though she really should have picked someone else. "So, first thing. We hit up all the event listings in the city. *Visit Austin. The Austin Chronicle. Austin American Statesman. Austonia.*" I click away at rapid speed. Laura chews on her fingernail, and I gently remove it from her mouth before continuing to type. "Okay. That should take care of the old people with money who still read the newspaper. Now Ig, TikTok, SnapChat, YouTube, Facebook, Twitter." I swivel the laptop toward her. "Type in your login info."

She stares at the screen.

"No way. You don't use any of them?"

"Facebook, sometimes," she says, embarrassed.

"Alrighty then. We'll create accounts for you." I walk her through each platform, choosing usernames and passwords that she can remember. Then we get down to business. "See these people? They're influencers. These over here? They care about social causes. I'll post a quote about the homeless, and then in the comments I'll mention your event. What's a good quote I can use?"

"Oh, um. Okay. How about a quote from Wayne, with his photo?" She grabs a few papers from the coffee table and looks through her notes. "Here's one: 'Some days I'm invisible. Others, I'm a freak. I want you to see me as something else. Or just see me. We can go on from there.'"

"Awesome. I mean, not that he said that, because that's super sad. But it'll definitely be sticky."

"Sticky? You learned all this in one class?"

"Well, my adoptive mother was the queen of philanthropic events. I know my way around party planning and wealthy donors. Okay, now we need video."

"I don't shoot video."

"*Everyone* under the age of thirty shoots video."

She shrugs. "Not everyone. I like stills. Everything already moves too fast for anyone to know what's really important. I'm a detail person. It has nothing to do with age."

I arch one eyebrow. "If you say so. But we've got to shoot something. How about you tell me about the show? Just start talking." I use my iPhone. I start recording.

She smiles. I watch the screen to make sure I'm keeping her in the frame. She gathers herself. Flexes her fingertips. Pulls her shoulders back, the way she did on the basketball court. As she speaks, I try to keep my hands steady. Her voice echoes in the loft, strong and self-assured. She gestures toward the portraits on the wall with a sweep of her arm, and I remember her fast break on the basketball court, the layup she made with the others watching her as if the points were a given. I study her, in a way I haven't—in a way I've wanted to, but couldn't because it seemed too intimate. The camera shields me in some way.

She has a hand on her hip, knees bent, a balanced stance that says *I can do this. Watch me.* But her fingertips drum, a nervous tic against her waist. I zoom in on her face. Her eyes dance with enthusiasm as she speaks—shining brown with flecks of gold—a gravel-shaped scar to the right of her brow. I realize she is right. I want to stop time—freeze the frame. I want to capture the expression on her face, the one that gives off such fierce warmth that I can't bear to look at it for very long.

"What next?" she asks.

I regain my senses. "I edit it and upload it. Then to make all of this keep going viral, you *have to* respond to any comments that come in, because it works as some kind of an algorithm, but don't ask me what that is." I sit in a chair and Laura stands behind me. "You're hovering," I say.

She sits, but her legs bob up and down. Her computer is running too slow to edit the movie file, so I click to see which applications are still open so we can close some of them to free up some working memory. Her email pops up. I'm about to close it when I see *Ben Rayner* in a subject line.

"What the fuck, Laura? Who are you emailing about this?"

"Let me explain."

"Jesus Christ. Un. Fucking. Believable."

She holds up a hand, stopping me. "It's not a big deal, really. I just filled out the paperwork to get Ben's death certificate from Texas vital records department, and—"

"You did what?"

"If Ben is dead, there should be a death certificate. And if there is one, you have your answer. But if there's not—"

"Why are you doing this?" I stand and grip the edge of the countertop. My knuckles turn white.

"Because you loved him, and he could be alive. That man could be him." She swivels her stool to face me, inches her head lower, beneath my own so I have no choice but to meet her eyes. "I'm sorry," she says. "I was going to tell you once I knew something definitive. I did it after I talked to Dr. Nez. I didn't see the harm in it."

"Oh my God, you're obsessed."

"I did it before the journal came. It's not a bad idea, though, right? I mean, admit it. There should be a death certificate."

"Sure. Brilliant."

She tilts my chin up. Her face inches from my own. "Why is it so hard for you to even consider the possibility that it could be Ben?"

I give up, let the weight of my chin rest inside her palm. "You want to know the reason I'm not on a bus to Arizona right now?" The truth. Heavy as a Texas rain. My voice quivers. "Because I know my brother. If he were alive, he would've found me. And if he's not dead, well, that's even worse."

"How could that be worse?"

"Because it means he gave up on me—decided his life was better off without me in it. I've been able to live with his death, just barely—but if he abandoned me—if he just threw me away . . ." I bite my lower lip, trying to hold it together as I finish my thought. "He was the only person who really knew me. And he fought for me, stood up for us when no one else would. Protected me. And I hold onto that because, just maybe, it means I was worth protecting. That he saw something in me that no one else sees."

She trails her fingers across my cheek before putting her hands together, almost in prayer. She dips her chin, rests it atop her fingertips. "Look, I hear you. You knew your brother, and if he didn't die, he would've come looking for you. But maybe there was a reason he couldn't. Maybe there's an explanation. I just think there's something to the missing pages . . . the section that's been ripped out. I skimmed that last page. He mentions sending you letters, never knowing if you got them." She takes my hand, sandwiches it between her own. "What if you could have a different ending than you were left with—for both of you? Maybe even a beginning?"

I stare up at the ceiling and then close my eyes. "Laura, I swear. I wish I had a ski resort to sell you in Amarillo."

A sly grin starts at the corner of her mouth. "Well, it does snow in Amarillo, and there's some pretty substantial elevation. Texans love to ski. I think you might be onto something."

I roll my eyes at her and heave a sigh. "Laura, pay attention to what I am saying. My brother, Ben, died. There weren't any letters. And once you get the death certificate, maybe you can just drop this whole thing. But for now, I'm begging you." I wriggle my hand out from between hers. "Please. Send the journal back to Dr. Nez and move on."

"Okay, okay. But you know who I am now. You've been warned."

I like that she says that I know her. And I do—at least the parts she's shown me—the dogged determination and big heart. Her struggle to keep boundaries, worse than my own.

"I still need your help. C'mon, forgive me." She takes one of my hands and raises it above the keyboard, jiggles it up and down like I'm a puppet—trying to make me type. I think about when I broke into her apartment, and the day I passed out on her futon.

"Forgiven," I say, and start typing, hoping that we are friends, and that we can finally put my brother to rest.

11

2019

I HANG A SIGN for the auction. Laura paces in front of her photos. I prop open the door to the stairs leading up to her loft apartment. She's dressed up in a sporty black Prana dress with spaghetti straps, her shoulders tense, lats tight, rock-hard lumps. She wrings her hands together, then shakes them out. Light jazz plays from a portable Bluetooth speaker. I set out trays with brie wedges and grapes. I fill glasses of wine, donated from a classmate of mine's father, who owns a Texas winery. As I promised him, I display and rotate the bottles so that the labels are clearly in view. I watch Laura adjust the pens and clipboards on a long table we borrowed from her office. Each clipboard lists the title of the image, along with a suggested starting bid. It's a silent auction. I realize I'm nervous for Laura—that I'm praying for people to start showing up.

And then, they do.

One by one, citizens of Austin, philanthropists, social workers, students, and art collectors fill the space.

Conversation hums. Laura works the room, smiling warmly at each person, touching their arm or their shoulder. I recognize a few of her teammates from the morning pickup game. I watch people as they stand in front of the photographs. At times it seems like they are in a church, observing the stations of the cross like I did during Lent—giving reverent time to each one. I wander over to the auction table and look at the bids on the clipboards. I stop at Wayne's. Someone has written in an opening bid, but nothing follows it. I pick up the pen. I double the bid. It doesn't matter that I can't afford it. It's worth more, and I want to drive up the price. I chew on the inside of my cheek. Either someone will outbid me, or I'll come up with the money. Providing I can keep my job. Lately I've been missing too many shifts.

I scan the room and spot Laura. Next to her, a woman, an older version of Laura, stands with a maternal arm across her back, straightening one of the straps of her dress. Laura places a hand on top of hers and rests it there for a moment. I look away quickly, as if I've intruded, even though the moment was public, set in a crowded room. I busy myself with setting out more hors d'oeuvres. Of course Laura has a mother. Everyone does. But I realize how little I know about Laura's life—and how much she knows about mine. I think about the file she likely has on me, pages and pages of notes—what she knows about me and my adoptive mother—Samantha Fielder—a woman who once looked at me the way Laura's mother is—like she was the greatest gift in the whole world.

The woman wears a neatly tailored suit, with a silk blouse and fashionable heels. She carries herself with assurance—her posture, her gait, all convey confidence. She seems almost regal. This, I think, is what Laura will look like in twenty years—and the thought warms me. I watch her break away from Laura and move toward the clipboards. I resist the urge to sneak a glass of wine. I'm trying hard to be good—if for no other reason than to be the kind of person who might be a part of Laura's life. I grab a bottled water instead and wander over to Laura's mother. I want to know more about Laura, and if Laura won't tell me, well, maybe her mother will.

I approach and say "Hello," just to alert her to my presence. I feel as though I've interrupted a conversation between her and the photo. And maybe I have, because her eyes never leave the image.

"This one," she says as I stand next to her. "I think it's my favorite." The image is of a Black woman, one shoulder strap of her dress down, nursing a baby, while the other child in front of her chews on the end of a plastic bag. The hem of a man's coat partially obscures the scene, as a dollar drifts toward the ground in front of her.

"Ah," I say, as if I'm an art aficionado. "Yes."

"Maybe because I was a single mom, trying to bring up that one," she points over her shoulder to Laura. "I wanted her to be a lawyer, like me. She's so smart, and I thought she was wasting opportunities I'd had to fight so hard for to achieve myself—that she could have so easily. We fought a lot over that." The woman reaches out her hand like she's grasping for something, before taking her hand and placing it thoughtfully against her chin. "But this—she was born for it."

"Hard to argue that," I say. I need more from her, some insight from this woman who raised Laura. And she seems willing—already opening up. "Do you think that's why she became a social worker? Because of your struggles as a single mom?" I'm prying, yes, but the moment feels almost like a confession in a cathedral—a place to share secrets.

"Mmm. Maybe. Though I had a bit of a love-hate relationship with people who worked for the county. There were a few good ones. I look back and I know she had to do the work. That heart of hers might as well beat on the outside of her chest."

"I bet you have some good stories about her," I say.

She runs a delicate fingertip along her collarbone. "We had an apartment with a fireplace. And one day she heard birds chirping. Then they were screeching. I told her to leave the things alone, but she became convinced that their mother wasn't coming back for them—that they were going to starve to death. So she opened up the flue and took those three scrawny, flesh-colored, featherless birds into her hands and placed them in a shoe box. She researched everything—what to feed them, how to keep them warm. But the mom hadn't abandoned them, and she came down the chimney looking for them and flew right into the window. It killed her instantly, and Laura cried for a week because she'd killed their mother. They hadn't needed her help. I told her that it didn't matter. Now they did. More than ever. She took on that responsibility like it meant life or death for her very self."

"Did the baby birds live?"

"Two of the three. She buried the third one next to its mom beneath a tree in the courtyard of our complex. Even after she set the two fledglings free, I'd find her under that maple, putting out flowers and singing songs. That big heart.

No way to rein it in. Even when she can't do a thing, or it backfires—try to tell her otherwise."

Laura's mom writes down a bid and walks away. "Nice meeting you," she says, though we never introduced ourselves. I glance at the sheet of paper. Her daughter has listed a suggested opening bid of $500.

Her mother has bid $5,500.

Laura moves to the middle of the room, clinks her glass a few times, and others join. The high ceiling of the loft makes it sound like wind chimes. When the room quiets, Laura says, "I want to thank you all for coming." She goes on to explain the wet shelter and the funds that the auction will help provide to build it. She lets everyone know that the auction will end promptly at nine PM. And when she is done, people go to the tables to up their bids.

I realize how worried I've been for Laura. How much I've wanted this to work for her. I am suddenly hungry, and I walk to the counter where I take a small plate and fill it with brie and grapes and crackers. I watch Laura and her mother, the ease between them. I envy it. I wonder what my mother is doing now—if she misses me at all.

* * *

The last of the guests have left and, after the door closes, Laura collapses into a heap on my shoulder. I prop her up and look her in the eye. "You did it!" I tell her. "How much did you make?"

She tallies up the sheets of paper. "Thirty-two grand and change," she says. Her smile stretches to her ears. "A fantastic start. Added to the grants we applied for, and we have enough to break ground on the annex." She throws a fist into the air, turns in a hopping circle. "Yes!! Unbelievable." She hugs me, and maybe I imagine it, but when I try to let go, she lingers there. A moment passes between us, but then she gives an extra squeeze, and says, "Thank you. I couldn't have done this without you."

"Sure you could have."

"No, not really. I didn't think anyone would show up. I was convinced my work wasn't any good. I didn't think anyone would buy a single piece. But you believed they would. I saw that you bid on one of the images. That changed everything."

"Thank God I got outbid, though. I have no idea how I would've paid for that!"

We laugh. "Oh, Biscuit, I'd have had you walking Bella for me, doing dishes, alphabetizing my books, creating a website for me."

"I'm happy to create a site for you," I say. "That's actually a fantastic idea."

"Alright, one thing at a time," she says.

Seeing her happy makes me happy too. I follow her around the loft, picking up plates and napkins. Bella vacuums bits of cheese from the floor, sniffing out those pieces that have disappeared from our view into cracks and crevices and seams. At the sink, I stand next to Laura as she scrubs silverware and glasses, and I dry them with a soft towel. Our shoulders touch. It feels so normal, so domestic. Just like I imagined.

"I met your mom," I say. "You guys seem close."

"Mmm. Wasn't always that way, but yes." She hands me a trivet. "How about you? I mean, I know you and your mom don't speak now, but I don't really know much about what happened or what it was like once they adopted you. You keep acting like I know your whole history, but I really don't. I don't have any files from when you were a minor. What was it like?"

I snort out a laugh and almost drop the square glass plate. "How much time to you have?" I picture my mother and her perfect life. "It was like they'd brought home a feral cat—and they immediately tried to declaw me to save their drapes."

"Tell me," she says.

I stop drying dishes and stare at the backsplash. When Laura senses that I'm frozen, she turns to me. Her eyes crease with worry, and I give a nervous laugh. I tilt my head back as if I want to keep my story from spilling out. "Honest truth," I say. "I'm afraid you won't want to have anything to do with me if you know who I am and what I've done."

Laura sets down the glass in her hand and takes my chin gently between her fingertips and leans my face toward her. For a moment I think she might kiss me, but she doesn't, and I can't tell if I'm relieved or disappointed. It's a ridiculous idea, unrealistic at best.

"Biscuit," she says. "Not a chance."

♦ 12 ♦

2008

Sky

I RODE IN A long black car and stole glances at the woman adopting me. Mrs. Fielder sat across from me, legs crossed, with a giant teddy bear occupying the seat next to her. She was tall and beautiful and smelled like lilacs. In a graceful motion, delicate as a butterfly, she swept her fingertips through her gold hair, swirled it into a loose knot, and secured it with a jeweled clip. When she caught me looking at her, her smile widened, and she looked at me like I was a present she'd just unwrapped.

Less than an hour before, the caseworker who had flown with me from Abilene to Dallas had pressed her hand against my lower back and encouraged me toward a couple waiting at airport arrivals. The woman, Mrs. Fielder, bounced lightly on her toes as if she might break into a run, before allowing me to come to her, where she rested her hand atop my head, as gently as a falling leaf.

"Hi, Sky," she said. "It's good to finally meet you."

Behind her, a short, thin man wearing glasses and a suit and tie cleared his throat. His angular face ended in a narrow chin with a crease down its center, and his eyes darted like a ferret's. He took a few steps forward and without looking at me directly, he took my hand and shook it. With his fingers curled loosely around my palm, he nodded as if we'd agreed on something.

Before taking a different car to work, Mr. Fielder had deposited us into the long black vehicle with a driver, where Mrs. Fielder and I sat facing one another. Huge buildings rose inside a swirl of highways, concrete, glass, and metal. Cars flew past us at dizzying speeds, and I sank in my seat watching them dodge between lanes with zero space between them. My first impression of my new hometown: Dallas was in a hurry to get somewhere, and it seemed like it wouldn't mind running a person over to do it. I gripped the armrest.

When we finally slowed down, the driver took a few turns, and with each one the homes became grand and monstrous. When we veered into a driveway and stopped at an iron gate, Mrs. Fielder leaned out her window, pressed a few buttons, and the doors slowly opened, as if they were taking their time deciding whether or not to let us in. A mansion appeared with a fountain and flowers and huge windows with balconies. "You live here?" I asked.

Mrs. Fielder reached across to me and squeezed my hand. "You live here now, sweetie," she said to me. "This is your home." I stayed quiet. She moved her hand to the top of my head. "Honey, we're adopting you. You know what that means, right? We're your parents. Your family." Her brows formed dueling question marks. "I'm your mother now, you see?"

Was it that easy? Could you become a family just by saying it? And if it was that easy to do, wouldn't it be just as easy to undo it?

The driver opened the car door, and I hobbled out. Mrs. Fielder handed me my crutches. She grasped the back of my elbow to steady me across the driveway, which had smooth, shiny stones, like the bottom of a riverbed, leading to the front door. I teetered, my crutches catching between the pebbles, but Mrs. Fielder didn't let go of me until we were safely inside.

I entered a room gleaming like the sun. There were so many shades of white, I had to squint to keep the brightness from hurting my eyes. The walls and stairs and ceilings were white. Everything sparkled: crisp and clean and shiny. I gripped my crutches to keep my hands occupied. In Abilene, they had an antique shop with glass figurines and collectibles. This was that: a "look but don't touch" kind of place that filled me with awe and dread. I followed along as Mrs. Fielder led me past the crystal chandelier in the foyer. Handwoven Tibetan rugs, she told me. A Botticelli painting. Custom carved banisters.

From there, we descended to a wine cellar, a room that had its own temperature setting for bottles, as if the bottles were living things who might be bothered by heat. At Mr. Fielder's office, she held the door open for me to see, but we did not walk inside.

"You aren't to go in here. I'm not even allowed most of the time," she said. "He pays the bills, calls clients, goes through the mail. He has a very important job, and he's a bit of an introvert to say the least. He enjoys his privacy." I peered in and saw a huge wooden desk, rugs made from animal hides, a mounted deer head over a fireplace, a wall safe with a wheel like a captain might use to steer a boat. "Does Mr. Fielder hunt?" I asked. I couldn't picture him with a rifle.

Mrs. Fielder laughed. "He hunted a long time ago," she said. "Just trying to fit in with his clients, never for food. He quit after we got married. I couldn't stand all those dead eyes staring at me all around the house. Now he keeps them in his study hidden from me. Out of sight, out of mind." She stared into the open room. "He's a good provider, generous, and truly brilliant—" She glanced down at me. "Though I admit he can come off as a bit awkward in social situations. He makes up for it in other ways."

A library on the first floor displayed floor-to-ceiling books with a ladder on wheels to reach the top shelves. Its earthy scent brought me back to Ben—to the public library where we'd spent so many hours, where he'd taught me to read, his callused fingertips tracing the letters for me as I sounded them out.

"First editions, some of them signed," Mrs. Fielder said, running her hands along the spines. There was something about the shape of Mrs. Fielder's mouth, the tilt of her chin, that reminded me of Mama. On the flight to Dallas the social worker had told me that a person couldn't run out of love the way you could with other things. I hoped she was right. Maybe love wasn't like food or clothes, where it seemed best to hold something back for later, just in case.

Mrs. Fielder brushed her hands down her dress, smoothing out wrinkles I couldn't see. "Would you like to see your room?"

Mrs. Fielder helped me up the staircase and then down a long hall. Behind a thick, heavy door, with my name on a balloon attached to the handle, my new room opened up before me like a surprise party.

The ceiling, layered in tiers and painted with delicate pink roses at its edges like icing on a birthday cake, towered over me above an expanse of floor that seemed poised for spontaneous dancing. The bed rose like a stage, centered against the back wall, so high off the ground I could barely climb into it. Four thick, carved white posts led to a billowing pink-checkered canopy stretched across the top; its sides draped like theater curtains. Across the room, a princess with golden hair rode an armored horse through fields of bluebonnets. The painted mural stretched from corner to corner. I held onto the bedpost, suddenly dizzy.

Next to me, Mrs. Fielder stared at the wall and said, "We gave a photo of you to a friend of ours who's a children's book illustrator. Your caseworker told us that you like horses. It turned out quite lovely." The girl on the wall did look a lot like me, except she was wearing clothes I'd never owned: a ballerina ruffled pink dress, sequined shoes, and a sparkling crown. And—she was riding a shiny, muscular stallion, not an old, beat-up ranch pony like the ones Ben and I had ridden on the Ramseys' farm. The horse was magnificent: his black coat glistened in the sun, and he wore gem-studded saddle, bridal, and reins.

Across from the mural, tall windows filled the space with light and double glass doors led out to a balcony with an iron railing. We stepped outside.

"Promise me you won't lean over the edge," Mrs. Fielder said. "I'd be sick with worry."

I peered at the courtyard below and inched back toward her, where she placed her hands atop my shoulders to steady me.

Another door led to a walk-in closet almost as big as the bedroom. Shelves and racks and cubbyholes brimmed with enough shoes and clothes to wear a different outfit every day of the month. I ran my hands along the wooden hangers, atop the rows of dresses in pastel colors with floral patterns. I hid my disappointment. I missed Ben's hand-me-downs—tough, protective boy's clothes. I forced a smile and eyed my Hello Kitty suitcase that contained the few items I had from the hospital. "Will I be getting back any of the other things I left at Miss Cindy's?" I asked.

Mrs. Fielders lips puckered. "Surely you don't need any of those things anymore. You have all this. It's all yours. And anything you're missing, we can replace for you." Mrs. Fielder leaned down and adjusted the bandage on my foot. She smoothed my hair back from my forehead. "You know, I heard the doctor say that your leg will heal even stronger in the places it was broken. Isn't that something?" I stared at the princess on the wall again, her long hair trailing behind her, a path back to where she'd been.

★ ★ ★

That night, we sat down for a meal at a long table with twenty chairs. Mr. Fielder took the seat at the head of the table. Mrs. Fielder and I sat next to each other on one side of him. The rest of the table remained as empty as a dirt road in front of us. Lupita, one of the house attendants, came in from the kitchen and filled our water glasses. No one spoke. She left and returned quickly with warm bread snuggled inside a soft cloth. I was about to grab a roll when she used a pair of tongs to put one onto the smaller plate in front of me, alongside two forks, a knife, spoon, and a larger metal plate. My stomach growled, loud enough that everyone heard it.

Mrs. Fielder said, "Honey, have you ever said grace?" I stared at my reflection in the shiny metal plate. "You make the sign of the cross first, like this," she said, and she touched her fingertips to her forehead, chest, and shoulders. I tried it. She folded her hands together. "Then we say, 'Bless us, oh Lord, and these Thy gifts, which we are about to receive, from Thy bounty, through Christ, our Lord.'" Mr. Fielder said the prayer with her. After "Amen," Mrs. Fielder crossed herself again and said, "Don't worry, sweetie, you'll catch on soon enough. That's what catechism classes are for."

I took a large chunk of bread. "Okay, sure," I mumbled while chewing. Lupita placed a salad in front of me.

"Small bites," Mrs. Fielder said, "like this." She tore off a tiny crust of bread and put it into her mouth. After she swallowed, she said, "And we always finish before trying to say anything. Right?"

I tore off a piece of bread, eager to imitate her, and placed it on my outstretched tongue, without asking why small bites were useful if you were starving.

When the plate of spaghetti and meatballs appeared, my hunger took over. I ate as fast as I could, shoveling down spaghetti using the fork, but also my fingers to get all the stray pieces. I picked up a meatball with my hands, careful to take small bites of it, and as delicately as possible, licked a bit of sauce off my index finger and thumb.

Mrs. Fielder's face blanched. Her eyebrows peaked. "Let's use our napkin," she said. She picked up the white cloth from the table and wiped my chin and hands with it before resting it in my lap. "There, now." She seemed proud of herself, like I was a job well done, even though the spit I used had worked better.

That night I lay in the bed, surrounded by silence, with tears streaming down my cheeks. Everything was too big and empty. At some point, Mrs. Fielder came into my room. She picked up the teddy bear, the one that she'd brought to me at the airport, and sat on the bed next to me with it. She said, "Bigley Bear and I are good snugglers, especially when someone is sad or scared." She opened her arms, and I let her pull me to her. I curled into the warmth of her body, and we sat like that for some time. "It's a lot, isn't it? Change can be so hard." she said. "But I'm right here. And I'm not going anywhere." Her kind voice was like the sun on my face after a long winter. Her hands, soft like doe skin, wrapped around me. She looked at Bunny and gave him a squeeze. "Tell me about this one," she said.

"My brother gave him to me when I was born. I sleep with him every night."

"He's special, then. I'm glad you have him." She held Bunny, turned him over in her hands before bringing him up to her nose. Her eyes widened with alarm. "Oh dear, honey." She sniffed again, ran her fingernail over a brown spot on the material. "This is covered in mold. It's all along the seams."

I yanked Bunny away.

Mrs. Fielder's face softened; the corners of her mouth turned down. "Don't worry, sweetheart. We'll get him cleaned up. He'll be just fine—good as new." She swayed with her arms around me, a rocking motion that quieted my thoughts. I leaned into the comfort of being held, inhaled the smell of lilacs. In time, when my breathing slowed and I stopped trembling, Mrs. Fielder asked if I wanted her to read me a story about a bunny, and I said yes. She pulled a book from the row of shelves in my room. It was called *The Velveteen Rabbit*, and I remembered Ben reading it to me in the library in Eden Park. It was about a stuffed rabbit that wanted to become a real rabbit but couldn't until a child loved him. A little boy finally did, and just after that happened, the boy got sick and everything in his room had to be burned in order to protect him from germs. But the boy had loved the rabbit so much and so well that when he finally had to say goodbye, the rabbit became real and hopped away instead of dying in a fire. I felt sad for the boy, but happy for the rabbit. Mrs. Fielder said that love had saved them both, so that they could go on without each other.

After she finished the story, she went to my bathroom and came back with a cool washcloth. She wiped my raw, tear-stained face, dabbing it in the tender places. Mr. Fielder knocked on the doorjamb. "You coming back down, honey?"

Mrs. Fielder looked at me. "Do you want me to stay with you for a while?" she asked. I nodded. "In a bit," she said to him, and he shuffled off. Mrs. Fielder tucked her feet beneath the covers and pulled them up around our chins. She pressed Bunny and Bigley into my arms. I turned onto my side, and she slipped her arm around me and pulled me to her. I burrowed my head into her chest, worn out from crying, and allowed myself to fall asleep.

In the middle of the night, I startled awake. Mrs. Fielder was gone. Her place next to me was cool beneath my hand. I couldn't go back to sleep. I tried, but the emptiness of the room frightened me. The air conditioner hummed, the floors creaked, the bed was too soft, and I had never spent an entire night completely alone. I held onto Bunny and grabbed Bigley. I stripped off the covers and dragged them into the closet. I took two pillows. I left the light on. I curled up with my toys, rubbing Bunny against my chin, waiting for the sun to rise, as it always had—the only thing in my life that hadn't changed.

13

When summer was over, I put on the uniform for private school. A pressed white shirt, pleated skirt, and shiny patent leather shoes that I could see my reflection in, like little black mirrors on my feet. There was a blazer with a design woven with gold thread into the left side of the material just above my heart. The design was a crest, a picture of a lion with the word *veritas* on top and *fidelis* beneath. Mom explained those words were Latin for truth and loyalty or faithfulness. I hated the skirt but loved the blazer, which made me feel like a spy on a secret mission—the 007 of St. Mary's Academy.

Wearing the plaid skirt was just one of many rules I had to obey: Attend daily Mass, say grace before eating, sit up straight, raise your hand before speaking. I broke the code of student conduct without knowing it until I was in trouble. And even though the uniforms were supposed to make all the kids look the same, the girls whispered about me and avoided me at recess. I never told Mom. I was afraid she'd agree with them.

A few weeks into the school year, everyone lined up for a special assembly outside our auditorium. The governor of Texas had a niece who attended the Academy, and he was slated to speak to our school. About halfway through his speech, I needed to use the restroom, but I was sitting in the middle of a row, and the man kept droning on and on. Even I knew better than to get up and interrupt him by trying to jostle out of my row. I tried everything: I crossed my legs and squeezed my eyes tight. I pulled at the elastic on the waist of my skirt so it wouldn't put extra pressure on my belly. As soon as everyone clapped, I left with my row and headed straight for the girls' bathroom. But everyone else had the same idea, and there was a line, a long one, with girls bouncing up and down. I did exactly what I would have done back at Miss Cindy's when I couldn't hold it anymore and someone was using the bathroom. I headed outside the building, looked both ways, pulled down my underwear, and squatted right next to an old oak tree. Of course, the politician and the people he had with him crossed the lawn right in front of me. One lady gasped. They all looked away. My face flushed red, and I let go a flurry of apologies while smoothing down my skirt. They walked much faster after that, as if my words were chasing them.

Mom came to school later, clutching her pocketbook to her chest, lips quivering. She avoided the other moms, though they called out hello to her. I recognized the look—she would run out of patience, realize she'd made a mistake. As I swung my feet beneath my chair inside his office, Headmaster Goddard spoke to my mom.

"Mrs. Fielder, we want to give every child a chance to achieve, but I have to be honest, Sky is quite far behind, and as we've witnessed today, not just in academics."

"We talked about this before Jack enrolled her. We've donated very generously to this institution, and Sky is very bright. Given her background, she might need some special attention, but that's what we pay such a premium for at private schools like St. Mary's, right?" The toe of her high-heeled shoe tapped against the hardwood planks of flooring.

Headmaster Goddard continued speaking about me as if I wasn't there. Yes, he said, but there were and must be minimum standards of etiquette. He gave examples, in case Mom needed them. I didn't raise my hand or stand beside my desk when called upon. I belched and expelled flatulence at will. I used my hands to eat in the dining hall, more than I used utensils. I shoveled my food and spoke with my mouth full. My uniform was sloppy for most of the day, with pencil or pen marks, dirt from recess, food stains from lunch. I played too rough with the other children and said things that were inappropriate. And apparently now, there was the pressing issue of my "unfamiliarity with indoor plumbing."

My mother's lip twitched at the end of each of his sentences, as if he were slapping her. When he was done, she pressed her fingertips against her forehead and shook her head. "Enough. I've heard quite enough." She stood up and pointed at me. "Do you know what my daughter has been through? You should be ashamed of yourself. She belongs here as much or more than anyone."

Headmaster Goddard opened his mouth but no words came out. Mom grabbed my hand and without turning back to him she said, "Just do your job, Jim. If you want to keep it."

While she often referred to herself as my mother, this was the first time I had heard her call me her daughter. I lifted my chin high walking out of the school. I was proud that she stood up for me, but that night she scrubbed me in the tub like she might wash off the parts of me she didn't like. I told her I didn't need any help, but she said that my baths weren't thorough enough. This confused me, because I bathed at the Fielders more than I ever had in my life, and I loved it. I usually sat in all the bubbles until they went flat, adding hot water whenever I wanted—because it never, ever ran out. I also never had to rush because there weren't any other kids in the house waiting for the bathroom or banging on the door. But scrubbing didn't occur to me. Where would the dirt go except into the water where I was still sitting, getting me dirty all over again? But I kept those thoughts inside my head and let Mom scour me to a bright pink.

That night, I sat at the top of the staircase eavesdropping on my parents below.

"I'm just trying so hard, Jack. If you had seen the way those other mothers looked at me . . ." Her voice quavered at the end. "What am I doing wrong?"

"Nothing at all. Not a thing." My father came up behind her and placed both hands on her arms, rubbing them as if she might be cold. "Honey, it's just going to take some time. Look where she came from."

Mom swatted his hands away from her and wheeled around. "You mean because she came from a poor background? She can't help that, Jack. I was poor, you'll recall—and an orphan. Money has nothing to do with this."

"Of course it does. People always like to pretend it doesn't. But money matters." He poured an amber liquid into a glass and took a drink, circling her. "Would you have married an awkward nerd like me if I didn't have money?" He set down the drink. "Please don't answer that. It's okay. I'm not a stupid man . . ." He pulled her to him. "I love you, and because I do, I'd give you anything." Jazz music played at low volume. The whine of a trumpet. A sad violin. He swayed with her in his arms, before twirling her outward in a dance that left him empty-handed. Free of him, she sagged onto the chaise lounge, draped her body across it. I could hear her crying—and knew it was my fault.

He joined her on the couch, took her hand in both of his and held it. "Sam, don't go there. This isn't the same thing."

"I lost them all," she said. "I must be doing something wrong—being punished in some way. I know she needs me, but I want her to love me."

"Is there a difference?"

"Of course, there is."

A grandfather clock chimed inside the room. "Sam, let's focus on what you have, right? You finally have the healthy, beautiful little girl you always prayed for."

I chewed on the inside of my cheek. There was a big pause before my father spoke again. "Look at me. You're a good mother. This is all going to be fine. I'll talk to Jim and send a check, make another generous donation to St. Mary's." He held her chin in his hands. "We've got that gala on Thursday. Lots of investors there. You love that kind of thing. You've got to hold yourself together. Please don't fall apart on me. I need you."

"She needs me too," Mom said.

"Of course, yes," he said. "Then do it for her."

She whispered, "I just thought this would be easier."

I rose from the steps, tears filling my eyes, and crawled quietly back into bed. I stared at the pink-checkered canopy over my head and the princess galloping across the wall of my room. That was who they wanted me to be. A perfect version of myself. The girl in the mural: she didn't have freckles across her nose, and her smile showed perfect, straight white teeth, where mine were crooked and stained by the water in West Texas. I thought about my parents' words and my classmates' whispers. There was something wrong with me, and I wasn't sure it could be fixed. My chest tightened, and I gathered the sheet to my chin. If I wasn't careful, they would send me back to foster care.

After I was certain my parents had gone to sleep, but before the alarm system could automatically set for the evening, I took the few things I still had from my life before that had come to me at the hospital in the Hello Kitty suitcase: a couple of sets of clothes from Miss Cindy's, a get well soon card signed by my foster sisters and brothers, a hair clip that Jasmine gave me, a Slinky, and some ripped coloring books and broken crayons the hospital staff had given me to keep me busy.

I found the seams of the clothes and tore at them until I ripped the fabric into strips. I crumpled the pages of the coloring book. I shoved everything back into the Hello Kitty suitcase and stared at my bed for a moment. Bunny rested against my pillow. He was a ratty toy, falling apart, with matted fur and missing one eye. I had a million Beanie Babies and Bigley Bear, all brand new. I took Bunny from the bed. I shoved him into the suitcase, and zipped it closed. I wiped away snot and tears with the back of my hand. I made noise without meaning to, but no one seemed to hear me.

Down the stairs and into the attached garage. I rested the bag at my feet. I opened the lid and stared into the black hole in front of me. I choked back sobs, thinking about Bunny lost and alone forever in the dark. Giving him up seemed an impossible task. He was the only thing I had left of my brother. I could change my mind. I didn't have to do this, but the answer was clear. I lifted the suitcase, dropped it inside, and closed the lid. I was Sky Fielder, just as it said on my newly minted birth certificate. My father was Jack Fielder. Mother, Samantha Fielder.

Sky Rayner was gone.

♦ 14 ♦

I SPENT THE NEXT eight Saturdays at cotillions, where I learned from Ms. Cassandra Lee that there was a right way and a wrong way to use a knife and fork, chew, drink, walk, and even sit—and that girls were expected to do things differently than boys.

We sat with our legs crossed at the knee or ankle. We walked gracefully, envisioning a thread pulled through from our feet to the top of our head and balancing a book there. Boys were to take our coats—or wraps—usher us to our seats, pull out our chairs, offer to get us refreshments, carry our packages, open doors for us. It was as if the mere presence of a boy meant that we became incapable of doing anything for ourselves. When we learned the dances, I was thankful for the white gloves; I didn't have to touch the sweaty palms of the boys leading me around the floor. The other girls seemed to like the fox trot and waltzes. I stumbled over my feet, wishing I could spend my Saturdays playing dodgeball or tag.

Ms. Lee made me her special project, which included a bucketful of insults every weekend, dumped on me despite my best efforts. She used me as an example of "what not to do." She would say, "So, what is Miss Fielder doing wrong here?" When I crossed my legs at the ankle or knee, I left too much of a gap between them, which made me look like a cowboy who'd ridden too many horses. I strode across the room like a football player instead of gliding. I slouched over my food like a farmer. And I kept trying to lead on the dance floor. My first instinct was always wrong, and I began to picture myself as someone else in each instance in order to know what to do: "What would Ms. Lee do in this situation? How would Princess Diana rise from the table and walk across the room? What would my mother do with her hands? How would the Queen of England remove the bit of gristle stuck in her teeth?"

After two months, I graduated. In the grand hall, I posed for a photo with my mother, the huge room making me feel small. Mom held one corner of my diploma, while I held the other. I kept my gloves on so I wouldn't smudge the cream-colored edges of my accomplishment. Sky Fielder was officially a junior debutante, and in celebration, Mom took me to the salon to get my ears pierced. Two diamond studs decorated my earlobes, which remained red and angry for weeks. To prevent infection, Mom helped me take the earrings out, cleaned them with a cold foamy liquid, and then put the studs back in place—warning me that I had to keep the diamonds in my earlobes for my body to accept them. "We don't want to go back to square one again, do we?" she asked, and she put the medicine back under my bathroom cabinet, close at hand, just in case.

♦ 15 ♦

2015

I RODE THE HORSE, a dappled Holsteiner named Cobblestone, over the series of jumps, collecting him at the mark and feeling him stretch beneath me, forelock and canon clear of the rail, neck supple and arched with a willingness to please. Again and again, without any faults, we sailed through the course.

Mom stood with her arms crossed next to the trainer. She wasn't a stage mom. But my accomplishments were her accomplishments. And I was okay with that.

"Awesome!" Alex yelled. I posted over to my best friend, reached my hand down, and let her high-five me. She smiled. I had wanted desperately to play softball or volleyball at school, but Mom believed those kinds of sports held no promise for young women, and she enrolled me in equestrian lessons, which was how I became friends with Alex. While we shared a few classes at St. Mary's Academy, Alex and I became inseparable once we started riding together at the Trinity Equestrian Center.

"My time?" I asked. Alex showed me the clock. I dismounted and handed the reins to the groomer. "Not good enough to win the Junior Championship."

"It might be," Alex said. "And so what if you don't win? We all want to win. It's not life or death, you know."

But two weeks before, I had found Mom lying on the couch in the library, eyes closed, hair matted, face smeared with makeup she'd neglected to remove the previous night. Foundation and mascara stained the cushion behind her head. She had skipped daily Mass. I called out to her from the doorway, approaching steadily, saying her name. When she didn't respond, I took her arm and lifted it. She groaned, mumbled for me to leave her alone, and rolled over onto her side, hiding her face from me.

"Did something happen?" I asked, knowing the answer—life happened. Still, I racked my brain to recall something I did or said that had caused this.

I called my father, who was out of town. I explained the situation—asked him if I should get an ambulance or a doctor to the house. But we weren't those kinds of people. Getting help would ruin her reputation. People would know there was something wrong with her or with our family. He said she'd snap out of it, but not to leave her unattended.

So I slept on the couch across from her. I brought her food and begged her to eat some of it. I took a wet rag and cleaned her face. She let me brush the tangles out of her hair and change her clothes. She was there, but not. With her vacant, hopeless stare, she reminded me of the dead deer mounted in my father's office. It terrified me. I depended on her—needed her. She couldn't just leave me.

Now, across the paddock, I looked over at my mother and waved. She managed a smile, though her cheeks quivered, and she clasped her hands in front of her, leaning against the railing to steady herself.

When Alex took her turn in the arena, I watched her stride over to her horse, mount up, and, as if she and the horse were both bred for this, run a clean course in a slightly faster time than my own. And even though I needed to win—I wasn't envious—I was in awe. Alex's limbs were long and graceful, not unlike the bay she used for competition, a sixteen-hand Dutch Warmblood. Alex was tall, beautiful, easily agile, curvy in places where I remained flat and squared off. She pushed me and I pushed her, and together we both became better riders.

Outside of the arena, she broke the rules, often, and got away with it—sneaking out after curfew, shoplifting lipstick at Saks, wearing her uniform rolled at the waist so it sat more than the required two inches above her knee. At daily Mass, she slipped notes to me or drew on the missalette, sketching horns, a beard, and a pitchfork onto the black and white photo of Father Richards.

My parents tolerated my friendship with Alex for two reasons: One, because Alex's parents were major investors in my father's oil fund. And two: I never broke the rules like Alex did. I made the honor roll every term, donated my time volunteering with Mom at various Catholic charity events, and dated the boy they'd picked out for me, a Hemsworth look-alike named Scott Prior who attended St. Mark's Academy.

After Mass one Sunday, Alex and I stole away to her room to listen to Lady Gaga and P!nk, while we painted each other's nails. Her parents never seemed to question my background, and in fact seemed to think I was a good influence on their daughter. A package of Oreos sat between us, and Alex made quick work of emptying a sleeve.

"I'm guessing Scott will be there tomorrow?" She rolled her eyes when she said his name. My parents were holding a dinner party for some of my father's largest investors, and both Alex and Scott would be attending it with their parents.

I nodded. "Mom wants us out of the way. We can hang out by the pool until it's time to change clothes. It'll be fun!"

Alex selected black nail polish from a bin she placed on the floor in front of us. "Why do you like him so much? He's basic. You could do so much better."

"I don't know. I like him because he likes me—and, I guess, because I feel like that's who I'm supposed to like."

Alex crossed herself in mock prayer. "Jesus, Mary, and Joseph . . . Sky, this isn't the 1800s. You're not Jane Austen." She held one of the cookies out to me, and I didn't take it. "I bet he kisses like a hummingbird." She narrowed her tongue and darted it in and out between her lips.

I grabbed a pillow from the bed behind me and shoved it toward her face.

"Have you hooked up?"

I shook my head, cheeks burning.

"Why not? Don't you want to?"

I shrugged.

She froze with the nail polish still midair. "You honestly believe all that stuff they tell us in catechism class, don't you? I swear, if God had only wanted us to have sex to have babies, he wouldn't have let us have orgasms."

"Oh my God, please stop." I took the pillow back, covered my face with it, and pretended to scream.

"Orgasm. Orgasm? Orgasssmmmm!" she belted out the word like a song and held the last note. I held my side and tears poured from my eyes. "Seriously," she said. "We'd just lay eggs and a dude would swim by and fertilize them."

After I stopped laughing, I wiped the corners of my eyes. Alex curled her legs beneath her. "Hey, do you think I should get ink?"

I shrugged. "What would you get?"

"I don't know, maybe something ironic or edgy. You know, like the dragon in that old movie, *Girl with the Dragon Tattoo.* Or maybe something tribal, like Rihanna has on her hand."

"I haven't seen *Girl with the Dragon Tattoo.*" I didn't remind her that it was rated R, and I wasn't *allowed* to see it.

She lowered the strap of her tank top and twisted her back toward me. "I'd put it right there on the back of the shoulder blade. That would be rad."

"Truly," I said.

"Oh, or I could get one like P!nk. She has a bulldog with a Bible verse, which is totally random. Also, she inked a razor blade across the inside of her wrist with the word Insecurite—spelled wrong, but probably the point. I mean, she's a badass." She unfurled her feet from beneath her, wiggling her toes.

"Your mom would let you get that?" I already knew the answer.

"They really don't care what I do. That's what happens when you already have four older kids and think you're done—and then, oops. Surprise! I was a mistake. They're tired."

"Where are they, your brothers and sisters?"

"Spread out across Texas."

"You close to them?"

"Yeah, they kind of all took turns taking care of me when I was a baby. I was spoiled rotten, really. Then one by one they graduated, went off to college, got married."

"That had to be hard," I said. I stretched out onto my side, supporting myself with an elbow. I never spoke about my family—the one I'd buried along with my past, the gaping hole I filled with other things.

"All of a sudden I was an only child. It got awfully quiet around here." She gestured with her arms wide. "That's why I make up for it with a little chaos now and then. Keeps my parents' brains active. I'm helping them stave off dementia."

"I'm sure they're very grateful." P!nk started rasping out a bass-thumping girl-power anthem. I mouthed the words, while Alex belted them out.

The smell of garlic wafted from the kitchen, and Alex looked at her watch. "Gee, five o'clock already? Time for the early-bird dinner special." My stomach growled. "Those old people eat early." Alex held out another Oreo toward me. "You're too skinny. One nibble won't hurt."

I shook my head no and watched her chew the entire cookie before baring her blackened teeth at me with a huge grin. "Don't judge me," she said with a mouthful of crumbs. After she licked her lips, she took my right hand and held it firmly between her own. She dipped the brush into the nail polish, covering my imperfections with gentle swirls, and blowing soft puffs of air against my fingertips to help the paint dry quicker.

★ ★ ★

On the morning of my parents' party, I walked into the kitchen, dressed in my bikini, a towel draped over my arm. Mom handed two platters to Lupita, who ran off to the dining room with them. "I'm glad Scott's coming over early," Mom said. "He's a good Catholic boy. So handsome, don't you think?"

"Don't start," I said.

"That family. Seriously, three generations at Ivy League law schools. But it's not just the money. Top of his class, captain of the debate team, and he plays lacrosse."

I groaned, and she tugged at the towel. "You look thin. I'm glad you reined in that voracious appetite of yours. Finally. When you were little, you ate everything we put in front of you. We were afraid you'd be four hundred pounds." she said. And then she called out after me, "Don't forget to put on sunscreen!"

I knew the routine, the role I would play that evening as my parents' perfect daughter. I'd apply my makeup, exactly the way Mom had shown me: foundation, blush, powder, eye shadow, concealer, eye liner, mascara, lip gloss with a hint of color. Nothing over the top. Conservative. My hair would be brushed, shine added, sparkly headband matching my dress. I didn't want to ruin the idea that Mom had taken a blob of clay and sculpted it into a masterpiece to display in their foyer. At this point in our relationship, I wasn't about to become a kindergartner's ashtray hidden in the attic. As for my father, at events like this one he let Mom lead the way. He knew he was less than eloquent—that the clients loved Mom—liked the reputation of our family—our devotion to each other and the Church. The clients, guests, neighbors all knew I was adopted—though certainly not the circumstances that led to my placement—and they worshiped my parents for it, talking about me at fundraisers and over cocktails when they thought I couldn't overhear them.

"How wonderful my mother was for taking me in."

"What a life they had given me."

"And she wasn't even a baby!"

My mom would reply, "No, we were the lucky ones. God blessed us with such an incredible gift."

⋆ ⋆ ⋆

Alex arrived before Scott with a blue streak dyed through a single strand of her long, red hair. I lay on a chaise by the pool, and she lowered her head over mine, tossing her hair upside down, creating a starburst of sun over the edge of her shoulder. "What do you think? Did it last night."

"It's kind of a peacock blue, right? I like it. My parents will love it, I'm sure."

"Your mother already saw me walk through, and I thought she was going to stroke out. I waved at her and kept going." Alex slid out of her T-shirt and shorts, kicked off her flip-flops, and dove into the pool. I watched her glide beneath the water, a kick-ass mermaid avenger with iridescent hair. She created her own current and rode it back the other direction, effortless and playful, as at ease beneath the waves as a dolphin.

Scott arrived next, taking the chair on the other side of me, placing me in between him and Alex. There was little connective tissue between the two of them, except for me. He gave me a peck on the lips, shed his shirt, and used the diving board to show off with an arcing swan dive.

The three of us basked in the sun in between dips into the pool to cool off. I asked Scott if he would put sunscreen on my back, and Alex rolled her eyes. Scott squeezed a few dollops directly onto my shoulders and used his palms to move the lotion around in self-conscious swipes.

"Amateur," Alex said, taking the tube from him. She put a dab of sunscreen into each hand, rubbed them together, and then kneaded my back, massaging in the lotion without missing a spot. Red blotches on Scott's cheeks spread like wine spilled on a church altar as he watched.

We took turns selecting the music streaming outside, and Lupita brought us lunch and lemonade so we would stay out of the kitchen. When it was time to change for the dinner party, Alex and I went to my room to shower and get dressed, while Scott used the cabana.

In my room, Alex stripped off her bikini, strode across the room, and grabbed her dress from the hanger in my closet, where Lupita had placed it earlier. I tucked my chin, looked at the rug covering the hardwood floor, watched her without meaning to. I envied the way she moved, without shame or embarrassment, completely and utterly naked. Her body was perfect. Breasts high and round, suspended like two raindrops above the smooth skin of her abdomen. Her hips curved out from a tapered waist; a soft triangle of red hair spread like feathers between her legs. My own body was marked with secrets. When I felt out of control, undisciplined for what I'd eaten or missing an easy question on an exam, I would hate myself later, would scratch thin lines across my breasts and beneath my bikini line where no one could see, until I felt punished and relieved—a kind of penance I kept beyond the basic Our Fathers and Hail Marys. Alex had no scars on her skin.

At some point, I realized she had stopped moving, and I lifted my eyes, knowing I'd been caught staring at her. I started to apologize, but she didn't look angry to me or even surprised.

She moved toward me, never breaking eye contact, and when I tried to look away, she raised my chin so my eyes would meet hers. She stood in front of me, our bodies separated by an inch, so close I felt the warmth of her, smelled chlorine, the sweet citrus of lemonade on her breath. She took my hands, which hung at my sides, and held them inside of her own. Then, soft as a whisper, her lips met mine.

The kiss never strayed from my mouth, yet it touched every inch of my skin. My body shuddered, and a deep ache spread from the pit of my stomach to my chest. When she pulled away, I leaned in, breathing her inside of me like air. And it felt that way, like I'd been slowly suffocating until that very moment. She placed a hand against my cheek before gently letting go and disappearing into the shower.

At dinner that night, I fumbled with my bread knife, spilled my water. I was certain the entire table knew what I was thinking and feeling—though I wasn't sure I knew myself. It was like I'd wandered into the deep end of the pool without ever being taught how to swim—and then suddenly realized that I knew how to tread water all along. Scott sat with his parents, and Alex with hers, spread out from each other and from me.

I sat next to my mom, with my father at the head of the table. I picked at my Cornish game hen, while others at the table delicately dissected the meal. Mom talked about my riding, complimented Alex and me on our dedication to show jumping, said she thought I'd go to SMU and pledge a sorority. They discussed cars their children wanted for their sixteenth birthdays. My mother favored the BMW 328i. My life planned out for me. She asked Scott about lacrosse, and he looked overly pleased with himself. He expressed optimism about the prospects for this season. The others chimed in with pleasant anecdotes and predictions of their own.

All I heard was static, a monotonous hum of conversation. My eyes kept veering toward Alex, and when she looked at me, it stole all the air from the room. Everything else—everyone else—seemed dull and flat in comparison. *What had just happened? What did it mean?* I couldn't roll back time. We had kissed. I couldn't unkiss her. And what scared me the most was that I didn't want to. All I wanted was to be alone with her again.

The dinner discussions turned toward the performance of the oil fund, the fact that it had been "sluggish" in recovering since the 2008 crash. I zoned out, my brain reliving the kiss, that feeling in my stomach, the ache it left behind.

Once dinner ended, the men left to smoke cigars and drink brandy in the library, and the women sat out by the pool. Alex left early, since her parents liked to get a good night's sleep, and Scott's took him home since he had practice at six AM. I overheard the women talking about me.

"She's just lovely, Samantha."

"You've done such a wonderful job raising her."

And my mother's reply, "She's such a blessing. God has been so good to us."

Guilt knotted in my stomach. I choked it down.

As soon as I was alone in my room, I called Alex, but instead of talking about the kiss, we talked about the stifling conversation at the table, my father's lack of social skills, and the Junior Equestrian Championships. I didn't care what we talked about as long as I could keep her on the line with me. I never wanted to let go.

⋆ ⋆ ⋆

Her hands were in my hair. Our bodies beneath the sheets. We kept the lights out. I wanted to look at her, but I couldn't bear to let her see me—my scratches, small breasts, all my imperfections. I kept my bra and underwear on, hiding the damaged parts of me that would make her run far and fast away from me. And yet, on instinct alone, my hips rose to meet her fingertips as they slipped beneath the fabric and found their way inside of me.

I knew what we were doing was wrong; guilt tore away at me, especially after Mass on Sundays, when I hid in my room, scraping and clawing at my skin until beads of blood appeared. After those moments, I swore to myself and God that I'd stop myself, that I'd tell Alex we had to just be friends. Instead, every Friday night, I rushed to pack my things to spend the weekend at her house.

Alex's parents went to bed every night at nine PM. Their master bedroom was downstairs at the other end of the house. My parents never questioned our sleepovers. But of course, I worried. My father, straitlaced and proper, said that gay people were mentally ill. Over Sunday brunch one morning, he pointed at a section of the *Dallas Morning News*. "We've got to do something about this. It's sickening, immoral."

He held out the page with marriage and engagement announcements. Two men in tuxes stood side by side, one with his head resting on the other's shoulder. "Do they think that putting it in the paper will make it seem normal?" my father asked, peering over the newspaper. "Next, they'll be saying intercourse with animals or children is okay too. Get married to your dog, why the heck not." He blinked hard twice before flipping the pages to the business section.

Mom took a sip of her orange juice and said, "And they're both so handsome too. Such a shame."

"They're not dead, Mom," I said.

She touched her napkin to the corners of her mouth. "Well, maybe that's why God created the AIDS virus in the eighties."

My mouth fell open, but no words came out. She continued, "I'm just glad we're sending you to Catholic school, raising you right. The world has lost its moral compass." I stared at the two perfect poached eggs on my plate, unable to think of anything except Alex's breasts. Mom looked at me. "You agree?"

"Of course," I answered, breaking the yolk gently with my fork but unable to eat a single bite.

It had to stop. Of course, I knew it had to. The thought of getting caught, of anyone at all knowing what Alex and I were doing, terrified me. Before Alex, I feared getting a bad grade or saying the wrong thing at a formal dinner. But now, I knew the truth: this thing, what I was doing with Alex, whatever we had become—would be unforgivable—if not by God, then certainly by my mother. Of course, the world was changing—but Texas wasn't. Neither was St. Mary's Academy or the circles my parents moved in. I hoped I'd grow out of it—get married to Scott or someone like him, have kids. My parents would come visit us at holidays. But every time I saw Alex, it was like orbiting the sun. There was no way to be near her without wanting to be a part of her. And the alternative? I couldn't honestly picture my life without her in it.

To divert any suspicions my parents or others had, I kept seeing Scott, encouraging public displays of affection: a kiss at the door, holding hands at the pool. My father often saw us and nervously darted away. Mother only smiled. I wanted to snap my fingers and feel more for him, wondered if it might be possible if I were doing the things with him that I did with Alex. But I had trouble picturing it.

Alex, on the other hand, didn't worry at all about creating a cover story. In fact, she seemed to enjoy the risk of getting caught. On a field trip from the school to a museum, we rode the St. Mary's Academy bus to downtown Dallas, and beneath the backpacks in our laps, Alex traced circles up my bare thigh. Later, in the girls' bathroom between classes, she reeled me in for a kiss, after searching the stalls for any straggling students. I stepped away and warned her. "We'll get expelled. My parents will send me to a convent."

"Well, that would be a mistake. I mean, it's a bunch of women rooming together who don't put on makeup and wear sensible shoes." The corners of her mouth turned down. "I don't care who knows," she said. "I'm not ashamed of it. I want to be with you."

"We could lose everything," I told her. "Don't you get that?"

"Yeah, I do. But this is more important to me," she said. She stroked my cheek and trailed a fingertip along my lips.

I pulled her to me and kissed her long and deep.

♦ 16 ♦

ALEX AND I SAT in world history class, our desks across an aisle so narrow that I could stretch out my leg and touch hers. She folded a note into a triangular, thick wedge and kicked it over to me. The teacher, Mrs. Shaw, turned toward the wipe-off board and drew a diagram of the countries involved in the conflict leading up to World War II. I coughed and bent down to pick up the folded paper. The marker squeaked. I opened the note. “I’m kissing you in my mind. Right. Now.” My face flushed with heat. I scribbled a note back. “My hands are up your skirt.” I pretended to wipe something off my shoe, hid the note beneath the sole, slid my leg over to hers, leaving the note on her side of the aisle as I returned my leg back to my own desk.

The teacher whirled toward the class. “How did each country decide which side of the war to be on? What made us allies or enemies and how did that change once the war ended? I’d like each of you to spend a few moments reflecting on this and write out a—”

I jerked my head up. Mrs. Shaw took deliberate, angry strides down the aisle toward me and Alex. She stopped at

Alex's desk and held out her hand. Alex hid the note beneath her binder. I stopped breathing. This could not happen. Alex made a futile attempt to rip a page from her notebook and hand that to the teacher instead. Mrs. Shaw lifted the corner of the binder, grabbed the folded note, and slipped it into her pocket. "Pay attention, ladies. For passing notes, you each owe me two pages instead of one on this topic." She dipped her narrow chin like a sewing needle to her chest before returning to the front of the room.

My eyes watered, and I felt sick. She would read the note. My life would be over.

When the bell rang, Alex and I scurried into the hall. She leaned in quickly. "We'll say we were quoting lines from the book *Lolita.* We found it in my parent's library and weren't supposed to be reading it. We thought those parts were hysterical and had been teasing each other by repeating them to see who could make the other laugh first." She squeezed my hand, let her lips brush my cheek. "It will work. Don't worry."

The day ticked down like I was waiting for a governor's death penalty pardon. Maybe Mrs. Shaw would throw away the note without reading it. Maybe she'd forget about it entirely and it would stay inside her pocket and disintegrate in the washing machine. Or maybe she would post it on the bulletin board for everyone to read or pin a giant red *L* to our chests, a scarlet lesbian letter for each of us. In between class breaks when we were allowed to access our phones, I texted Alex.

Had she heard anything yet? Been called to the office? Seen Mrs. Shaw in the hallway and gotten any idea whether she'd read the note yet?

No, no, and no.

I would rather kill myself than have my mother know what Alex and I had been doing. As much as I didn't like hearing it, Mom had taken me in when no one else had. I owed her more than this. As the last class of the day wound to a close, I promised God that if He let me get away with this, I would stop seeing Alex. It would end that day.

Before the final bell rang, an announcement came over the PA summoning Alex and me to the office. As I rose and walked the hallway toward the front of the building, I pulsed with the need to scratch at my skin, to get relief from the shame and guilt building up inside of me with no place else to go. Oblivious students skittered around me. Student council election posters scrawled in thick marker lined the walls. I clutched my backpack to my chest like a shield. This secret felt worse than the others, the ones I kept about who I was and where I'd come from. With Alex, I'd been complicit. I couldn't help where I'd been born, but I'd chosen to be with Alex—to do the things we did together.

⋆ ⋆ ⋆

I entered the office, and my mother was already seated in a chair in front of Headmaster Goddard. I knew that Alex had already seen him, that her parents hadn't shown. Headmaster Goddard had our note on the desk in front of him. He dipped his reading glasses and read the exchange aloud. When he was done, I blurted out the word "Lolita"—like a password. I stuck to Alex's story. The book *Lolita.* Yes, I was ashamed of reading it, and it was silly and improper for us to pass notes like that. I would go to confession tomorrow, receive my penance. Apologize to Mrs. Shaw and stop writing notes in class. My mother seemed to believe our lie.

When my father came home that night, I listened to their discussion from my perch on the stairs.

"Why would she do this to me? Does she have any idea how embarrassing that was for me?" She paced in front of the couch, the click of her shoes punctuating her anger. "I knew better than to let her spend time with that girl. Her parents don't watch her at all." She rubbed her arms like she was cold. "And if I thought for a moment that it was true . . . that Sky had written that note to her, that she was that way . . ." I waited for the rest. "I don't think I could live with it. No daughter of mine . . ."

"She's dating Scott," Father said. "Have you watched the two of them lately? I'm more concerned about that, to be honest." A bottle clinked and a cork squeaked.

Mom's fury ebbed, receded toward sadness, and turned inward. She slumped, boneless, onto the couch and put her head in her hands. "Is it me? Am I a terrible mother? I must be."

"No, Sam. She's just a normal teenager. If you think it's necessary, you could send her to one of those conversion therapy programs."

I held back a scream. I'd heard about the tortured "pray the gay away" facilities.

"No, Jack, that would just be admitting that it's true, and I refuse to believe it. We've brought her up right."

"If it is true, you can only do so much," he said. "They told you in the adoption training that she might have attachment disorder. What was that other one . . . oppositional defiance? It could be trauma or genetics, but it's not you."

"It doesn't matter. Everyone will think that it is. Everyone always blames the mother."

"Let's just not make a big deal about this, okay? She's going to confession. She said she was sorry, right? And she's not going to hang out at the Coles' anymore, right? Problem solved."

I threw myself on my bed. I texted Alex. There was no way I could end things in person. I deleted and retyped several times before I finally allowed myself to hit send. "I can't do this anymore." Three dots appeared and disappeared several times. I pictured Alex sitting cross-legged on her bed deciding what to say. While I watched those dots, tears filled my eyes. I let them fall onto my phone where they blurred the thread, the words she typed back: "I know." Three more dots appeared and disappeared, and then nothing.

* * *

At the stables the next day, I avoided Alex, and she avoided me. But I watched her when she wasn't looking. I ached to hold her in my arms, feel her breath against my neck. The times we stood near each other or passed each other in the tack room, I could smell her lip balm and the sun on her skin, which made me want to kiss her.

In the jumping arena, Mom hovered along the railing, her eyes keen as a hawk's. Could she tell what I was thinking? Did she notice my eyes lingering on Alex? I thought about what Mom had said about AIDS, about my father's comments about gay people. My hands grew clammy holding the reins. My body hummed with confusion. To distract myself, I convinced the trainer to set up bigger jumps. I worked the course, felt

Cobblestone gather beneath me, and proceeded to knock over the top rails with every pass. My mother called out a warning. "Be careful. Pay attention." Was Alex watching me? Did she still want to be with me? My mind tangled with thoughts of her, and I hated myself for it. I lacked focus and discipline. I choked up my hands on the reins. If I could control a thousand-pound horse, I could control my emotions.

I pushed myself harder. I rounded the corner toward the advanced jump, something I'd never cleared with Cobblestone or any other horse. I surged forward. Five, four, three, two . . . Cobblestone rose up, his body vertical, an inconceivable angle. I gripped along his neck, my thighs and knees clutched his backbone and torso. We sailed over, just clipping the rail, which teetered and fell behind us.

As Cobblestone plunged down the other side, I struggled to hold on, propelled forward out of the saddle and onto his neck. His front hooves slammed into the dirt. I braced for impact but lost my balance. Cobblestone nailed the landing, but I went airborne. I whimpered and tried to flip and roll to soften the blow, but my head hit the ground hard. I groaned. Mom was the first one there, followed by the trainer. Alex came next, eyes shimmering. I lay there for a moment. Those faces above me, hazy with worry—and anger. Mom looked angry. "What were you thinking? Now look what you've done."

I rose to my shins, unsteady. Deep pain pulsed just behind my eyes and forehead, a bass drum pounding. I dipped my chin and curled my head to my knees.

"Can you feel your hands, feet? Is anything broken? What hurts?" The trainer assessed me, running her hands over my limbs and neck before removing my helmet. I moaned, and Mom helped me to my feet. The trainer slung my left arm around her torso, and Alex moved to the opposite side. As she reached out to support me, I nudged her away, allowing my mother to slip in between us, and I lifted my arm and placed it behind my mother's neck. With my mother and the trainer's forearms overlapped and encircling my waist, I wobbled toward a bench along the fencing. The trainer looked me over again, checked my pupils for signs of a concussion. Alex gave me a watery smile from a few yards away. Mom rubbed my back in small circles. My head throbbed. My heart broke.

* * *

That night, I lay in bed. Mom came and checked on me every two hours. She pressed a cold rag to my cheeks. "I'm okay," I told her, pulling a corner of the washcloth away.

She sat on the bed, put her back against the headboard, snugged a pillow onto her thigh. "Look at you. All you've accomplished. You've made us so proud." She patted the pillow.

I leaned to the side before inching myself over to rest my head in her lap. She smoothed my hair. She wiped the tears that leaked from the corners of my eyes. She often said she loved me, and I was even sure she believed it. But she didn't know me. And I was okay with that—with her loving the idea of me.

"I can't help worrying," she said. Her mouth twisted; her hands fluttered atop the sheet. "You're all I have, you know that?"

"I'm sorry," I said.

She rested her forehead against my own and closed her eyes. "I lost so much before God blessed me with you." When she pulled away, her cheeks were mottled, and her shoulders rounded. For the first time, I thought about all the miscarriages she rarely spoke about—how hard that must have been. In some way it explained why she wanted so much from me—why she made me feel as if I could never fail her. But it was an impossible task. No matter what I accomplished or how good I tried to be, the ghosts of those dead babies lived with us. And even though I had chosen my mother over Alex, it didn't stop me from wanting Alex, from thinking about her every moment, which was a problem I couldn't seem to solve on my own.

Mom brushed the hair back from my face. "Sweet, beautiful girl. You call me if you need me." She stood and left, cracking the door so she could hear me. Her footsteps echoed and faded down the hall.

17

On Sunday, I entered St. Mary's Church. I dunked my entire hand in the holy water and let it drip from my forehead, chest, and shoulders. I resisted the urge to tuck in my shirt and sneak some inside my skirt to the place where it might do the most good. I entered the confessional. I could see the shape of Father Richards through the holes in the screen. I knelt. "Bless me, Father, for I have sinned. My last confession was two weeks ago." I took a deep breath and started with the small stuff. "I lied. I took the Lord's name in vain. I had impure thoughts about a girl. I disobeyed my parents. I said curse words."

"Let's go back to the girl," Father said, clearing his throat. "Sexual thoughts?" he asked.

"Yes." And more, I thought, but didn't say. I vowed to double my penance to make up for it.

"You know that God made Eve from Adam's rib. That the holy sacrament of marriage is between a man and a woman. In Leviticus, it says that if a man lies with another man as he would with a woman, that both have done what is detestable and their blood shall be on their own heads."

"Yes, Father."

"Sometimes it's best to remove temptation, if it's possible to do so. If I were on a diet, I wouldn't stare at donuts, even if they were right in front of me. I'd make myself go over to the produce aisle and pick out a carrot. After a few days of eating healthy carrots, maybe I wouldn't even miss the donuts."

I pressed my folded hands to my lips to keep from laughing. All I could think about was calling Alex to tell her that Father Richards had just used donuts and carrots to describe women and men. She would absolutely die. It made me sad that I couldn't—that I would have to keep this story to myself.

Father Richards gave me ten Our Fathers and ten Hail Marys and forgave me. "Go in peace, child, and sin no more." And as funny as I found his donut and carrot analogy, I knew that he was right—that I needed to replace one set of impure thoughts for another to know if it could be done.

★ ★ ★

Scott picked me up, on time and well groomed. Hair product, aftershave, creased khakis. I wore a summer dress, low-cut in the front to show what little cleavage I had. He assumed it was just another date, at least at first. He let me choose the movie, and after very little debate, we snuck into a steamy, R-rated thriller that—as advertised—contained both sex and nudity. After the lights went down, I opened my purse and took out a bottle of scotch I'd stolen from my parents' bar in the library. Scott leaned in and whispered into my ear, "I'm not sure what's going on, but I'm not going to ask any questions." We passed the bottle back and forth along with a bucket of popcorn and candy. If I was going to break the rules, I was going to do it all at once.

During the movie, I leaned against his body over the armrest between us. When he held my hand, I moved it to the hem of my dress. I initiated a kiss. Twisted my left leg around his right. I pretended to be the woman in the movie, seducing a stranger at a bar.

Two hours later, we stumbled out of the theater and drove to a popular make-out spot, next to a locked gate overlooking White Rock Lake. In the back seat of Scott's BMW, we fogged the windows. The place was dark, secluded. Scott's narrow tongue flicked in and around my mouth, and his hand rubbed the spot just beneath my left breast. His breath smelled sickly sweet, a mixture of whisky and Milk Duds. He ran his fingertip along my collarbone, up to my chin, and around to the back of my neck. I took his other hand and placed it on my thigh. He inched it slowly upward, leaning in, pressing his hips into me. I tried to concentrate on the sensation of being touched, the rhythm of movement. My mind veered toward Alex, how different her body felt against mine—the soft, long curves. Her red hair, the scent of rosemary and lavender shampoo. I felt my pulse and a warm wet quickening between my legs.

Five minutes later, wedged into the back seat, with Scott's foot stretched against the dashboard, Scott unzipped his fly. I hadn't expected it to hurt. My insides seared like a brand. Scott rocked gently at first, then lost himself in the momentum of the act, moving on top of me with all the grace of a mechanical bull. His hands caught on the fabric of my dress, snagging it along my hips. His face chafed my cheeks, chin, and lips, leaving them red and raw. He shuddered and came, pulling out at the last minute to spurt a warm, sticky liquid down my leg. He used his shirt to wipe my leg. Zipped up his fly. Adjusted my dress. It was over, and I wanted it to be.

"I've heard it gets better for girls after the first time," Scott said. "We could try again sometime, maybe?" He smiled sheepishly. "Was it okay?"

I nodded. But it wasn't okay. It was an experiment, one that had failed.

* * *

Over the next few weeks, we tried it twice more. But it didn't get any better for me. I felt nothing, even though I desperately wanted to. He wasn't Alex. And yet I would settle for him—make it work. No one could know I was gay, because I would simply choose not to be.

♦ 18 ♦

2019

I SEARCH LAURA'S FACE for a reaction: condemnation or affirmation or something in between. She sits next to me on the futon; our bare thighs almost touch just below the edge of our dresses, which we still have on from the auction. One inch separates us, but there might as well be no space left between our skin. A familiar ache builds inside me, and I don't know whether to allow it to grow or to shove it away. I've lost so much already that the possibility of her rejection seems an unthinkable risk. And yet I'm paralyzed. I want this to be enough. Just to sit close to her. There's so much energy crackling between us that it's about all I can handle anyway.

Breaking the silence, my stomach rumbles—low, deep, and loud, and I clutch it, mortified, until Laura bursts out laughing. Before I know it, I'm laughing too, even though neither of us seems to be clear about what's so funny. "Thank God I didn't fart," I say, which makes us double over until Laura slips to the floor, with tears streaming down her cheeks. Bella jumps and licks her face as she tries to figure out what the fuss is all about. It feels good to laugh like this, like a life jacket thrown to a woman overboard.

Laura clutches her abdomen and sputters, "It's like I just did eight hundred crunches. I can't even sit up." She gathers herself and takes a deep breath. "Okay, so sorry." She dabs at the corners of her eyes with the back of her wrist. "Wow." She looks at Bella and then at her iPhone. "Oh, I almost forgot."

She stands. I brace myself. She will make an excuse, ask me to leave now.

Laura walks toward the door. She grabs Bella's leash from a hook, and Bella goes nuts, tugging at the middle of the leash, leaping in the air, and shaking her head like she's killing a snake. "Okay, okay," Laura says. "We're going." She motions to me. "Come on."

There's an almost full moon, of course there is. We walk down the sidewalk with Bella leading us. Unhurried. We take Congress Avenue, past the people congregated there to watch the hordes of bats beneath the bridge, to the boardwalk overlooking the skyline and crossing Lady Bird Lake. The path is a newer addition to the trail system, one I've yet to explore. Along the way, we stop to look at a metal strip affixed to the top of the railing. It's part of an art installation, one of thirty-six sculpted western-style belts with lyrics from a Texas musician etched into the bronze, which is tinted to resemble leather. The first one we read is Patsy Cline's, "Crazy for cryin', crazy for tryin'," which is a sign if ever there was one. I almost laugh out loud. The next is "I'd be working in the Kremlin with a two-headed dog." So much for omens.

"What does that even mean?" Laura asks. "And what does Russia have to do with Texas?" I shrug. Laura holds Bella's leash with one hand, but hooks her other arm through mine, so that we are joined at the elbow. We stroll. I'm not sure I've ever strolled with another human being, and I decide I like it. *Look at us*, I think, strolling along arm in arm.

Lights glint off the water. We take a seat on a bench beneath the patinating belt with Lyle Lovett's lyric: "Me upon my pony on my boat." One of my favorites. I'm relaxed and nervous at the same time, which seems impossible, but true nonetheless.

"So you never told your mom you were gay? You just decided *not* to be?" Laura asks. "Did it work?"

I wonder how much more to tell her. She's still here, after all. "There's a bit more to the story," I say.

"I can take it," she says. "Tell me."

We stare at the skyline. I pet Bella. I decide to go all in.

* * *

2015

Sky

A few weeks after I won the equestrian championships, I was supposed to be at school, but I complained about a headache and a queasy stomach, and Mom agreed I could stay home. Mom had an appointment at the spa, and my father insisted she go to it.

The minute Mom's car left the drive, my father knocked on my door. He cleared his throat. "How many times have you thrown up this morning?" he asked, unable to meet my eyes. He had one hand behind his back.

"Twice," I said.

He held out a paper bag. "I've been watching you and Scott, and . . ." His voice trailed away, he blinked several times. "I'm not sure you have the stomach flu." He pressed the bag into my hands. "So read the directions. Use both of them. Show me the results."

I closed the door and opened the bag. Inside, I found a purple box labeled *e.p.t. 2-pack*, and beneath the large letters, *early pregnancy test.* I crumpled the bag inside a fist. Oh God, no. I couldn't be pregnant.

Scott and I had only been together a few times, and we'd been careful, hadn't we? I counted back in my head. When was the last time I had my period, one month, two? They were never completely regular, so it was easy for me to lose track.

Don't panic, Sky. Take the test. It will be fine. It has to be.

I read the directions carefully. Peed on the stick where it told me to. How much urine did I need to get on the stick? Was it bad if most of it ended up on my hand? I set the stick on the counter and stared at the tiny windows that would reveal my fate. All around me: the crisp white towels, white walls, cabinets, marble floor. How many different shades of white could there be? A faded smear of lipstick stained the sink basin. White showed everything. You couldn't hide from all this white.

I waited. Prayed. Waited. If I was pregnant, what would I do? What could I do? My parents didn't believe in abortion, and yet there was no way they'd let anyone know that their sixteen-year-old daughter was pregnant.

I looked at the plastic stick again. And there they were: two blue double parallel lines. Positive. My father knocked on the door and I jumped, hitting my ankle against the hard porcelain. "I'm not done yet!" I screamed, shrill panic in my voice. His footsteps retreated down the hall. Oh God, oh God. It was wrong. It had to be wrong. I fumbled with the box for the second test, for the backup one that would surely tell me that all of this was a mistake. This time, I peed into a cup and dipped the wand into the urine. Again, I waited. Two lines appeared; a highway divide you couldn't cross. The box claimed a ninety-nine percent accuracy rate.

Oh my God.

I held onto the stick and stared. My stomach rolled and I jumped up and twisted around in time to puke into the toilet. Father knocked again. I had to open the door, what choice did I have? He would demand to see the strips. I could buy time. Tell him I did it wrong and needed him to buy another package. I could let the new tests read negative. Run them under water or something. But then what? It would become obvious in a few months. This was something I couldn't hide. Was abortion legal in Texas? I had no idea, and even if it was, I was fairly certain I couldn't go through with one. "Sky?" my father said.

I slid the tests underneath the door without unlocking it. "Oh no," he muttered. "No, no, no." Then, almost as a whimper, "Do you have any idea what you've done?"

"I'm sorry," I said. "I'm so sorry. I didn't mean to . . ."

"This will destroy her. If I lose your mother . . . I honestly don't know what I'll do." He cracked the door open and held out his hand. "Give me all the packaging. I'm going to toss it in the outside bin so your mother can't find out about it until I'm ready to tell her." He took the box and plastic wrapping from my hands. "It will be better if she finds out from me."

I wanted him to yell at me or slap me, but he didn't. His hands shook as he gripped the packaging. "Please promise me you'll tell no one about this until we figure out a plan. Not Scott or your mom, not even during confession. I'll figure out what we're going to do and let you know." He paused before leaving. "Maybe keep your door closed or play some music so Mom can't hear you throwing up."

When I was certain he'd gone, I slipped out of the bathroom. I willed my legs to move toward the bed, where I collapsed, face down, sobbing. A baby. Impossible.

I rolled over and put my hand over my abdomen, which was as flat and hard as the walls of my room. The air conditioner hummed—white noise against my shame. Beneath it, the aftershocks of my father's worry shook the house. His nervous and frustrated footsteps echoed through the halls. There was no way to repair this. No do-over. And why had I thought it could turn out any other way? What if I had told them I was gay, instead of sleeping with Scott? Which was worse: being gay or getting pregnant? And did it matter, since both were true?

⋆ ⋆ ⋆

After my father told my mother the news, a week passed, and she still hadn't spoken to me or come out of her room. I wanted to knock on her door, but my father told me to give her some time and space. Every day, I stood outside her bedroom, listening to her cry, sometimes sob, knowing that I was the cause of it. My father had Lupita bring her meals, which ended up uneaten on the other side of the door later in the day. When my father was finally able to get her to talk to him, I could hear them behind the door discussing what to do next about my "situation." Calls were made. More quiet and whispered conversations.

⋆ ⋆ ⋆

Two days later, my father collected me from my room and sat with me at the kitchen table. I waited for my mother to appear, and when it became clear that she wouldn't, I asked, "Is Mom going to be okay?"

He stared at my shoulder, folded his hands. "Honestly, I don't know." A truck pulled up in the circular drive; lawn crews unloaded their equipment.

"What's going to happen to me?" I asked.

He cleared his throat, tapped his hands against the glass. "We're sending you to Hope of St. Catherine's in Austin. They're a Catholic institution providing housing and adoption services for pregnant teens," he said. "It's not so bad, honestly. A good place."

He seemed to be waiting for a response from me, but a lump in my throat prevented me from speaking.

"While you're there," he continued, "you'll keep working toward your high school diploma. You'll have the baby, and it will be adopted. There's really no other option. You can't raise a child, and we can't raise one for you." He stared at his hands, but I could see sympathy in his eyes. "I feel badly for you—I do."

The blood rushing inside my ears made them buzz, and I was finding it hard to get air. "I won't go. You can't just toss me away like that." It terrified me to think that I would start over yet again, alone, and do something as adult and painful as having a baby with no one who cared about me there to see me through it. I wasn't equipped for this. I couldn't do it.

Outside the window leading to the backyard, our gardener pruned the rose bushes. He stuffed the last of their blooms into the plastic sack he carried.

"You know, she loved you so much, maybe even more than me."

Past tense. Loved.

"That's it, isn't it? You can't stand how much time and attention she gives to me. Admit it." My voice pushed through the tightness of my throat. "You've always hated me. You never wanted me anyway."

He stared at the glass table in front of him. "I don't hate you." Tears built behind my eyes. "But you're right," he continued. "I never saw myself with children. But Sam did, and I love her and our marriage, so here we are."

"You're not my father."

His eyes dimmed, pity darkening them. "Look, I may not have tucked you in or taught you to ride a bike, but I provided for you. You've never had to be afraid of me. I've never spanked you—never so much as raised a hand to you."

"And I should be grateful for that?"

"I've been here for you—so has your mom—and neither of us deserved this." He gestured into the air—and it was unclear whether he meant me in general or the pregnancy. "You can't blame us for this. Take a little responsibility."

He was right, even though I wouldn't admit it.

"If this gets out," he said. "we'll lose our clients, our reputation, our community—everything your mother and I have worked so hard for."

"Really? You sure about that?" I sneered, aiming to wound him. "Can't you just say, 'Gee, she was adopted, we could only do so much'?" I said. "After all, I'm not really yours. Girls my age get pregnant in rural West Texas all the time, and no one sends them away."

"You can do this, because you have to. You don't have another choice."

"What if I have an abortion?"

"Please keep your voice down," he whispered.

I choked out words—getting more desperate. "Or I could tell everyone. Scott's parents. Your investors. Then the secret would be out, and you couldn't send me away. Everyone would know and they'd think you were horrible for not helping me."

His neck flushed bright red, tendons swollen along the length of it. His anger frightened me. "We *are* helping you. You just don't see it that way. And after all the trouble your mother had keeping her pregnancies, I can't believe you'd even consider ending the life of your baby. She would never forgive you for that. Never. Abortion is murder. God creates life and only God can take it away. You made a bad decision, but I know you're not a bad person."

"You're helping yourself."

"The people we know—the circles we run in—they would do the exact same thing."

And I realized the truth of it when he said it. Yes, of course they would.

I pinched the back of my arm as hard as I could. They both cared more about how my pregnancy made them look than about helping me get through it. But I had to think my mother would change her mind. She would forgive me. Help me. The gardener dragged the bag of dead roses toward the curb. "When do I go?"

"Friday," he said. "We're telling the school and anyone else who asks that you're attending boarding school in Maryland."

"This Friday? Why do we have to leave so quickly?" He stared out the window, which answered my question. The longer I stayed in Dallas, the easier it would be for someone to find out our terrible secret. They wanted me gone. Now. "Will Mom come?"

He shook his head. "This is going to take some time, I think. But she'll come around."

I swallowed hard, pressed my fingernails into my arm, leaving crescent moon shapes along the skin. I had to know. "After I have it—" I couldn't say baby, even though I was having one. "Will I come back home? Does she want me to?"

"Right now, she's not saying much of anything. But yes, that's the plan—for things to go back to normal."

19

A NUN, DRESSED IN a black robe with her habit trailing behind her, mowed the grass, steering a John Deere tractor and waving at all who passed. Hope of St. Catherine's sat on a five-acre campus with several buff-colored limestone buildings scattered along the lawn. I expected St. Catherine's to be silent and oppressive, with daily floggings for girls who had joined the secret society of those who have sex out of wedlock. Yet, at least from the outside, it seemed peaceful, welcoming even.

My father did little more than drop me and my bags at the reception area. He didn't say goodbye or to call home when I got settled. He left, and he never so much as glanced back in my direction as he slid into his convertible and sped away—home to Mom, who he had all to himself again. I felt like a defective Rolex he'd bought for his wife, only to find out its warranty had expired. I watched him go with a mixture of fury and relief.

My room, painted a cheery canary yellow, allowed space for the few items I brought and little more. I unpacked my suitcases. I took my time, neatly folding the items that would still fit me for a few more weeks. I moved in a fog. Step by step. One foot in front of the other.

⋆ ⋆ ⋆

Around twenty women in various stages of pregnancy or motherhood lived at St. Catherine's, along with babies and toddlers under the age of two, plus any of their older siblings. Several rooms in one building were set up with cribs in them, but mine had only contained a twin bed, dresser, and little else. My building, the Joseph House, was for girls planning to give up their babies for adoption. No need for a crib in our home, which seemed sad in a way—a preparation for loss instead of life.

The Virgin Mary watched over us from every corner of every building. She appeared in the forms of life-sized statues, posters, medallions, figurines, refrigerator magnets—even candy dishes, soap dispensers, and office supplies. We were there without our own mothers, so in a real sense, she instilled a feeling of love in each of us, with her soothing and maternal presence—draped in blue robes, with her arms out and palms up in graceful serenity.

In the playroom of the main house, a nun in a chair held one baby in her lap, reading to him from a thick picture book, while using her foot to rock an infant in a carrier on the ground in front of her. The nuns watched the babies and older kids while their mothers attended school. In the mornings, our housemother packed a lunch for us, and we headed to another part of the campus for charter school, which offered an accredited high school diploma program taught by laypeople, as well as some of the nuns. If you walked into our classroom at any given time, you wouldn't notice that this was a school for pregnant girls, unless you tallied up the number of trips we took to the bathroom or peeked beneath the tables where we sat with our hands resting on our swollen bellies.

The community kitchen smelled like burnt toast and ketchup, even though all of us had mandatory cooking lessons. I was three months pregnant, hungry all the time, prone to the pee pangs (as I called them), and my face had broken out into an angry case of acne. I looked like I'd been attacked by killer bees. I read about my baby's development, out of curiosity, boredom, and because I wanted to make sure I wasn't giving birth to an alien that no one would want to adopt when it came out. For my twelve-week ultrasound, the doctor gooped gel all over my stomach and used a gadget to slide across my skin to send images to a screen next to my bed. At first, I couldn't figure out what I was looking at, but then there it was: the outline of a face with a nose, the curve of a belly, feet, and hands—a baby, nestled and sleeping—completely unafraid to be in this dark place inside of me, a content bear cub in a den. My emotions skidded and whirled like bumper cars inside my head. For weeks I had known I was pregnant, but it hadn't seemed real until those double lines on the EPT test had an actual heartbeat. I was responsible for this baby growing inside of me. Whatever I did to myself; I did to the baby. I didn't want to be responsible for anything or anyone, but it was a part of me now. Wherever I went, it went. Whatever I ate, it ate. I thought a lot about God, especially at the chapel in the mornings—that if God really knew me—he would never have trusted me with any living creature, let alone one supposedly created in his own image. Why on earth would he allow a teenage girl who couldn't even remember her locker combination to grow a human life inside her belly? It seemed like a horrific design flaw for fertility to begin before a girl had conquered acne or gotten all her permanent molars in.

After Mass one morning, I mentioned this to Sister Mary Margaret, who was quickly becoming my favorite nun at St. Catherine's, and she smiled and said, "How do you think Mary felt? She had never been with a man, she was just a teenager, and suddenly—she's pregnant. Must have been quite the shock!" I laughed and then quickly covered my mouth, afraid I might offend her. But to my surprise, she joined me, until tears rolled down our faces, and we toppled over onto the pew. I hadn't laughed that hard in what seemed like a lifetime, and once released, it just came pouring out of me. I let down my guard. I felt safe and cared for—even though I was temporarily—I hoped—motherless.

I called home every week, wanting to speak to my mom, and usually getting Lupita. I thought that if I gave Mom a little time, she would forgive me, would help me through this after all. One afternoon, my father answered. He sounded rushed and impatient. A car horn sounded in the background. "Look, Sky, your mom can't handle this. She's just . . . broken from it. I don't know any other way to put it. I've had to send her to a private outpatient facility. She's getting the care she needs. That's really all I can tell you."

After the call, I skipped class and stayed in my room instead of eating lunch or dinner. I resisted the urge to scratch myself, though I desperately wanted to. It was as if this baby were forcing me to be kinder to myself.

Sister Mary Margaret came to check on me. A pile of tissues lay crumpled by my face, and I curled like a caterpillar beneath the covers. She said nothing. She sat on the edge of the bed next to me. She smoothed the top of the sheet, leaving her hand pressed against it.

In between sobs I croaked, "I had two families and I managed to lose them both. Who does that?" I thought she'd tell me to pray about it or remind me that I was a child of God. But instead, she said that Jesus was adopted too—that his parents didn't always understand him. That he surely must have felt lost and alone, abandoned by his father, even at his death.

"Why is life so hard?" I asked. "I don't understand why a God who loves us would let us suffer so much."

"Hmmm." Sister Mary Margaret looked around to make certain no one was eavesdropping and whispered, "My views on this have slowly been evolving." She adjusted her habit and put her index finger to her temple. "Let's say a wildfire starts and burns through a neighborhood. You pray for your home to be spared. Your neighbor does the same. After the fire, your house is gone, and your neighbor's is still standing. Did God ignore your prayer? If he was all-powerful, couldn't he have stopped it from burning? People will say yes, God has a divine purpose that is beyond our understanding. But here's what I think: *I, Sister Mary Margaret, a mere mortal human being*, would do everything in my power to stop your house from burning, and I refuse to believe that I have more compassion than the God who created me in his image.

"God doesn't cause or stop suffering, maybe because he can't." She put her hand over her mouth and gasped beneath it. "Sacrilege, I know." She touched my arm. "Okay, perhaps I'll allow the idea of a random miracle here or there, but for the most part, the time of miracles is over, or else he'd be doing them every second of the day! One person's prayers don't outweigh another's. God doesn't save one child from cancer and allow another to perish. No. I think life happens, and we make choices. And much like a good father, our God is there to listen, to help us grieve, to guide us in our decisions, to help us feel at peace. He can't fix it for us."

"So I can pray to him to comfort me, but not for my mother's forgiveness?"

"You can pray for whatever you want, dear. But your mother's forgiveness will have to come from her—if there's anything to be forgiven."

I lowered my head back down to the pillow and closed my eyes, and Sister started singing. It was a song I'd heard at Mass a hundred times before, but the first time I'd actually listened to the words. "He will raise you up on eagle's wings. Bear you on the breath of dawn. Make you to shine like the sun and hold you in the palm of his hand." Sister stayed with me, singing in a sweet, soft voice, layering the words on top of me until I fell asleep beneath them.

* * *

Five months later, my water broke in the middle of algebra class. I'd been having twinges of pain earlier that morning, but I was a few weeks from my due date, so I hadn't thought much of it. I was solving a word problem about a motorcycle and a bus moving at different speeds toward the same location and felt a warm wet stream soak my pants and the chair beneath me. For a moment, I thought I'd peed myself, but then I remembered the video I'd watched about going into labor. "Oh" escaped my lips. Not sure what to do, I stood and walked to the front of the class, one hand on my belly, leaving a trail of water on the floor behind me liked I'd just stepped out of the shower.

"Okay, girls!" Sister Agnes clapped. "It's time. One of you run get Sister Mary Margaret!"

The contractions came slowly at first, like a freight train trying to move forward, inching along with a heavy load. Someone rang the bell by the chapel and the buildings emptied out with girls and nuns hurrying to the front circular drive to see who was in labor and see her off. The nuns moved around me, their creamy white coifs swirling in the black coffee of their habits. They got me into one of the cars and wished me "Godspeed," while the other girls waved and yelled out good luck to me. A special rosary would be said in the chapel that night for me and the baby.

At the hospital, Sister Mary Margaret held my hand as they wheeled me to the delivery room. The last time I had been in a hospital, I had been eight years old. The contractions picked up speed, massive and unstoppable—a train bound for a destination I'd bought a one-way ticket for months ago. I sweated and screamed and pushed, my thighs and stomach and eventually every muscle trembling and exhausted with effort. The doctors and nurses were all business. Practical, which gave me confidence. While I had never done this before and swore I would never do it again, Sister Mary

Margaret had seen babies born all the time, and went about the task as if it were no more than part of the morning rosary. She wiped my forehead, gripped my hand, prayed. The pain was unbearable. I cursed and swore, apologizing to Sister between four-letter words and gritted teeth, and willing this baby to be out of my body—all the while feeling self-conscious and exposed with a grown man peering between my thighs. I wondered if I might die. I read about women dying in childbirth. Was my body able to usher another life into the world? Because it seemed like I was splitting in two.

Hour after hour. No relief. No comfort. Where was my mother? How could she have left me to do this alone? I had been worried about her, but had she worried about me at all? Anger fueled me through the next set of contractions. It wasn't okay. It wasn't right.

In between bearing down and sweating from every pore, I begged the doctor, Sister, the nurses, "Please, just stop this. I can't—I can't take it anymore."

I was about to let loose with a string of obscenities when something inside of me gave way. The pressure eased and a head and body slid into the hands of the doctor, who lifted it in the air like a rare and precious work of art. It was a girl.

I felt relief and then worry. How could anything survive all those violent hours of pain? Surely the baby had felt it too. I tilted my head up and sputtered, "Is she okay?"

A wail pierced the room. "Hear that?" the nurse asked. "She's got a healthy set of lungs. Everything else too."

I closed my eyes. It was done. It was over. Thank God.

* * *

After the nurses cleaned up the baby, Sister Mary Margaret carried her over to my bed and held her out to me. "You can hold her, if you'd like. It's your choice, dear. Some girls don't want to, and that's okay. There's no right or wrong to it."

I nodded and Sister placed the infant on my chest. Her fingers, perfectly formed with tiny nails and soft wrinkles, wrapped around my own. She had a swath of blonde hair and dark, cobalt blue eyes, with a feathered birthmark along her forearm like the stroke of a paintbrush. I remembered my brother, the snowflake blotch of skin on the back of his shoulder, the way my hand fit neatly into the pattern. We were all still connected in some way.

I leaned down and pressed my lips to her forehead. I inhaled her scent and tried to memorize it. "You are perfect in every way," I told her. "Which is why I can't keep you." My voice broke and my tears fell onto the blanket swaddled around her. Her mouth moved and I put my finger into her open palm. As painful as childbirth had been, it couldn't compare with this—"I'm no good. I ruin everything. And I would mess things up for you. I would never be a good mother. I could never give you the kind of life you deserve. So."

Her eyes opened to small slits, and her mouth moved in tiny ovals. I pressed her to me, and her taut body relaxed with a sigh. Her soft head, with a little knit cap, nestled in the space beneath my chin, where my heart pulsed against hers.

Sister Mary Margaret stood beside me. "She's beautiful. What a precious gift."

And she was.

I second-guessed my decision. It was impossible not to. This entire time, I had thought of my pregnancy and this baby as a disaster, something to move past, so I could get on with my life—so that my mother might forgive me, take me back. But where was she? And why did I care so much? That was the question. But this—this was my life. If everything I had ever done had led me here, to her, then it was all worth it. It all made sense. My breath caught in my throat. "Is it too late to change my mind? To keep her?" I glanced up at Sister, who had tears in her eyes, the wrinkles around her mouth quavering.

"This is the hardest part. You have to be sure. You're sixteen. I'm not saying you can't do it, but I'm telling you that it won't be easy."

"Nothing in my life has been easy. I've had a crash course in hard."

"Mmm. I've seen a lot of moms come and go in this birthing room," she said. She sat next to us on the bed, adjusted the cap above the baby's eyes. "You can't go into this thinking it will give you purpose in life or try to keep her because you think you won't forgive yourself if you give her up. This isn't about you anymore. It's about her—what she needs and wants. Whatever you choose, it will be the most selfless thing you'll ever do." She smoothed back the hair from my forehead, matted with dried sweat.

And I knew, of course I did. I had no degree and no job. My parents wouldn't allow me to come home with a baby. They would disown me. I already loved this baby. But love was irrelevant. It wasn't even part of the equation. Love wouldn't feed us. I didn't want this child to have to fight to survive, to wonder where her next meal would come from or if she'd freeze to death. Those were the things that mattered. A person could live without love. What this baby needed was someone who knew how to be a mother—and I didn't have the first clue. I looked at my baby one last time, my heart shattering, and handed her back to Sister. "I know I can't do it; I just wish I could."

⋆ ⋆ ⋆

The adoption, arranged months ago, was a closed adoption, because I wanted it that way. I was too afraid to know where my child was or who her parents were—afraid I'd be consumed with following or finding her—and that doing so would ruin her life.

I named my baby Hope.

⋆ ⋆ ⋆

The day I left St. Catherine's, the nuns and the girls gave me a send-off. Along with a cake, they gave me a card and a present, some picture frames encouraging me to fill them with new memories—assuring me that the best part of my life was ahead of me. Sister Mary Margaret had written a special note she handed me on my way out. It read: "Sweet child, God has given you a pair of sturdy wings and tested them well. It's time for you to fly."

• 20 •

When I returned home, it was evident that nothing and everything had changed. As a family, we ate dinner at the same table. Said the same prayers. Attended Mass on Sunday. My parents had me promise I would stick to the story of a semester at boarding school and a summer spent abroad. Evidently, lying was okay, but sex before marriage wasn't. Plus, it didn't matter what people believed or didn't. Inside I still felt different—other—isolated and damaged. And then there was Scott, who I couldn't even look in the eye. My parents had always talked about the "sanctity of life." So what about Scott's? Didn't he deserve to know that he had a daughter in the world somewhere? And while it seemed unfair and wrong that Scott didn't know he had a child, it was equally unfair and wrong that his life had gone on blissfully uninterrupted, while mine had been upended. He had a great relationship with his parents and had gotten a lacrosse scholarship to play at Notre Dame. I seethed staring at his picture in the paper on signing day. I vowed to do better, be better, win my parents over.

I continued to pursue equestrian. Alex tried to reach out to me in different ways, and I hardened myself against her. She was the reason I was in this mess. If she hadn't kissed me, I would never have slept with Scott. But my heart knew otherwise. It broke every time her eyes met mine. But I doubled down. I wouldn't let her distract me. I shunned Alex. My parents had given me a second chance, and I wasn't going to blow it. I had lost their trust and I would win it back.

My parents fought, often. And while it seemed to be about money, I couldn't help but think it was about me. During my absence, my father had sold two of our vacation homes, which was just as well, since we never used them. They seemed to be a status symbol, rather than a family getaway. And what was left of our family seemed to be in tatters. I was more than happy to avoid Martha's Vineyard or St. Barts, where I'd have to go sailing in a one-piece swimsuit to hide my stretch marks.

I focused on school, knowing my mom had once had dreams for me to go to SMU, to join a sorority, to graduate summa cum laude. I threw myself into my coursework, studying for the SATs night after night. I won the equestrian championships for the second year in a row. I lost the pounds I'd put on, until I weighed less than I had before my pregnancy. I researched possible topics for college essay applications and roared with laughter at the prompts:

How have you learned from obstacles?

Talk about a long-held belief you've recently challenged.

Share your story.

Yeah, not a chance. I ended up writing my college essay on the sport of equestrian, its roots, and my own relationship with show jumping. Then I waited. It seemed as if life itself depended upon the results of those applications. If a college accepted me, then perhaps my mother would too.

When I finally got my acceptance letters, I brought them to the dinner table and unveiled them with a flourish. I had been accepted into SMU, Rice, and the University of Texas. I leaned over my mom, fanning out the letters in front of her, the official seals of each institution gleamed with embossed metal foil. I was certain this would be the culminating event that would bring her back to me. Instead, she barely looked at the letters. She mumbled, "Congratulations, sweetie," as if I were a toddler who'd mastered stacking blocks or learned her colors. She lifted the fork to her mouth carrying a small sad bite of roasted okra and lowered it without eating.

I sagged in the oversized chair across from her.

I waited. I stared at her.

Her fork clinked against the plate. The antique grandfather clock in the hall chimed. My father squirmed in his chair, watching us both. And then the trapped fumarole of rage burst through to the surface.

"Nothing I do matters, does it?" I said. "You got into college, *but* . . . You made the dean's list *but* . . . You won the national championships . . . but, but, but . . ." Tears came, bitter and angry. Mom glanced up; her mouth twisted. I could see the truth of my words on her face. "There will always be a fucking asterisk by my name."

My mother winced at the curse. Then dabbed at the corners of her mouth.

"What do you expect us to do, Sky?" my father asked, quietly. "We're trying here. We really are."

"Are you? Because it doesn't feel that way." I shoved my plate away. "You'll never be proud of me. Ever." Both of them lowered their eyes. "So why not cut to the chase? Why not admit the truth? If I'm so unlovable now, what if I told you it was all true? That note Alex and I passed in class that day, the one Headmaster Goddard read to you? Everything I wrote, I meant. We had sex. Not just once, either. All the time."

Mom dropped her fork against her plate. Her eyes hardened and she flinched.

"That's right. I'm gay." A laugh burst out from me, tinny and wild. "I only slept with Scott because I wanted to be this perfect person! Hah! The irony of it all. I wanted to, but I can't. You hate me anyway, so what does it matter?"

Mom whispered, her voice a hiss, but her words unmistakable. "You are not a lesbian. This is just another phase. Why must you continue to hurt us? I won't have it. Not under my roof."

"You've done quite enough, Sky."

"You haven't seen anything yet," I said. I erupted from the table. I stomped upstairs. I had no idea where I was going, but I knew I couldn't stay there any longer. I gathered up my things into the same bag I'd brought home from St. Catherine's. I didn't bother folding anything. I shoved my belongings into every space, including jewelry, and anything I thought I might sell for money to live on. While

I was grabbing my toothbrush and acne medication, Mom appeared in the doorway.

"All I ever wanted to be was a good mother," she said.

My mind reeled with the question: A good mother, or *my* mother? "Are you going to try to stop me?" I asked. Though I looked at her with hatred, I wanted her to beg me to stay.

She folded her arms across her chest. "It seems like you've made up your mind. Where will you go?" Her eyes shimmered, but she didn't blink. Her gaze firm as stone.

"What do you care?" I shoved by her out the door of the bathroom and back into my room. "You never loved me for me. You loved the idea of me. So you could pat yourself on the back for saving me. You're not my mom. You never were."

It was a slap of words, as surely as if I had raised my hand to her. She recoiled, eyes blistering with pain. A small, pitiful sound escaped her lips, and she turned and ran from the room. She wasn't strong enough to deal with someone like me. But I was beginning to wonder if anyone was.

I didn't have a car or a license, but I did have cash. I took the bus to Austin and showed up back at St. Catherine's begging for room and board in exchange for work.

There, I finished my high school diploma, and with Sister Mary Margaret's help got access to state mental health services to process the trauma that had happened in my life and to heal from my parents' rejection. I was diagnosed with ADHD and PTSD, as well as depression and anxiety disorders. I was back in the system, assigned a caseworker and a social worker and a therapist, with ongoing Medicaid until the age of twenty-one. Navigating the options available to me, filling out forms, and making phone calls to agencies with acronyms I couldn't keep straight became an obsession and a full-time job of its own. I had no idea how someone in a more compromised state could ever get through all the red tape without giving up. If it weren't for Sister Mary Margaret's encouragement and knowledge of resources, I might have given up.

Instead, I ended up at UT on a tuition waiver, supplementing government aid with a college work program, and living on SNAP food and housing assistance. As for my mother, I thought I'd never hear from her again.

21

2019

THE MOON OVERHEAD SHINES off the water while Laura and I sit on the bench overlooking Lady Bird Lake and the Austin skyline. I cross my arms to shield myself from Laura's disapproval. She will hate me for what I've done—for who I am. I sense that she is looking at me, but I can't turn my head to meet her eyes. I'm too afraid what I will see in them.

"Biscuit," she says. "You might just be the strongest person I know."

I breathe again, but I still can't look at her. "Why are you still here?"

"Because I've truly never met anyone like you."

"And that's a good thing?"

"The best," she says.

I allow our legs to touch. She leans against my shoulder, and we sway a little, side to side in a gentle rocking motion. Perhaps she is just comforting me after the story I've told her, but every part of me heats up. *Am I misreading the situation? I am a client. She might not be gay. If she is gay, she might not feel the same way about me as I do about her.* My thoughts scramble like ants in the shadow of a heavy boot. I turn my head and she is staring at me, a soft, knowing look that goes straight to the center of me. Without thinking, I lean forward and kiss her.

Her lips press into mine. Her hands move to my face, pulling me in. Every inch of me responds. I reach my hands to her face, too. I cradle her chin. And then just as quickly, she is inching me away.

"I can't," she says. "It's just—sorry—I—"

She can't look me in the eye. She dips her chin. Laces her fingers together and touches them to her mouth, lowering them in a way that suggests she is wiping away what just happened.

Inside, I shatter. Embarrassment. Anger. Then denial. I force a smile and wave my hand in dismissal. "Chill, Laura. It wasn't anything," I say. I laugh, but it disappears into the night.

The corners of her mouth quiver and hurt dims her expression. "Oh, okay. Well." She pets Bella, gathers up the slack in her leash, and rises slowly. "We should probably head back."

I want to fix this, to rewind and start again. I stay on the bench a moment longer. "Wow, no need to make a big deal about it. Forget it happened." I feign nonchalance, but there's a hard edge to my words. Her back is toward me, and she rolls Bella's leash around her hand. Her shoulders tense, but she doesn't speak.

I try to read her body language. Is she angry? Repulsed? Are we still friends or have I blown it? We walk back in silence. There is apparently nothing more to say. We part ways at the bus stop. But I decide to walk home instead.

I'm unable to get the kiss out of my head. I can still feel her lips on mine—the soft way she leaned into me. Or maybe I imagined that she kissed me back? I don't know and now it seems I'll never know. I check my phone to see if she's texted me. But she hasn't.

I keep my mind occupied by creating stories about the cars at the stoplights. A woman in a minivan. Her kids, around ten years old maybe, are glued to the video playing in the back seat. They are twins. They rarely get along. The only time she gets a moment's peace is by driving around in the car. She hates her life. Next, a luxury sedan. The man has one hand on the wheel, and his other one is holding the hand of the woman next to him. I imagine they've just eaten at Ruth's Chris Steak House—that he is a plastic surgeon who was raised in the Northeast, but he fell in love with a Texan during his residency in Austin and never left. She runs a flower shop downtown and plays piano—badly, but without realizing it. They are trying to have a baby. Tonight, when they get home to their tidy Craftsman, they'll try again. In between cars, I'm alone with my thoughts again. The main thought I have is that there's no point to any of this.

I pass several bars and decide to embrace who I really am—a fuck-up—and by God, lean into it. I have my last three exams tomorrow, and I don't care. They just don't mean anything. I feel like I'm fighting against a rip tide that keeps pulling me under, and I'm tired of swimming. I text Keegan and ask him where he is.

Thirty minutes later, I open the door to a dive bar called the Dirty Nelson and walk into a swarm of neon lights and bouncing bodies. The place reeks of beer and sweat. It's alive with drugs, hormones, and an alternative band whose bass shakes the walls and floorboards. I recognize a few classmates and spot Keegan in the back. He hugs me. He's a nice guy, but I only want him for one thing tonight. I give him the bit of cash I have on me. He slips a baggie into my palm. He's a trust-funder, and he likes me—so it's enough. He just wants everyone to have a good time, and he likes being the center of it.

I take two Oxy and wash them down with a tequila shot from the bar. I flirt with a guy named Ryan, and he buys me another round. The band starts another song and the drums pulse through me. I lose myself in the bodies and the music and the lights and the melting haze that smooths all of it out into one numb, blissful disappearing act. Everything is suddenly okay and no big deal and nothing to worry about. It is lovely not to care about anything except how good I'm feeling—how happy I am to be with these people—moving together as one giant heartbeat. This wave. It carries me. Ryan offers me another Oxy. I don't really know Ryan, but I don't care. My mind is soft and protected. I will only take one more and that should last me the rest of the night.

⋆ ⋆ ⋆

"Sky? She's coming around now." I recognize the voice, but I think I'm dreaming it. She cannot be here. I don't want her here. A nurse comes over. I reach a hand toward my forehead, just above my right eye, which has gauze over it. "Where am I? What happened?"

"You overdosed on opioids, likely laced with fentanyl. Sixth one we've seen this weekend."

"My head?"

"You fell and cracked it on the floor. Someone revived you with naloxone. We called your emergency contact. You'll need someone to drive you home when we release you."

Mom walks over to the bed and leans forward. I try to look away but my head sears with pain. "You lost the right to care what happens to me," I say. "You shouldn't be here."

"Maybe so," she says. "But here I am."

I close my eyes. I wish her away. She has no right to step into my life now, because when I needed her the most, she abandoned me. My head pounds and I disappear into it.

⋆ ⋆ ⋆

When I wake again in the hospital, my mother is gone. I wonder if I've imagined her. Instead, a large, elderly woman with gray hair that curls around her ears sits in the chair across the room. She senses my confusion and walks over to the bed. "Hi, Sky, I'm Helen. The state assigned me as your new caseworker." My *new* caseworker? Did that mean . . . had Laura gotten so freaked out about the kiss that she'd reassigned me to someone else? Yes, well. Of course. What had I expected? My eyes sting with sadness, despite my anger willing the tears away. "I have to ask you some questions," she says. "I'm afraid they won't be easy."

I nod. I don't care. I have no more secrets. What's the point in keeping any?

"Was your overdose intentional? Were you trying to kill yourself?"

"No, but I kind of want to now." Concern floods her cheeks and I rush to say, "Just kidding. I mean, I shouldn't joke about something like that. Sorry. No. I didn't mean to hurt myself." The minute I say it, I wonder if it's true—if on some subconscious level I was trying to end it all. She has a small notepad in her hands. "Please, don't write that down." That's all I need, to be on suicide watch in the loony bin. "It was just a mistake. I thought I was being offered M&Ms."

Helen frowns. "To continue receiving services, we'll need you to be clean and sober. That will mean drug tests."

Perfect.

"The hospital will release you today, and your mother will drive you home. I'll be following up with you twice per week for the testing and to check on your general welfare."

"Why can't I Uber home?" I ask.

"Because you had a head injury, and it's hospital protocol."

"What if I don't want my mom to take me home?" I sound like I'm five years old.

"Okay, well, is there someone else I can call for you?"

I think about Laura. "No," I say. I turn my head toward the wall. "It's fine."

A nurse comes in and helps me back into my clothes from the night before, which have specks of blood on them from my head injury and reek of body odor. I have a white hospital bracelet on my wrist with my personal info on it, and another that's bright orange and reads: Fall Risk. The irony, I think. That's me: a fall risk. I snort while reading it, which causes the nurse to stare at me. "Don't worry," I tell her. "It's altogether possible I'm losing my mind." Her response to this is, "Okay, dear," as if I've just told her I've decided to have eggs for breakfast. She steadies me while I slip on my dress, and I realize that I don't have any of my things. "Do you know where my phone is?" I ask.

She looks inside the plastic bag where my clothes were. "That's all you came in with."

I rummage through the bag and come up with my school ID, a debit card, and two dollars remaining in cash. But no phone. I'll have to contact the club to see if they found it. I hope no one stole it, because I can't afford to replace it. For fuck's sake. What next?

The hospital attendant wheels me out to the curb where my mother is waiting. She has the passenger side door open. I don't recognize the car, so perhaps it's a rental. She moves toward me and holds onto my elbow as I stand and lower myself into the seat. I want to yank my arm away from her, but I don't. All I want to do is get back to Manor House and take a shower and find my phone.

I give her directions to Manor House, and she insists on accompanying me inside my room. I'm embarrassed for her to see how I'm living, when I should be proud. I'm making it on my own, without her help. I touch the line of stitches on my forehead and wobble toward the edge of my bed.

Yes, I'm doing beautifully, thank you.

I see her take in the room. The stained ceiling. Rumpled clothes on the floor. A package of ramen on a dresser. A half-empty pill bottle. Her eyes land on the photo on the cardboard box I use for a nightstand—the fake family in Paris that came with the frame. She doesn't say anything for a while, but the corners of her mouth turn downward and her eyes glisten. "Maybe I could help you to the shower," she says.

"I'm fine. It's okay for you to leave." I give her permission, but I don't tell her she has to go. I wait.

I'm as surprised as anyone when she moves away from the door—away from her escape route and toward me. She sits next to me on the edge of the bed. "Sweetheart, you almost died." She reaches out her hand, tentatively at first, and then committing to it, she sweeps her fingertips over my forehead to move the hair from my eyes. She's careful to avoid my stitches. She still smells like lilacs.

She walks alongside me as I trundle toward the bathroom in the hall. Her hand is poised at my arm, ready to catch me. I have a waterproof Band-Aid to place over my stitches, so that I can wash my hair without getting them wet. "I'll be right here outside the door," she says. "Yell if you need me." After I close the door, she says from the other side, "Otherwise, I'll burst in if I hear a thud." She's trying to make the situation lighter, and I appreciate it. It's not her style to make a joke, which makes me wonder how much she's changed over the last few years.

Once I've showered, I admit to her that I've lost my phone. I use hers to contact the Dirty Nelson to see if it's turned up. It hasn't. They have someone look again while I stay on the line. No. Mom watches my face, listening to my half of the conversation. I wonder if she'll offer to buy me a new one—for the birthdays and Christmases she's missed with me, or the car I didn't get, for kicking me out of the house. If she offers, I decide I will pick out the most expensive one. But she doesn't offer. Instead, she takes me out to eat.

It's awkward. We sit at Magnolia Café facing each other, nibbling on our food. While I had wanted to order chocolate chip pancakes, instead I pretend to be an adult, ordering a salad topped with grilled and blackened mahi mahi. At first, we catch up with each other in a stiff way. I tell her about college, my classes, my job. I want her to be proud of me, even though I hate myself for wanting it. She asks questions and shows interest. It seems genuine. It's something. She tells me about Dallas, about the house, Lupita, father's business. "He's stressed all the time," she says. "He's always been such a reserved person, but lately he's been so angry and hot-tempered." I nod, politely. "Oh, and I know you just lost your phone, so now it might be a moot point. But I got a strange call the other day. A doctor in Arizona looking for you. Did she get in touch?"

My pulse quickens. "Um, yeah, she did. But wait, how did you know where I was living?"

She blushes. Her fingertips flutter around her necklace. "You're still my daughter. I've always known where you are. And even though I'm a dinosaur, I still know how to use Google and social media."

I take this in. I'm floored that she's known where I was this entire time. I don't know whether to be flattered or furious. I try not to react either way.

Mom takes a small bite of her salad. "What did she want?"

"Who?"

"The doctor."

"Oh. She has this patient who's unconscious but had some of my brother's belongings. They're trying to figure out who he is and let his family know about his condition. I told her that Ben died when I was little, but this patient had his journal and this photo of us together before I was adopted. I got to see the journal, and it was definitely his, but there were these pages torn out, and then he mentioned sending me letters." I feel foolish asking, but I have to know. "I know Ben's dead. I know it. I didn't hit my head *that* hard. But did any letters come to the house for me that you guys kept?"

"Not that I'm aware of. But I'll check with Jack and Lupita. Your father always got the mail and took care of the bills." She pauses, moves her hands to her throat. "I'm sure that was hard for you, getting a call like that."

I shrug. Her compassion somehow hurts *and* heals: a bite and a salve. It makes me angry. Furious even. She's lost the right to care about me. In between swallows of arugula, I blurt out, "Just so you know, I'm still gay. I haven't become less gay since you kicked me out of the house."

I watch her face. Her mouth twitches. She looks around at the other tables and takes a sip of her water. I think she might try to shush me or tell me to lower my voice, but she doesn't. In fact, she looks confused. "I never kicked you out of the house. You chose to leave."

I press my palms against the table. "Bullshit," I say. "I was there. You gave an ultimatum. You said, 'Not under my roof,' or have you forgotten that?"

"You still had a choice. I wouldn't allow you to sleep with a boy or a girl in our house, under our roof."

"But you don't get it. It's not about sex. I'm still a lesbian. It's not something I do, it's who I am. It's my identity."

Her mouth twists at the word lesbian, as if I've told her I have a contagious disease, but she seems to take this in. "It's just very confusing to me," she says. And I can see that it is. I almost feel sorry for her, but then I remember St. Catherine's and the baby I gave up.

"You abandoned me," I say. "When I needed you most, you weren't there. I had to give birth without you. Say goodbye to my daughter, your granddaughter, without you." My voice breaks at the edges of my words. "How can I ever forgive you for that?"

She grips the string of pearls around her neck. "I didn't plan it that way. I was in and out of the hospital myself—because of you. If we're being honest, I've struggled to forgive you for the way you upended our lives. You snuck around behind our backs. Had sex with that girl and with Scott. Even if it hadn't ended up with a pregnancy, you disobeyed us and the Church, and—"

"Enough. Just. Stop. So, *I* caused your nervous breakdown? Seems like you had a few of those before I came along. Whatever. I don't need to be lectured again about all the ways I let you down or what kind of terrible person I am. I get it. You've made yourself perfectly clear."

"Have I? You think this is all about me being judgmental? That I was so worried about what other people would think that I sent you away? Is that it? Let me tell you. I wanted to protect you."

"Oh my God! You can't be serious. From what exactly?"

"From the world—from yourself—from everything! What kind of life do you think you'd have trying to care for a baby at sixteen? From that moment on, for the rest of your life, you'd be putting your own dreams aside, struggling to meet that baby's and your own basic needs—without a college degree. How would you have felt facing your classmates or friends while you were pregnant? And whether you were gay or straight, how difficult do you think it would be to find someone who wanted to marry you when you already had a child? And as for being gay, well, you think I'm being too harsh, too condemning? You live in the Texas Bible Belt. No matter how well you do in school or at your job, you could be fired for being gay. Oh, they won't say it outright, maybe, but it will happen. Or they'll see a post on social media, and you'll be interviewing for a position you're more than qualified to get, and they'll pass you over. Or worse, some crazy person could kill you, like they did that poor boy in Wyoming—Matthew Shepherd, or those people inside that club in Orlando. You're my daughter—you will always be my daughter."

She's crying now. And I almost buy it. Especially when she says, "I had thought maybe this could be a new beginning for us."

I narrow my eyes at her—wanting desperately to wound her the way she's wounded me. "Why? Because I forgot to update my emergency contacts? If you knew all this time where I was, how come you never reached out to me?"

"I thought you'd call me when you were ready. You were seventeen. You left. You ran away. You didn't want me to find you. I figured that if you did, you'd let me know. I might have disapproved of some of the things you did, but I never went anywhere, Sky. I still have the same address. I let you go, but I never abandoned you. There's a difference."

22

MY MOTHER DROPS ME off back at Manor House. She puts the car in park and starts to get out, but I tell her I'm okay. I tell her I have to study, which, although true, is unlikely to happen.

"I can stay a few more days if you'd like. I have a hotel." I can tell that she wants me to say yes, but I can't. It still doesn't feel like she wants to take care of me because she loves me or because she can suddenly accept me as I am. It feels like obligation. I close the door and walk away without looking back. But once I'm inside my room, I allow myself a good cry. I wallow. It's a soaker. And when I'm good and done, I go toward the pill bottle at my bedside, open it, and find it empty. While I was in the shower earlier, my mother, who doesn't love me, must have snuck back into my room to quietly save me from myself.

Buoyed by anger and resentment, I rally. I actually study. I actually go to class. I had missed three of my exams, but because I can prove I was in the hospital, they allow me to make them up. I retake them over the next two days and actually try to get good grades. I'm tempted to get a refill on my Adderall prescription to stay energized, but instead, I swig Monster drinks one after the other. I refuse to become what everyone seems to believe I already am. I will get my degree and I will get a good job and I will not end up homeless and on the streets and hungry.

After forty-eight hours straight, focusing on nothing but my classwork and exams, I collapse onto my bed at Manor House. I pull the covers over my head and close my eyes. In minutes, I'm drifting off, when there's a knock on my door. I've forgotten about Helen and my drug test. I fling open the door asking, "How many more weeks will I have to do this?"

But Helen isn't on the other side of the door. Laura is.

At first, there's relief on her face. Then anger.

"How many more weeks will you have to do what—ignore me?" Laura asks. "I don't know; you tell me." Her arms are crossed over her chest. She pushes past me into the room. "What the hell? I've been calling and texting. You just ghosted me."

"You ghosted *me*! Reassigned me. I have *Helen* now!"

"Yes, and if you'd listened to my messages, you wouldn't have been surprised by it. And you would've known why." She places her hands on her hips, unyielding. A woman down the hall yells out, "Y'all shut the fuck up!"

Laura and I stare at each other and start laughing. The tension breaks like a hunger strike that's ending.

I lower my voice. "I lost my phone," I say. I sheepishly add, "And I fell, a little."

Laura's face softens and she runs her fingertips over my stitches. Her touch reminds me how much I've missed her. "Biscuit," she says. "What the hell."

I catch her up on the last couple of days, and when I'm done, she says, "I didn't know you were in the hospital."

"I would've thought Helen would've told you."

She looks at the floor. "I haven't spoken to Helen."

Then I swallow. "Oh no, you didn't get fired, did you? Over me? Because I kis—"

"I quit. I quit DHHS."

"What? Why?"

She sits on the edge of my bed. "It's complicated, but the truth is, I wasn't cut out for it. I can't help people the way I want to with all that bureaucracy and miscommunication. I like rules. I need rules. But theirs don't make any sense. And they move so slowly, I honestly don't see how anyone gets anything done." She rubs her eyes. "I'm just tired, Biscuit."

"Me too," I say. I join her on the bed. She leans against me and sighs. "So what will you do now?" I ask.

She shrugs, folds her hands in her lap. "I'm not sure, but I think I'm going to work on my photography. I didn't have confidence in it until after the auction, but now, maybe . . ."

"You should totally do that. You're so talented."

She bumps her shoulder against mine. "Thanks for that." The shower down the hall runs and the pipes rattle and moan. She waits for the noise to lessen and asks, "So what were you up to before I stormed in here?"

"Sleep," I say. "I crammed for the rest of my exams and just finished them. Not sure how well I did, but at least I was clean and sober for them. I'm just glad they're over."

"I've been really worried about you."

I wonder if we're ever going to talk about the kiss, but I also don't want to make her uncomfortable or have her disappear again. She doesn't have those kinds of feelings for me, and I'm okay with that. Her friendship is more important.

★ ★ ★

Later that evening, Laura and I go out to a music venue. While she is unemployed at the moment, she has two free tickets from a friend who couldn't use them—and she invites me. The small theater is intimate. The lights dim. A woman comes out with a guitar. There's no band behind her. She seems completely exposed. A single spotlight. Laura grips my hand, as if she's nervous for the woman. And I realize that I am too. But then a voice comes out. Unexpected and filled with emotion. The woman's name is Brandi Carlile. She seems to be singing about me. The lyrics in her song strike at something central to the moment, about how our life stories don't mean anything if they can't be shared with someone else.

I'm glad the lights are down, because I feel like a spotlight is shining directly on me. Laura's grip loosens on my hand, but she leaves it on top of my own. I'm not sure if I can do this. She's such a physical person, demonstrative, big-hearted. I crave that affection, and I also can't afford to. I slowly pull my hand away and scratch my chin before placing it in my lap, where it stays for the rest of the evening. After the concert is over, I still don't want the evening to end, and maybe Laura feels the same way, because she asks if I want to go to a coffee shop nearby to split a slice of pie. I hedge a little, and she urges me on. "Biscuit, when was the last time you ate anything? C'mon. Dutch apple, Baby, with a scoop of vanilla."

"Hey, you're out of a job now," I say. "You're going to need to rein it in a little."

"I'm okay," she says.

"Alright then. You had me at pie," I tell her. It's corny and I blush, but she doesn't notice. At Common Grounds, we sit side by side on stools at a coffee bar, our faces reflecting in the mirror behind the barista. We talk about the music and different people in the crowd. It feels normal to be with her. We are two young women in our twenties hanging out in Austin. Two friends. I take a sip of my mocha.

"Tell me more about you," I say. "Now that you're no longer my caseworker, I want to know where you grew up, brothers and sisters, all that stuff."

"Well, you met my mom. She's amazing, truly. No brothers or sisters. I grew up in Louisiana, along the bayou. Mom had me at eighteen. My dad was a high school basketball star. He got drafted into the NBA and skipped college to play ball for the New Orleans Hornets. They're called the Pelicans now. He did okay there, not great. Solid from the bench. But my parents . . . you've never seen two people more in love. The whole high school sweetheart thing . . . totally real for them."

She's never mentioned her dad, and her mom mentioned raising her on her own, so I assume he left them. I try to urge her on gently. "So your parents are divorced, or your dad had an affair?" I ask.

She laughs at this. "Never. Dad was awesome. My BFF. Taught me how to play the game. Set up a hoop in the driveway that was adjustable. I still couldn't reach the rim on its lowest setting, so he'd lift me up and let me dunk it.

Then he bought me a little trampoline to use to do it on my own. Mom about had an aneurysm over it! He was just a total goofball. Always smiling and positive. I'm sure that's where I get it from."

"So what happened? Where is he now?"

"When I was nine, Hurricane Katrina hit. We evacuated at the last minute to the Louisiana Superdome. But we had a boat, so Dad stayed behind to help rescue people from their homes. We didn't know how to reconnect with him. Mom kept telling me he was fine—that we just needed to stay put until he came back for us. Weeks went by. But the infrastructure was so broken that it was impossible to know what had happened to anyone. No one could get around. People were trapped by debris or impassible roads. We were in the Superdome for five days, and even though Mom tried to shield me from the worst of it, I still remember how horrific it was. Temps at ninety degrees. No power. Rancid food. No working toilets. Sewage flowing into the arena. The roof ripped away. Fresh water running out. Rioting. When 400 buses finally came to start evacuating around 30,000 of us from the dome, five people had already died there. Mom panicked because she couldn't figure out how to get word to let Dad know where we'd ended up. How do you find someone in a city of 1.5 million people with communications cut off? We stayed in a FEMA trailer for another week. When we finally got to see a news broadcast, they were tagging and loading hundreds of bodies into refrigerated makeshift morgue trucks and trying to identify people. The heat and the water exacerbated every effort; bodies were decomposing. I didn't look for my dad among the dead. I was looking for him among the workers, the people cleaning up the streets and helping get victims to safety. I refused to believe that anything could happen to him. He was invincible.

"After two months, we finally got word. Dad's body had been identified through dental records. He drowned trying to get an elderly woman out of her basement apartment when a levee failed in the 9th Ward. As excruciating as it was to get that news, we were the lucky ones. Because here's the thing: today, there are still people who died during Katrina who have never been identified and people who are still missing. Their families are still waiting for some kind of closure.

"After we buried Dad, we left New Orleans for good. Insurance wouldn't pay to rebuild our home. Everything in it was destroyed. A friend of Mom's in Austin let us stay for a while until Mom figured things out. Once Dad's life insurance paid out, she used it to get her college degree and then went on to law school. She did it for me, but she also did it for her. Still, I feel a little sad that she's never really dated anyone that I'm aware of since then. He was the love of her life.

"As far as money goes," Laura points to the pie we're splitting. "The Pelicans set up a trust for me after Dad died. I was able to access it when I turned eighteen. It's doled out monthly, enough to live on—not to splurge on a Ducati. Thank God someone realized I wasn't good with money. Still, I'd give every cent away if it would bring him back."

"I had no idea," I say. "I get why you do what you do now. Why you wanted that man in the hospital to be Ben." I watch her reflection in the mirror. The press of her lips into a half smile. Resilient, this one.

"Speaking of," she says. "They still haven't found a death certificate. I know, of course, because I keep checking."

"Of course you do," I say. I lean toward her, and she rests her head on my shoulder. And I lay my head against hers. We stay like that for several minutes—me taking her in for what seems like the first time.

♦ 23 ♦

For the next two days, Laura and I are inseparable. I have a week off now that midterms are finished. I call in sick to work, and Laura and I spend our time watching kayaks ply the water, and I join her on photo excursions throughout the city. Everything I do with her seems new and exciting. We take Bella for walks and play Frisbee. Laura cooks fake bacon for me in a half-hearted attempt to convince me to be a vegetarian. I show her examples of websites she might like for her photography. As a surprise, she drives me into the Hill Country to a place called Enchanted Rock. It could be Skeleton Canyon's little sister, with its slick limestone and red dirt. We hop out of the car and into a blast of wind. I hold onto the door of the car so it doesn't slam closed. "I hate wind," I tell her, squinting my eyes to avoid a swirl of dust.

"How about heights?" Laura asks, and she points toward the top of a vertical slab. Climbers with ropes cling to the face of granite, like drops of water on a dirty windowpane.

"I am not doing that," I say. I give her a sideways glance. "Did you ever do that?"

"Course I did. But you have to have a climbing partner, and mine moved."

"Can't you climb a mountain solo?"

"Some mountains. But the climbing that they're doing, you need someone to lead the route and someone to belay you. The person below holds the other end of the rope and cinches it up as you go so you don't fall."

"Um, yeah, I have too much ADHD to belay anyone. Look! Something shiny. And whoosh!"

Laura laughs. "Don't worry, we're hiking to the top. There's a trail that goes up behind it. She does a quick inventory of her daypack before hoisting it onto her shoulders. She's prepared. Two water bottles. Snacks. Sunscreen and bug repellant. Reliable as ever.

I let her lead the way, watch her surefooted steps, even along a portion of the path with a razor-thin edge. I was never afraid of heights. But when I look below, my stomach drops, and I feel dizzy. I stare at the back of Laura's shoulders instead, ready to grab onto her pack if I lose my balance. There's something unsettling about the terrain and its resemblance to the place where I grew up. All that open space makes me feel vulnerable and exposed. But there's a familiar beauty to it as well. I'm out of shape, but Laura's barely breathing. I'm grateful when she stops and looks up toward the summit. She lifts her arms above her head and sighs. "I feel so free when I'm out here. No stoplights or traffic. No buildings or concrete. You can just *be*, you know? Don't get me wrong, I like the city, but I grew up along the bayou, and it's part of me. Maybe the best part."

We keep walking, and I stagger when a gust of wind knocks me off balance. I stop. Wait for it to die down. Purse my lips and squeeze my eyes shut until it passes. When I open my eyes again, Laura is still walking and has gotten much farther ahead of me. She has her arms stretched out, parallel to the ground, letting her hands ride the air like a pair of wings. Of course she does, this person who is open to everything and everyone.

It takes us an hour, and when we get to the top, I'm dripping with sweat. I try discreetly to catch my breath, wandering over to read a posted sign about the trail we're on. There's a map and a "you are here" star marking our location, which is 2,000 feet above the ground. Laura walks over to me. We watch a paraglider take a few running steps before launching into the void below. "Damn," I say. He disappears before rising again. "No way in hell."

"I know, right?" Laura says. "But there's something to be said about using the wind instead of fighting against it. Smart. I mean think about it. Turbines create electricity. All that force. The power of it."

"Mmmm," I say. "Yes, all the damage it leaves in its wake. God, I mean, Hurricane Katrina?"

Her shoulders slump. "Biscuit, you're not getting it." She lines up next to me, shoulder to shoulder, facing forward, toward the place where the paraglider jumped. "Close your eyes." I stand there. "C'mon, trust me."

I shut my eyes, but I leave the left one open a tiny bit so I can peek through my eyelashes. She takes my hand, and steps forward, trying to take me with her. I stay planted. Through clenched teeth I say, "If you think I'm going to Thelma and Louise off this rock with you, you've got another thing coming." I ease my hand away from hers. She laughs and takes another step forward without me, closer to the edge of the cliff, but not dangerously so. Still, my stomach lurches. I picture her plummeting to the ground below. A powerful gust hits me in the chest and I react by dropping to all fours. Debris and dust pelt me in the face, and I close my eyes again and turn my head. When I open my eyes, Laura is still closer to the edge than I'd like, and she is leaning forward, full-bodied against the wind, at an impossible angle, with her head tilted up and her eyes closed. She trusts the wind to hold her there. And it does.

24

FORTY-EIGHT HOURS SPEED BY in a blink but also feel like an entire lifetime I've been missing. I'm getting dressed to meet Laura for breakfast, when a package arrives FedEx overnight for me at Manor House. I recognize my mother's handwriting and the return address. At first I think she's sending me a care package, that I will open it up and find chocolate chip cookies or maybe even a replacement iPhone. Instead, I find a letter from her, printed on scented stationery, paper-clipped to a sealed envelope inside a box layered with tissue paper. I unfold her note, which reads:

Dearest Sky,

As you requested, I asked your father if he had received any mail for you over the years that he had neglected to give to you. I truly had no idea that these letters existed or that your father was aware of your brother's whereabouts this entire time. He hid these inside the safe in his office. Apparently, he kept them in case he needed them as proof that your brother had broken the no contact order imposed by the courts after his arrest. It's no excuse, but your father was desperate to keep your brother away from you and out of our lives. He was the one who asked the hospital social worker to break the news to you about your brother's death. He told her that we couldn't bear to do it and begged her to help. Evidently he was fairly convincing. Even though the adoption was "closed," he still worried that your brother would show up on our doorstep, kidnapping you again or asking for money. He was trying to protect us. At any rate, I found more than I bargained for inside that safe, and it will take some sorting to get through the rest of it.

I've had quite a bit of time to reflect on our last visit together. I realize I haven't been the best mother to you. I never had much of an example myself. So I did the best I could. None of this will be the explanation or apology you need. We talked about forgiveness while I was there. I've realized that you don't need to forgive me or love me. That was never your job. You didn't choose me. I chose you. As your mom, it was my job to love you unconditionally, without expecting anything in return. And though you'll find it hard to believe, I did, and I do.

All this reflection had me digging through some of your childhood things: memories and photos and other mementos I kept, and when I came across this, I thought you should have it again. The night I found this, you had been noisy and heartbroken, and, even back then, a part of me realized that some things simply can't be replaced. I'm hoping in the end that despite our differences, you'll decide that I'm one of those things too.

Even though I didn't know your brother was still alive, I certainly played a part in keeping him from you—in trying to make a new life and family for you in place of the one you had. But we are all a part of you. And there's more than enough love to go around.

Your brother is alive, and these belong to you.

I love you, always. Mom

Tears blur my vision. I wipe them away and set the note on the bedspread next to me, along with the envelope. With the box in my lap, I pull away the tissue paper. My hand reaches inside, touching something soft and familiar. I lift Bunny into my arms. That velvety, well-worn stuffed toy from my childhood. I hug Bunny to my chest. He smells clean. His ratty tears and loose seams have been mended; his missing eye replaced. This is the only thing I have left from my childhood, and my mother has saved it for me. I want to hate her. To scream at her, though she isn't here to hear it. I want to hold onto my rage, the belief that she didn't love me, she loved the idea of me—that she wore me like a jeweled necklace—an accessory—until she realized I wasn't valuable. And yet.

I press my cheeks to Bunny's soft fabric, into the comfort and safety of it. While my mother and I may never be able to find middle ground, it is impossible to deny that love is beneath all of it. And I have to admit my own failings: that I have been so afraid of being abandoned by her and everyone else, that I abandoned myself. That's on me. No matter what the future holds, I can't allow myself to do that anymore.

Your brother is alive, and these belong to you.

My hands tremble. I pick up a large envelope addressed to me, with no return address, stuffed with pages torn from Ben's notebook. Already, I have wasted so much time.

I shove the envelope and Bunny and a few other things into my backpack and catch the bus to Laura's. As soon as she hears about the letters, she's on the phone with Banner Hospital and Dr. Nez, trying to get an update on the patient's condition. A nurse confirms that the man is still a patient at the hospital, and Laura is put through to voice mail, where she tells Dr. Nez that the man is Ben Rayner and that Sky Fielder is his sister, that this is the best number to reach Sky, and that Sky is on her way. We jump on the computer and search same-day flights from Austin to Tucson, and they are booked solid, except for one flight leaving late that evening, which costs almost $1,000 and would get me there later than driving. Within the hour, we are packed up into the Prius, with Bella in the back seat, heading west.

As we drive, we wait for a phone call from Dr. Nez to get the update on Ben's condition. We have twelve hours on the road, so I open Ben's letters one by one. I read some sections out loud to Laura and summarize others. I'm immersed in his story: in what he says, and what he doesn't say, with my mind filling in the blanks of how he lived and what became of him after the accident. The pages aren't really letters, as much as they are torn out journal entries. But I'm hoping they'll tell me what kind of life he's had over the last decade and how he ended up in that hospital. As I put together the narrative, I search for answers. If he was alive, and he knew where I was, why did he go to Arizona? Why didn't he come and find me instead?

I spent my fifteenth birthday in a juvenile detention center in Pecos, Texas. Harrison came to see me, but I yelled at him, called him a traitor and a few other words I won't repeat here. His job was to take care of us, and he'd fucked that up big time. How could it be the best answer, the only option the man could find, to separate us—after everything we'd been through?

Before we crashed, Sky had said that she hated me, and I couldn't really blame her. I almost killed her, and it made me feel like a monster. The last thing I ever wanted was for her to be afraid of me—and in the truck, she looked terrified. Harrison assured me that she'd recover from her injuries, which was the only good news I got.

The court convicted me as an adjudicated delinquent for illegal weapons possession, auto theft, trespassing, obstruction, and kidnapping. I received seven years in juvenile prison, to be released sometime before my 22nd birthday. Seven years. Harrison of course told me I was lucky, that sometimes they tried teens as adults. But the worst blow was the no contact order. I would have no visitation and no contact, supervised or otherwise, with Sky while she was a juvenile. I was a threat to her safety. I couldn't write or call, even though I knew the address and phone number, or I'd get more time added to my sentence. And even though she hated me, I wanted to tell her I was sorry—that I'd do better—be better when I got out.

★ ★ ★

"Inmate Z85521, sign here." An officer shoved a piece of paper across the desk to me. "Remember the number. We don't use names here." Thick walls surrounded me. The faint smell of urine. Static inside my head as the officer kept speaking. "You'll need it to sign for your mail, to check out books, and get class credit." I picked up the pen using both hands and scribbled my signature.

At the next station, they took my fingerprints. A woman removed the contents of my backpack. Catalogued the items inside. My sleeping bag, my books—items I had with me at the scene of the accident.

"What happens to my things?" I asked her.

She leafed through the pages of my journal, shaking it upside down, before handing it to me. The photo of me and Sky fell out and I leaped for it. The woman flinched but let me keep the photo. "You can have the rest when you get out. Officer Reyes will escort you to the search area."

A short, Hispanic man with a coarse black mustache and beady eyes led me by the elbow into a room containing several other kids and male guards. He unlocked my cuffs and shackles and said, "Strip down." I hesitated. "Now, inmate!" Reyes shouted.

I took off my shoes and socks. I unbuttoned the shirt Harrison had given me to wear in court. I caught one of the other boys looking at the white blotches on my shoulders, knew without even saying a single word, I was marked as someone who'd be easy to make fun of. Finally, I dropped my shorts and boxers. Embarrassment burned my face. I cupped my hands in front of me.

"Raise your arms above your head. Show me your armpits." Reyes commanded. "Run your fingers through your hair and shake it. Lift your genitals." I didn't move. "Lift up your penis and testicles. Do it now, or I will do it for you."

My eyes stung, anger building up behind them along with tears. I grabbed my junk, gave the perv a good look, wanting to rip his head off. This was new a new type of anger, raw like blistered skin.

"Bend over and spread your cheeks." A few boys ahead of me were already on this step of the processing. I heard several self-conscious coughs and stole looks at those in front of me. We were

boys—an assembly line of bare asses, acne, and struggling body hair. I bent at the waist. I pulled my cheeks apart. "Wider. Squat and cough twice." I did as he said, but in my mind, I went someplace else.

I followed the others naked to the showers, where they sprayed our heads, underarms, and pubic hair, what little some of us had, with chemicals to kill lice, whether we needed it or not. They handed me red cotton pants and a cotton shirt that looked like hospital scrubs, a loose V-neck pullover without pockets or buttons. Elastic waistband with no drawstring. The socks and underwear were threadbare and stained. We wore plastic shower shoes, stretched out and cracked, but easy for the guards to hose off. I worried I might puke. I was the smallest guy in line, a head shorter than anyone around me.

The hall echoed with our feet. We filed into an empty cafeteria and were told to take a seat. A white man, with a military-style haircut, shoulders the size of a steer, spoke to us.

"You are now the property of the state of Texas. I am your mommy, your daddy, your priest, and your executioner. The staff here has the authority to use any means necessary to maintain the safety of others in this facility, including your fellow inmates and guards. You are here because you have been deemed a danger to society, and in the interest of public safety, you have been removed from your fellow human beings. You've lost your freedom because of your decisions. You will eat and sleep and study and work when we tell you to. You get an hour outside in the morning and another in the afternoon. Other privileges you earn, like extra television hours and more days receiving visitors. You can make collect calls to the outside world once per week. You cannot receive phone calls. Do anything illegal, and your sentence can be extended. If you age

out of your sentence here, you'll finish your time in adult prison. Gang activity is strictly prohibited, which doesn't mean it doesn't exist. My only advice is to keep your eyes open and hide any sign of weakness. The guards are not your friends. They have a job to do, and they will do it."

★ ★ ★

I ignored the other kids at school, work program, and meals. I spent my time looking at the ground, at my feet, anywhere but in another person's eyes. It was like Papa used to tell me about predators and aggression. Never look a wild animal in the eye or it will take it as a challenge.

In the rec yard those first few days, I watched groups of prisoners, separated by race, orbit each other. The Mexicans would claim a picnic table, the Black guys grouped together under the basketball hoop, the white inmates hung out along the back wall. I tried to understand the rules for a game I never wanted to play. I convinced myself I could stay safe by keeping my head down, acting tough, studying my environment. Still, eyes in the courtyard ran over me, jutted chins, whispers. Danger crackled.

♦ 25 ♦

"HEY, PECKERWOOD, YOU GOT something in between your teeth."

The words came from behind me, just as I left the lunch line. I tried to ignore them, to pretend they were meant for someone else.

"Hey, you deaf, fuckhead? I said, you've got something in between your teeth."

I whirled around and into the fist of one of the BGF members, a Black guy twice my size. The punch knocked me backward a step, but I held my ground and my lunch tray.

"My fist. My fist is in your teeth, get it?" he said. Five of his buddies stood behind him laughing like this was the funniest thing they'd ever heard. I ran my tongue along my lower lip and tasted blood. I knew what I had to do. In my counseling session two days ago, they told me to "make good choices," but there weren't any choices, not in here. In here, the color of your skin determined where you belonged, which side you were on, and the rules of engagement—like chess pieces on a game board.

I grinned at the guy, repositioned my carton of milk, and swung the tray full out at his head, aiming for the bridge of his nose. The others swarmed me then. Fists and feet and elbows connecting with my face and gut and balls. Food from our plates went airborne, covering us. We slid across the greasy floor, a tangle of bodies, watered-down spaghetti sauce, cooking oil, sweat, and spit. The guards dispersed us with blasts of pepper spray and dragged me away in a choke hold. My tooth remained in a puddle of blood on the floor.

At dinner that night, I took my place in the back at a table by myself so I could see the room. The other guys from the BGF and the Mexicans from the EME murmured, stared, probably plotting their next moves against me. After I sat down, the Aryan Brotherhood of Texas members picked up their trays and joined me. One by one, they introduced themselves. The leader, a man who went by the name of Spider, jutted his chin at another guy by the name of Doc, who slid his portion of fries over to me. "You handled yourself well today, man. Six on one. Showed those toads you weren't going to be anybody's bitch." Spider stood around six foot three, bony arms and legs, like his nickname, with a shaved head and a pointy, jet-black goatee. A scar like a dry riverbed stretched from the corner of his eye to the bottom of his ear.

I gummed a French fry with my injured mouth and waited.

"You know who we are?" Spider asked. Instead of waiting for an answer, he told me. "We are a dying breed, that's who we are. Our race is our nation, and all the inbreeding, immigration, and desegregation threaten to make us extinct. Understand? Our way of life is under attack." He stared at me hard without blinking and stood up. He raised his voice like he was speaking to the entire room, not just me. "We stand for the purity of the Aryan race and the advancement, power, and financial gain of our people."

Echoes of "fuck you" and "sit down, motherfucker" filled the room. A guard shifted closer to our table. Spider sat and placed a hand on the guy next to him. "I'm assigning Sleet as your sponsor in the ABT." Sleet reached across the table and shook my hand. It seemed an odd gesture, like I'd just been hired for a job. Sleet's tattoos—interlocking triangles, the letters AB, double lightning bolts, an iron cross—raced up and down both arms and up onto his shoulders and the square of his thick neck. He sported a quarter-inch, platinum-bleached mohawk down the middle of his shaved skull. It bristled like a dog raising its hackles. Spider continued, "Decide to be with us, and we've got your back. No one will mess with you in here. But it's your decision. You can always go it alone and see how that works out for you. But you're either with us, or you're our enemy too. Ours—and theirs."

I glanced around the room at the other tables. I had just turned fifteen. I was 5'6" and 120 pounds. My voice cracked when I spoke. The older guys in here were men, broad-shouldered, muscle-bound, and tatted up, with dead eyes masking everything but their hate for each other and now me. I wasn't a skinhead. But that didn't seem to matter anymore. In here, even the Blacks and Mexicans expected me to be racist, whether I was or not.

I nodded, clenched my jaw to look edgy and tough, and when lunch was over, I heaved up the few fries I'd eaten into the nearest trash can.

⋆ ⋆ ⋆

I shared a cell with Sleet, who was the scariest guy I'd ever met. I never caught his real name. Everyone inside had a nickname, and the guys in the ABT called me Sweetwater, since that's where I'd come from. A few months older than me, Sleet took up most of the room with a body like a rhino. Solid layers of compact muscle covered every inch of his frame. He stood at least four inches taller than me, with quads and biceps squared off by time, discipline, and ego.

Our room had two bunks, each tastefully decorated with a thin gray blanket, pillow, sheet, and stained mattress, separated by a couple of feet at most. Above each cot, a long shelf held any personal belongings. A shared desk and chair, both bolted down, provided a place to study. A stainless steel, single unit sink and toilet combo faced outward into the room. Take a shit, and everyone could watch you.

Sleet adopted me as his special project. The ABT was surprisingly well organized, like a foreign country with its own government, where you studied to become a citizen. Sleet quizzed me each night on the constitution and bylaws of the ABT, explaining anything I didn't understand. At times, Sleet would get frustrated with my lack of attention or enthusiasm, and he'd hurl a shoe or pillow at my head. It made me thankful they had so many rules about what they allowed inmates to keep in their cells. One night while we hung out in our cell after dinner, I got to a section I didn't understand and asked Sleet, "What's 'blood in'?"

He sat on the edge of his cot, which sagged beneath him. "It's what you've got to do to get into the ABT." He crossed over to my bunk and stood next to it. "It's an act of violence ordered by the ABT to show your loyalty. Think of it as your final initiation."

I hesitated, but I had to know. Just how violent were we talking about here? "What was yours?"

"I got the order to hit one of the EME gang members. But the guy ran, so I couldn't get to him. Instead, I took out his entire family. Tied them to chairs and burned the house down with them in it."

My mouth fell open and the color drained from my face.

"Man, don't look at me like that. The guy deserved it—fucking coward. Worst thing you can do is run. Once I get out of here, I'm going to find him. Might take years, but I'm patient."

"How will you find him?"

"There's no escaping us. We cover the whole Southwest. We're everywhere, man." He wiggled his fingers, then poked me in the chest. "And don't feel sorry for that motherfucker. He'd done some serious shit. Plus, I saved the family's dog. I'm not a monster or anything."

My tongue sat heavy on the floor of my mouth. He laughed at me and flopped back down on his bed. I curled onto my side, facing the opposite wall, reading the rest of the rules, and wondering what I would be asked to do for blood in—and worse, what would happen to me if I refused to do it. I thought about the day my parents died. No way to forget a second of it. But this was different, wasn't it?

The day I killed our Papa, it was Sky's fifth birthday.

That morning, our parents had come up empty-handed, once again, without a present for Sky. Any money we ever had went toward drugs—though Sky still thought it was their "medicine." That morning, Mama could barely get out of bed, but she did, and she gave Sky a birthday squeeze before measuring Sky against an old doorjamb we brought with us whenever we moved. Then she measured me. It was a tradition we'd kept ever since I could remember—measuring each of us no matter whose birthday it was. She notched our heights and the dates into the soft wood and commented on how tall Sky had grown since last year. Still, when Sky realized Mama and Papa hadn't gotten her a present, she started sniffling, and Papa lost his temper.

"Hey, little miss," he told her. "You have everything you need. Don't go thinking you're something special. The things you want in this life will own you. Get that through your head." His hands shook and his mouth twitched, and we knew better than to say a word to him. He grabbed his hat and went outside to check on the

chickens. After he left, Mama said she'd make a cake later and for Sky not to pay attention to Papa, that he was just grumpy and wasn't feeling well—that we should go ahead and take our hike while she got the cake going.

I led Sky up the wild game trail in Skeleton Canyon. We picked our way over limestone and shale, leaning into a steep hillside carved out by wind and water. Sky kept up, until she couldn't. I could see her out of my peripheral vision as she plopped down on a slab of rock, her hair as wild and white as a dandelion puff. I wished I'd had the guts to mouth off to Papa. It wasn't wrong for a five-year-old to want a new toy for her birthday—one she'd picked out—or a party, or friends, or even a goddamned pony. Might be different if she demanded it or hadn't gone to sleep hungry half the time.

"No shame in going slow," I said. I twirled a piece of grass between my thumb and forefinger. "You know what I do when I've got a long hike ahead? I think about one step. That's it. Just taking one more step. I concentrate on the next place I'm going to put my foot, and then the one after that. Then before I know it, I'm there."

"I already tried that," Sky said, panting. "Tell me 'The Legend of Skeleton Canyon' to keep my mind off of it," she said.

I groaned. "You could tell it to me by now."

"Not if you want me to keep walking."

I sighed. "Alright. But only because it's your birthday." In truth, I loved the story and telling it—especially since I knew that one day she'd stop asking. I pulled her to her feet, picked up a small rock, started walking up the trail again. After I told her the story, she got excited about the possibility of us finding the treasure, that maybe it would happen because it was her birthday.

We reached a section of the gulch with a cave large enough to stand in carved into the side. I took off my jacket and let the sweat beneath it dry in the cool air.

"Is this it?" Sky asked. I nodded. "Is this where the treasure is?"

"Could be," I humored her. I didn't have the heart to tell her that even if treasure existed, people like us would never be the ones to find it. "We have to search every one of these caves. And this place and these trails, our backyard," I said, arms sweeping wide, "goes for hundreds of miles, through Texas, across New Mexico and Arizona, all the way down into Mexico."

She peered into the darkness of the cave. "Are there ghosts in there?" She tucked her chin to her chest to hide the fact that she was scared.

"Toughen up, Sky. You're five now. You wanted to come with me." I tried not to get irritated with her whining since it was her birthday. "Besides, you'll never find that treasure without taking some risks."

"I'm as tough as you are, if you'd ever give me the chance to prove it," she sulked. Then, without sounding very tough, she said, "I'm hungry."

I sighed, opened my pack, and took out strips of old venison jerky I saved for our hikes. Sky sat cross-legged and gnawed on a slice of it. I stood at the edge of the cave looking out over the canyon and the river floor. I stretched my arms to the sky, inhaled deep and long. When I exhaled, my breath hung in the air. I tucked my hands deep in my pockets. The days of running barefoot were over, and the tough calluses of summer wouldn't protect us much longer. Soon we'd be cooped up inside with each other, and that trailer would feel more like a prison than a home—a place you'd want to escape from as often as possible.

I swigged from the water bottle, held it out to Sky, who did the same. I wiped my mouth with the back of my hand.

We stayed in the cave for a few hours, enough time for the sun to move across the sky and create hard shadows across the walls of clay and stone. A part of me wanted us to stay there, live in that cave, make it our own personal hideout. The other part knew it was time to go back home, see whether it had turned out to be a good day or a bad one, and be a man about it.

Scrambling downhill took half the time it had going up, and we had fun doing it. I worked with Sky on riding down the scree, sliding sidestep, letting the loose gravel carry us while trying to remain upright. Sky braced herself with a hand on my pack when she lost her footing.

When we reached the junk garden near the house, we stopped, hands on knees to catch our breath. A raven perched on the lip of a metal oil drum, which lay rusted on its side, enveloped by weeds and soil, becoming one with the earth again. I felt the pulse of my heart in my hands. "You're getting fast," I told Sky, who flushed with the compliment. I placed an arm across her shoulders as we walked across the field. A yelp drifted on the wind. Coyote, maybe, but then, no. I heard Papa's voice, then Mama's, high-pitched, pleading. Sky exchanged a look with me, her brow knotted. I lowered my arm in front of Sky's chest like a gate at a railway crossing to stop her from walking farther. I listened again. Over the ripple of the creek, I made out the scattering burst of words.

The crack of splintering wood followed by a sickening silence propelled me toward the house. A slow jog turned into a sprint as I yelled over my shoulder to Sky. "Do. Not. Move. Not one step from where you are. I mean it, Sky." I shed my pack without breaking stride. "Not one inch until I come back."

I burst through the door, slamming it against the wall. Papa spun toward me with spit and sweat flying off him like a rabid dog. He had the rifle pointed at Mama, who lay on the ground. He jabbed it at my chest. I held up both hands. Mama whimpered, rising up to her hands and knees, her forehead bleeding, glass shattered and crunching beneath her palms. The air vibrated with adrenaline. "Run, Ben. Take Sky!" The words came out as a guttural moan, more animal than human. "Go! Please, go!" She inched toward me, and Papa placed the toe of his boot against her shoulder to stop her.

I opened my mouth, tried to speak, but couldn't.

Papa said, "Bitch stole money in my own goddamned house. Ingredients for a fucking cake."

Mama shook her head, "You used it up. You don't even know because you're so out of your head."

My dry mouth hung open. My feet rooted to the spot. Papa moved toward Mama, aimed the rifle at her, and without even hesitating—pulled the trigger. I jumped at the sound, hands over my ears. "No, no, no . . . please . . . no." But it was too late for begging.

Papa turned toward me, looked over my head out the open door and yelled for Sky to come to the house. When he stared at me again, his eyes were cold and black at the center, and I knew—there would be no good end to this—Papa would kill us. "She's got nothing to do with this," I blurted. "Just let us go."

Papa either didn't seem to hear or didn't care anymore. He bent his head sideways to make his shout heard outside. "Sky! Now!"

When I didn't move and Sky didn't answer, Papa held the gun out to the side and used his other hand to shove me away from the doorway. I stood my ground, leaned in toward Papa, refusing to budge. My whole body convulsed with the effort.

"So this is how it is? You think you're a man now?" Papa said. He thrust the rifle toward me and laughed when I flinched. "That's what I thought." Papa made a move to step by me, but I grabbed the barrel of the gun and held tight. "You best let go now, boy. It ends here."

Papa yanked, but I used my other hand to grip the stock. We wrestled the rifle between us, until Papa jabbed it at me, throwing me off balance. I reeled backward but kept from falling.

Papa laughed and struck me with the butt of the rifle at my temple. I blinked at the flashes of light in between my eyes, and then I lunged. My legs wobbled and gave way. I fell into Papa, tangling our feet, and sending us both to the floor. The gun fired. For a moment we lay still on the ground. I waited to feel pain or to see Papa raise the gun and finish me off. But Papa wasn't moving. Dust hung in the air around us. I shifted from beneath Papa, my ears ringing, the gun on the floor where it had come to rest. I stumbled to my feet, teetering over Papa, who I gripped by the shoulder and rolled over slowly.

I stared at Papa's face, now all but unrecognizable. The blast had blown apart his jaw and cheekbones. His eyes remained wide, staring at me, maybe through me. I staggered sideways, surveyed the room, and saw my mother move. I dove toward her, skidded on my knees to her side. "Okay, okay," I murmured, trying to think. I placed my palms against the gunshot wound, which made her cry out. Blood ran in rivers from her abdomen, through my fingers, braiding out and around, a relentless current. She shuddered; her breath ragged and wet. "I'll get help," I said. I started to stand, but Mama rested her hand over mine, stopping me. She shook her head side to side. She knew.

As gentle as a breeze after a hurricane, the life left her. I held onto her, rested my head on her chest. No, no, no. Please. "I'm sorry. I'm so sorry." I whispered it over and over, half confession, half prayer. From my knees I rose and looked at the room. What was left of our lives had splintered to pieces. I heard my breath, taut and wheezing. Particles of dust floated inside a sliver of light like embers from the last of a dying fire.

Our parents gone. Sky, waiting for me outside. She would come looking for me. She couldn't see this. I grabbed a bucket of dishwater from the counter, poured it over my hands into the sink, hurried to wash away the blood. Afterward, I wiped my eyes with the back of a sleeve, took a last look in Mama's direction. There, next to her feet, a small bird sat staring at me. How long had it been there? Surely it wouldn't have stayed through all the noise and violence that had happened. I didn't necessarily believe in the afterlife, but I couldn't dismiss it entirely.

"You can go," my voice broke. The bird twitched its head, considering. A sob caught in my throat. "You don't have to worry anymore," I said. "It's okay. We'll be alright. I'll take care of us." The whispered promise hung in the air. I took careful steps toward the bird, reached out my hand, felt the brush of feathers and the air of a wingbeat as she disappeared.

I gathered myself, took a deep breath, and went out the door to find my sister. She was hiding inside an old empty oil barrel, shaking like an earthquake. I reached out to her, smiled, told her everything would be okay, and then threw up in the grass. I ended up walking her over to the Ramseys' farm, a quarter mile, a place Mama left her sometimes when I had been in school, and Sky was too little to go yet. I told Sky and the Ramseys that our parents weren't feeling well, and I needed to take care of them.

Papa had dug a new pit away from the arroyo for us to bury any animal parts we couldn't use after a hunt. We called it the bone pile. It seemed undignified to bury them there, so I tried to start a new hole, quickly realizing there was no way I could do it on my own. The ground was too hard, and it would take too long. So I buried our parents at the bottom of the bone pile in a grave my father had ended up digging for himself, while taking our mama with him. I spent the rest of the day covering the pit back up with dirt and cleaning the trailer. If I live to be a hundred, I'll never forget how hard that was—will never stop seeing all that blood. And because I didn't want to spoil Sky's birthday for the rest of her life, when I came to get her from the Ramseys, I told her Mama and Papa were at the hospital, that they were real sick but being taken care of.

I waited two more days, and when she came home from school one day, I told her that they had died and showed her where they were buried. We planted some flowers and said a few words, and I made Sky promise not to tell anyone that we were on our own. She cried for a while, but we got back into a routine, and time smoothed out the rough edges. We still were fighting for our survival, but at least we didn't have to factor our parents into that equation anymore.

♦ 26 ♦

2019

LAURA PULLS OVER TO the side of the road. Rain pours around us. Bella has joined me in the front seat, in my lap, and I stroke her fur for comfort. "I guess some part of me knew what happened to our parents," I say, watching raindrops leave trails down the window and tracing them with my fingertip. "I just packed it away. It's so unfair that Ben had to live with that. He protected us, but it's obvious he felt guilty. I don't think he'll ever forgive himself. He was already a hero to me—larger than life, my big brother. But now, well . . ."

"He must have been so scared at Danville. Those places are horrible. Worse than adult prisons, I think, because the kids are so vulnerable." A thunderhead forms on the horizon with lightning illuminating it from the inside.

"It's hard for me to picture him there. I like remembering him swinging from the tire swing in Skeleton Canyon, not joining a gang and . . . hurting people."

"If he did, he had no choice." A couple of trucks pass us, spraying our small car in their wake. "Do you know where we are?" Laura asks. I shake my head. She hands me her phone, which is mapping our route. "We are six miles from Skeleton Canyon."

And even through the rain, I see the changes in the terrain. The red dirt. The pitted landscape. Cactus brush and arroyos. Mesas rising that will yield to deep rifts. The land is suddenly alive, taking shape and form. I expect to feel swallowed up by it, but instead, I feel drawn to it, like it might hold all the secrets and answers I need to become whole again. For my brother, too. "Our beginning and end," I say, without really thinking about what I mean, except that I know it goes on and on . . . that the canyon connects three states and another country. We were only a small part of it.

"We could go," Laura says. "It's not really out of the way."

I consider this, but the canyon isn't mine. It's ours. "No. I'll wait. It doesn't seem right to go there without Ben. It was our home, but without him, it's just soil and sagebrush." There's no real beauty to the land without my brother in it—because he's as much a part of Skeleton Canyon as the creeks and pinyon and yucca. And even though it's magical thinking, a part of me thinks that if I wait, if I do this one thing, he'll be able to go back with me.

We keep driving and Laura's phone pings. Dr. Nez has left her a voice message. Cell service is intermittent at best. Laura plays it back on speaker so I can hear it.

"I got your message, and I'm glad to hear that Sky is on her way. Ben's condition is deteriorating. I'll try to keep you posted on any ongoing developments, but I'm hoping Sky can get here soon. You have my number."

My brother is getting worse. Laura presses the accelerator. We keep moving in the direction of Ben, skirting the edges of Skeleton Canyon, the past and future colliding like a Texas thunderstorm.

★ ★ ★

When I wasn't worrying about my initiation, I settled into a routine—something I hadn't had in a very long time. You could count on things at Danville: breakfast, school, exercise, lunch, work program, dinner, lights out. The food tasted like garbage, but it came at the same time every day and there was plenty. We had access to computers, though most sites were blocked. In my spare time, I wrote in my journal. Sometimes I did it to document things; other times, I envisioned Sky reading it—hearing about what had become of my life. Despite all the gritty parts of it, it made me feel better—like I was talking to her—even though the conversation only went one way.

Beyond three squares, rec activities, and school, inmates got television privileges in the main room, though the set was typically set to the National Geographic channel or something designed not to get us riled up with sex, drugs, or violence. I pretended to hate it, to complain that programs showing lemurs and bear cubs were lame—but I loved them. Watching nature shows was like going home. No other way to put it.

Fights broke out every other day. A guy from the BGF used a spoon to dig out the mortar between the bricks in his cell until he finally got one loose. He cracked the skull of one of the ABT guys with it. Another guy from EME hung himself with his shirt and pants tied together and twisted into a rope. At night, I yanked the pillow over my head to muffle the screams.

I didn't trust the guards—you couldn't. I'd seen them beat a kid half to death, choke inmates, piss on them, and worse. I tried to be brave, to shake off feeling like a scared little boy instead of a man. Hanging with the ABT was the only time I felt safe and protected. And then I met Micro.

Chaplain Mike, Micro as he was sometimes called because of his short, featherweight build, looked to be in his forties, short Afro, neatly trimmed soul patch with a bit of gray, dressed in Levi's and a polo shirt, Vans slip-ons, carrying a messenger bag. Tattoos peeked out from beneath the cuff of his short sleeve, a silver cross dangled from his neck.

For weeks, I'd waved the man off, not wanting to talk, especially about God—but today, I was on edge. The reality of my situation was setting in, and I was terrified I was becoming someone else. Someone I hated. Someone my sister would hate.

Micro paused at my cell, saw me looking at the messenger bag, and said, "I carry this instead of a briefcase. Briefcases make people nervous, like I'm going to serve them papers or something." He smiled, bottom teeth capped in silver. "What's on your mind today? You alright?" He glanced at Sleet's empty cot. "Mind if I sit?"

I jutted my chin at the bed as a yes. "I don't believe in God; you should know that first off." Micro didn't flinch, which softened me a little. "I mean, maybe there's something out there greater that created trees and rivers, but I'm not sure it's some dude with a beard in white robes who pulls puppet strings."

"That so? I kind of picture him as a righteous Black man who looks like Michael B. Jordan, but to each his own." Micro laughed. "Just so you know, it's not a requirement that you believe in God or any religion or any of that for us to talk. I've

been where you are, and sometimes it just helps to know that someone on the outside cares."

I shook my head. "What do you mean, you've been where I am? Dude, I'm in jail."

He folded his hands and leaned forward like he was letting me in on a secret. Scars that looked like cigarette burns dotted his forearms. "That's exactly what I mean. I was in and out of juvenile facilities, and when I got out I studied theology—went into the seminary—got ordained."

I considered this, weighed my skepticism against the need to blow off steam and talk about what was happening. I crossed my arms over my chest, trying to hold back.

Micro continued, "Also, anything you say stays with me. Unless you're planning to hurt yourself or someone else, I'm sworn to secrecy." He leaned back. Sleet's bedframe squeaked. Somebody down the hall yelled out, "Motherfucker!"

My chest tightened. Maybe telling someone what I felt would ease the pressure cooker inside my head. Writing in my journal was one thing, but it couldn't replace talking to an actual human being. I studied the man, wondered if I could trust him. "You're Black," I said.

"You noticed."

"So how does that work? I'm affiliated. ABT, you know?"

"In here, you could say I've earned a certain amount of respect. For one, yeah, I'm Black, but hey, wouldn't you know it, my mama was white. Second, I'm the only pastor who comes here. I get a free pass on all sides. Sort of an unwritten truce. I don't give anyone up, never have—and everyone here knows it. The second I do, I'm done here. No one would trust me again."

Micro's aftershave, cleaner smelling than anything in Danville, wafted over to my bunk. I was sure it was Old Spice or something, but to me it was nothing less than the tidy scent of freedom. I glanced around to the empty hall and whispered, "All that white supremacist stuff is bullshit."

"Glad to hear it, but it wouldn't change my job in here. And, just so you know, you're not the only kid in here who feels like they don't have a choice. Every guy in here is just trying to survive."

I chewed on my thumb, stared at my feet, and started talking. A few sentences in, the words burst out of me like water spewing from a burst pipe. It was less about trust and maybe more about having no room left for the garbage inside my head. I told him about the court order and about the Fielders, how they were crazy rich. Micro listened, nodded his head every now and then. "Who knows what her new parents have told her about me, likely nothing good. They'll poison her against me. By the time I get out, she won't even want to see me." I popped my knuckles. "I just don't want her to forget about me. I was thinking maybe I could have someone on the outside from the ABT check on her for me or sneak a message to her. I have the address."

Micro, who had been sitting quietly listening, held up both hands. "Stop right there. You want to get her killed? Worst thing you can do in here is let anyone in here know who you love and what you care about. Plus, you said the Fielders are rich. All red flags, my man."

"Well then what the fuck am I supposed to do?" I realized the swear and apologized for it.

He swatted it away like a mosquito. "Let's break this down. Stay with me. What can you do from in here, other than get into more trouble or put Sky in serious danger? Deep down, she knows who you are and what you mean to her. You'll have to trust that—or convince her otherwise once you're free. For now, your sister needs someone to raise her and keep her safe. She's a little kid. She needs parents."

I rubbed the top of my head. "So you're saying that me not being in her life at all is for the best."

Micro crossed his legs, cradled one knee. "Yeah, crazy as it sounds, that's exactly what I'm saying. You said your job was to take care of her, to keep her safe. Maybe you do that best by doing nothing."

"Please don't give me the whole 'If you love something set it free' speech. I'm so tired of hearing that shi—stuff." I swallowed the knot in my throat, the tangled-up emotions that wanted to be tears.

"I know, man" he said, his mouth in a tight line. "I know."

After Micro left, I stared at the photo of me and Sky. She had a life with the Fielders, not with me. I pressed a fist to my forehead. The world was going to move on without me, and I'd go insane if I kept obsessing about things I couldn't change. I slid the photo back into the journal. My life outside these walls had been put on hold, but life inside had just started.

♦ 27 ♦

ABOUT THREE MONTHS INTO my sentence, as I lay on my bunk reading a Star Wars graphic novel I'd borrowed from the library, I got the direct order from Spider for blood in. I thought it would be against the BGF, but it was against one of our own. Doc had been green lit by Spider for tipping off a guard about illegal contraband we planned to use in a hit against the BGF.

When the commissary delivery came, Sleet stopped doing push-ups in the middle of our cell and handed me my package. Inside I found a razor blade wedged inside a package of ramen along with a folded square of paper. I handed Sleet the note. He slapped me on the back.

"You got this, Sweetwater," he said, like I was about to make a game-winning free throw. "I'll be right there with you."

A smear of words in orange crayon read: "Meet in the yard at 10:35am. Bring the weapon. Use the razor to remove Doc's patches and strip away his affiliation with the ABT." I stared at Sleet, confused. "Patches?"

"You're going to skin him, bro. Shear off his gang tats." He returned to his push-ups. Sweat hung in the room. I stifled any reaction, choked it down with the bile in my throat. "Keep it quiet

too. If the guards know, they'll isolate him in the SHU to keep him safe. If we can't get to him, we'll go after his family."

I held the package at my side.

"Hey, you know, you always have a choice, even if one of them is dying. Free will and all that shit."

I thought about the Fielders. Rich people. The different path my sister was walking. "Maybe, but other people seem to have choices that don't have anything to do with life or death. Like whether to order eggs Benedict or a Frappuccino."

"Nah, even the Wall Street dudes with penthouse suites sometimes hurl themselves off high-rises. Death is always an option—or the result of inaction, which, in my opinion, is still a choice."

I had been in prison for months, but I hadn't felt truly caged until that moment.

⋆ ⋆ ⋆

The next morning Sleet, Ajax, Doc, and I hung in a tight group, smoking at the west corner of the basketball court. I liked Doc and tried not to think about that. If he had any clue what was coming, he didn't show it. At the scheduled time, a guard paid off by the ABT disappeared from the yard. Sleet grabbed Doc from behind, and Ajax shoved a dishrag into Doc's mouth. Doc's expression shifted from surprise to recognition to panic and terror. Sleet yanked both arms behind Doc's back and I heard a sickening pop—Doc's muffled scream—then a second crack and the crunch of cartilage tearing from bone. With Doc's shoulders dislocated and hanging useless by his side, Sleet and Ajax spun him and dragged him by his heels out of view of the security cameras. Doc wiggled his torso like a worm that's been stepped on, trying to free itself from the pavement. His arms trailed behind him, fingers grasping at loose dirt. Sleet and

Ajax laid him on the ground. Sleet sat on Doc's legs while Ajax stripped off Doc's shirt. The gag in Doc's mouth muffled his words, but as soon as he saw the razor in my hand, he bucked and tried to kick out at me. His eyes widened and he clawed at the cement. I pinched the razor between my fingertips, fumbled it, and dropped it into the dirt.

"Jesus, man," Sleet said. "You're wasting time."

I grabbed the blade again and pressed the sharp edge against the pale skin of Doc's chest. I jabbed the point beneath the black outline of a swastika, felt the flesh catch and puncture. I channeled my guilt onto that symbol of hate. I applied more pressure, twisting it until the layers beneath it gave way. Doc's lips curled around the rag in his mouth and his shrieks escaped from the gaps in tortured bursts.

"Sorry, man," I said.

Sleet punched me, "The fuck you are, goddamned pussy."

Doc thrashed beneath all three of us. I peeled away the top layer of skin like a surgeon, ignoring the stench of urine and sweat pouring off Doc, slicing my own hand as I worked—my own blood and skin mixing with his. I avoided Doc's eyes. I rose above myself, watching it happen.

In the end, I removed three tats in all. We left Doc bleeding and moaning next to the clotted piles of his flesh. If you asked me who had done such a thing, I would have told you I didn't know, and I wouldn't be lying.

⋆ ⋆ ⋆

A few weeks later, they voted on me as a member. I chose an iron cross with skulls behind it for my tattoo, placed it on my right shoulder, and made it as small as possible. Sleet looked at me like he was proud—even though we both knew I had gotten off easy. My "blood in" was more than a test of my loyalty; it was a warning: The ABT wanted me to know what happened to snitches or guys who didn't obey orders. When my initiation was over, Sleet slapped me on the shoulder and held onto the back of my neck. "Welcome to the family, Sweetwater," he said. "We are brothers now."

• 28 •

2010

I ROAMED AWAY FROM the rec yard out to the edge of the wire fence, around the corner and out of view of the others. A gravel road encircled the prison compound; beyond that lay an empty wooded lot. I could still hear the clank of guys lifting weights and the bounce of a basketball.

I opened my book from the prison library to identify the birds I saw. There were raptors, songbirds, grouse, owls. I tilted my chin toward the sun and caught sight of a Cooper's hawk hunting from a tree. I'd read about the Cooper's hawk: "a fierce, carnivorous bird with red eyes" who had no problem eating his own—smaller birds, in addition to the occasional rodent. He had a narrow head, eyes hooded beneath a gray cap of feathers, and a chest marked with mottled patterns of caramel and white. He adjusted himself on his perch, fanning out his gray and white striped tail. That slight movement alerted a bird below to his presence. A spindly-legged plover of some sort hopped up from the edge of the gravel path, where she'd been perfectly camouflaged minutes prior. At first, I thought the bird must be stupid. Why make yourself known with a predator hovering over you?

The Cooper's hawk, moving only his head, focused on the smaller bird. The plover's legs wobbled, a bent wing dragged the ground, and it teetered off balance. I winced for the bird, hoping for a swift end to her suffering. The hawk dropped like a missile to the ground, a dagger of talons extended in front of him. The smaller bird dodged the strike by flying forward a few feet. She dipped her wing again, flattened herself to the ground, trilled loudly. At first I thought maybe she'd been hit. The scene replayed itself over and over, the hawk no closer to getting the plover after several attempts. When the hawk gave up, the plover, miraculously healed, flew over to a depression in the gravel, a pothole really, where I made out the shape of a nest containing three speckled eggs.

I flipped pages in my book until I found the section on plovers. This one was called a killdeer, a bird famous for protecting her young by faking injury, typically a broken wing, in order to lure predators away from her nest. The more the predator chased her, the farther she drew him away from what was important to her. Brilliant, really. "Well played," I told her from the inside of my cage, and she became one with the rocks again, disappearing right before my eyes.

I was reading about birds when Micro found me in the yard. Before he even sat down, I told him what had just happened, and then what I'd just learned about homing pigeons. "These biologists put these pigeons inside a soundproof, air and temperature regulated cylinder, and transported them a thousand miles away. On instinct, they found their way back." I shrugged at the wonder of it. "Couldn't be anything else. The researchers made sure they couldn't hear, see, or smell the outside world while they traveled from one place to the other. Crazy, right?"

He peered over my shoulder. "That's something," he agreed. He sat on a patch of dirt across from me. He wore his signature checkered Vans and a grin ear to ear. In his hands, he held an envelope, which he set down in front of me.

"I'm hoping that smile means you got me early release," I said.

"Next best thing," Micro said. "But first, how are you?" He leaned forward. I liked that this was the first question he always asked me and that he genuinely seemed interested in the answer. I didn't have to say "fine" because the man had been where I was, and he would know that was a lie. He never dug for specifics, anything that might get me in trouble.

"More blood in," I said. And that was enough. I wiped my hands down my pants, surprised they didn't leave a trail of dirt down the fabric.

Micro nodded, "Hard. I feel you, man."

"It's like a noose that keeps getting tighter." My hands shook atop my legs. I chewed at a cuticle, watched the blood bead up along the nail bed. My voice broke as I put my thoughts into words. "I think maybe I'm not meant to be here. I keep watching these birds—maybe that's what death would feel like. Free. Flying." A guard in the courtyard yelled at one of the inmates. His voice echoed against the cement. "What's the point anymore, really? I'm doing nothing in here, other than becoming someone I never wanted to be."

The sun flickered through the limbs of the tree. Micro nudged the envelope closer to me. "This might help," he said. "Just because you have a no contact order doesn't mean you can't have access to public information. The biggest sentence in prison is being kept from those we love—not knowing how they are. If I can take that pain away from you—give you something to hold onto—I'm happy to do so." A sly grin stretched across his face, bottom silver-capped teeth gleaming. "That's the purpose you've given me, so hey, thank you."

I opened the envelope and shook out the contents. Newspaper clippings and printouts from the Dallas Morning News *slid onto the table. One was about Samantha Fielder hosting a fundraising gala to benefit a Catholic charity for unwed mothers. Another had a photo of Jack Fielder in a suit with a hard hat on next to some other guys at a new land-leasing ceremony for an oil company. The third took my breath away. Sky. Dressed in ivory-colored tights and a blue dress, holding a certificate with white gloves. Hair perfect. Eyes beaming. A junior cotillion debutante. It took me a moment to recognize her. But it was her—still.*

I wiped my eyes with the back of my hand. "Man, thanks. Really."

"No problem. Just be careful. Hide them if you can. The less information the ABT has on you, the better."

I nodded, bit the inside of my lip. "She looks okay, right?" I held up the clipping, gently by the edges.

"Seems like it," Micro said.

I opened my journal, slid out the old photo of me and Sky, held it out to him. "Up until today, this was the only photo I had of her."

He studied it with a sad smile. "I can almost picture the two of you, running wild somewhere."

I leaned back onto my elbows. "I named her, you know. Papa was in jail, and I was there for the birth. Mama and I had been staying in a women's shelter. I was six, so I went to the hospital with her when she delivered. I got to hold her, even before Papa. I gave her this stuffed Bunny she sleeps with—slept with. Who knows if she still does? Anyway, I named her Sky. Once she got older, she complained about her name, said it was silly. I told her she got lucky because I was only in kindergarten back then, and I could've named her puppy or pancake."

Micro laughed, turned the photo over in his fingertips.

"You know, the only thing I was ever any good at was taking care of Sky. She doesn't need me now. I mean, look at her." I choked back sobs. "There's no way our two worlds overlap, not after this."

"Hey, man, you're seventeen. Even if that were true, you don't know what else you're going to be good at. Didn't you ever dream of something—for yourself, beyond being a big brother to Sky?"

"Writer maybe," I said, without meeting his eyes.

"There you go." He looked at my journal. "I hope you're keeping track of all of this, because, trust me, when you get out of here, you'll have one heck of a story to tell."

"I write pretty much every day, and sometimes I add a sketch or a drawing." I set my jaw, tucked the photo away in my journal, slid the newspaper clippings back into their envelope.

"Hey, remember, there's an end to all of this." He motioned to the razor wire and fencing. "Don't get any more time added. Focus on keeping yourself busy."

"It's not going to work. I think I'm done."

Micro leaned in, put his hand on my shoulder, then took it away. Then he did something unexpected. "You have that address for Sky? I might be able to dump off a little mail. Just once. You could be writing fan mail to Cardi B for all I know, right?"

I blinked at him several times before jumping into action. Without another word, I ripped out a section of the journal, starting from the day of the accident, scribbled a note to Sky at the top, hoped she could make some sense of it. I handed Micro the pages and he slipped them into his bag.

"I can't put a return address on it," he said. "And I'm going to mail it from another county to get a different postmark on it. If she

figures out how to make contact with you, it's got nothing to do with me, you hear?"

I nodded.

He rose to leave, and I hugged him. His strong grip surprised me. When he pulled away, he held onto my shoulders and stared at me. "You got this. If ever I saw a man of purpose, brother, it's you. You're like that pigeon. Once you're free, you'll find your way home again. I'll see you in a couple of weeks."

Other than the fights I'd been in, I hadn't been touched by another human being in months and hadn't realized I missed it. Strength at Danville meant violence, posturing, drugs, cursing, ink, affiliation. I'd almost forgotten there was another kind of strength that a body could convey: hope.

* * *

2015

Sleet sorted through what was left of his commissary stash: a protein bar, some deodorant, a pack of cigarettes, a bottle of Pepto Bismol. He tossed me items he no longer needed from the pile. I missed catching them because my arm was still in a cast. A week ago, I got into a stupid fight with a guy on the basketball court, and while my right hand was on the pavement, another dude stomped on it. I broke three fingers and tore a tendon in my wrist, but the prison doc said it would heal. Until then, I keep trying to write with my left hand, which is slow and messy and frustrating.

"Won't miss prison food, I tell you that, Sweetwater," Sleet said, slapping my back. "First thing I'm going to do is hit Taco Bell." I placed the things he gave me onto the shelf above

my bunk. "So here's the address, bro." He handed me a scrap of paper. "Houston. Two other brothers there already. Nice apartment, near downtown. I already have a job set up for us."

When I didn't ask more about it, he said, "Don't you want to know what it is?" His brow furrowed.

"I'm guessing it's not flipping burgers at McDonald's."

"You're a riot, Sweetwater. No, not McDonald's. A meth deal. Best part is, we've got access to weapons now—a whole new world out there."

I nodded, but my lack of enthusiasm must have shown.

"Hey," he ground his knuckles into the middle of my chest. "The ABT saved your ass in here. Don't forget that. You work for us now—and you can do that outside or in. If I were you, I'd be working hard to prove to us that you're more valuable once you're out of jail than in it." He tossed me a bag of potato chips and a candy bar and turned his back. "And just to remind you, you don't want to get on the wrong side of this. I'll see you in Houston."

♦ 29 ♦

THE DAY OF MY release, I collected my belongings and signed off on each item in Danville's logbook as I stuffed them into my pack. Micro had left me a card. On the cover was a charcoal rendering of a cabin in the woods. Inside he wrote, "Our whole life is startlingly moral. There is never an instant's truce between virtue and vice. Goodness is the only investment that never fails. —Thoreau." Then he added something totally corny that I admit made me choke up a little. "You might not believe in God, but I have it on good authority that He believes in you."

The county gave me "exit clothes" to wear, a T-shirt and jeans, along with some generic brand sneakers, plus $200 for bus fare and incidentals. I used some of the money for food—a two-piece Kentucky Fried Chicken dinner, followed by a cheeseburger at Burger King and topped with a swirly dipped cone at Dairy Queen. After that, I pocketed the rest of my cash and hitchhiked north, trying not to puke in the semi after all the greasy food. The trucker didn't ask me any questions or make small talk, which was a relief. Inside the cab, a pine tree air freshener swung back and forth in rhythm with the swaying of the rig, unable to mask the diesel smell when it wafted inside. The man's wife and kids stared out at me from photos *taped to the bottom of the windshield. A bobble-head Jesus nodded every time we hit a bump. A sticker reading "God, Guns, and Good Beer" peeled away from the edges of the dashboard. I asked the man if I could open the window, just for a little while, and he said he didn't mind.*

Outside, a loud, shocking, colorful world whizzed by. Roadside bluebonnets painted the hillsides an unreal shade of violet. Fresh-cut grass on the medians scattered like a hatch of insects in the truck's wake. A couple of dogs wrestled in a front yard. A boat bobbed on a lake. Sidewalks bustled with joggers, bikes, strollers. I stuck my hand out the window and let it ride the wind. Everything vibrated with life. I'd almost forgotten that a world outside of Danville existed. All those years: the same sounds, smells, tastes. Same fucking walls. The hell of it all was what a person could get used to. The world out my window shook me awake, and I hadn't realized I'd been sleeping.

As the miles and hours passed, I thought about what I was risking. How many days would it take Sleet to realize I was on the run? Could they trace me back to Sky? I didn't think so. I never spoke about my family to the ABT and never had any mail or visitors. I didn't want to put Sky in danger, but there was no way I could move on with my life without seeing her again—which was how I ended up in Dallas.

It was dark when I made camp at White Rock Lake. The light of a new moon crested the canopy of live oaks towering above me. Ducks tucked their beaks into feathered wings, nestled into the night. A chorus of crickets hummed beneath blades of grass. It wasn't wilderness, but it was as close as I could get in the middle of a city the size of Dallas. I wrote in my journal using the glow of headlights that swept the edges of brush from an overlook where teenagers parked to hook up. You could see the silhouettes and steam beyond the windows. Most of the guys at Danville talked about how they were going to get laid the second they got out, though they used slightly different vocabulary. It was their main priority. Of course, I noticed women, thought about sex, but it did no good to dwell on it. I'd been locked up with men for seven years. I had no experience with girls. None—and if I was honest about it, I found the idea slightly terrifying. So I focused on my immediate goal: going to see Sky. The Fielders might have provided a nice life for her, but I was her brother. And even if Sky hated me, I wanted her to know that I was here for her—that I'd never forgotten her.

There was no way to sleep. I was nervous as hell about the day ahead. For hours on end, I rehearsed what I might say or do, so when the sun rose, it surprised me. I'd gotten used to mornings beginning with the clank of forty cell blocks unlocking at once, instead of the warble and trill of wrens and sparrows. I shook out my sleeping bag and stowed my things. I used the public bathroom in the park to clean myself up. In the mirror, I ran a hand over my hair, which still looked like the standard-issue Danville buzz cut. While I waited for it to grow, I wore a skullcap, pulling the edge of the beanie down to the top of my eyebrows. I had also quit shaving a few weeks prior to my release. I hated the beard. My face itched constantly, like I was wearing a wool ski mask. But I couldn't be too careful. My gray T-shirt already had a grass stain on the sleeve and smelled like B.O.

I groaned, pulled it off, shoved it in the sink with a squirt of hand soap. I soaked it well, holding it under the faucet and rinsing it several times. When it seemed like I'd done a good enough job, I wrung it out and left it hanging on the edge of the basin while I worked on cleaning up the rest of me. Using paper towels, I scrubbed my face, pits, neck, chest, ass, balls, and stomach. I did the best with what I had available. I put the T-shirt back on wet, thankful it was summer; the fabric would dry quickly in the sun.

Walking out of the park, I checked the newspaper clipping one more time, just to make sure I had the address correct. I shouldered my backpack and thumbed a ride. Before long, I sat, smiling and nervous, humming in the passenger seat of a Dodge Ram *pickup on my way to see Sky after seven long years.*

The driver let me out at the entrance, pulling up to the crisp white line of fencing. A banner announced the event: The Junior Equestrian Championships. Shade trees lined acres of grass so green they should have a new name for the color. Sun danced across the paths where people walked to the bleachers. I felt eyes on me, knew I didn't belong, and felt shitty about it because I had actually tried. I yanked up my jeans, which sagged at the waist. I sat at the far end of the stands away from the other groups of people. I studied the schedule, the bios of the riders. At first, I looked under the letter R *for Sky Rayner, before remembering to look under* Fielder *instead. The listing didn't say much. In fact, there was more information on the horse than the rider.*

SKY FIELDER, DALLAS, TEXAS. COBBLESTONE: GRAY—HOLSTEINER, GELDING, 16.5H, 7 YEARS.

I knew zero about fancy horses or show jumping, but it seemed like everyone here had a giant stick up their ass: straight posture, raised chins, starched clothing. I fidgeted with the edge of the program, jiggled my legs. A welcome breeze dried the sweat from my face. I sniffed. The place smelled like fresh grass and sweet oats, not hay or horse manure. I lit a cigarette. I would quit, but not today. I spit a piece of tobacco off my lower lip to the ground below.

Riders filed out and stood in a line in front of us and the announcers introduced each competitor. I rolled the edges of the program between my fingertips, pressed the skullcap down, scratching the hair beneath it.

Seven years. And there she was.

Sky strode into the arena, third in line. She wore the same outfit as the rest of the riders, white high-collared shirt covered by a short navy blue blazer, cropped pants, tall black boots, smooth helmet, gloves. But she was different, anyone could see that. More athletic than the rest. Despite the polished posture, her shoulders tensed—and she was thin, too thin. I couldn't take my eyes off her. Beneath the lip of her helmet, her eyes beamed with the bright blue I remembered. But she wasn't a little girl anymore. The newspaper photos couldn't prepare me for that. She was a young woman. Her face had sharper angles now, her lips fuller, set into a tight, determined line. She stood shoulder to shoulder with the others, about my height now, I guessed. Of course, she had grown up.

When the riders filed back out to wait their turn to compete, I wanted to go to the stables and wish her good luck, but I knew that wouldn't be fair—that my sudden appearance would throw her off. I would wait until she was done. I had waited this long; I could wait a little longer. Plus, I was worried. I honestly had no idea how she would react to seeing me. She was still a minor, maybe a junior in high school. Would she turn me in for talking to her because of the court order? Would she slap me or throw her arms around me? I dropped the cigarette to the ground below and gripped the program in both hands.

A horn sounded and the first couple of competitors rounded the course. The horses looked nothing like the ones in West Texas, and neither did the riders. You could see your reflection in the shiny coats of both animal and human. Braided manes for the horses and a single long braid for the girls kept fly-away strands of hair in check. Polished boots, hooves, saddles. Uniformity. Precision. The horses and riders were elegant. Fluid. Watching them was like sitting beside a river flowing over smooth rocks. I didn't understand the rules of the competition, but I tried to follow along—anything to keep my mind occupied. The waiting. All but impossible.

When Sky's turn came, my pulse spiked, adrenaline coursed through me. She entered the arena atop a gray horse. She looked poised and confident, even though the beast she was on seemed huge and powerful. I instantly wanted to protect her. Cobblestone's mane rose in a stiff, knobby column, like vertebrae on a spine, cresting the arcing slab of muscle on his neck. His walk was somewhere between a prance and a trot, like he knew he was something special. I rubbed the stubble on my chin, wrapped the arm with the program across my stomach, nervous for Sky. She took a deep breath and the horn sounded. They ran the course, leaping rails and water obstacles. This girl—the same one determined to make it to the top of Skeleton Canyon with her big brother—competed with assurance and grit. Slight changes in her hands, legs, and posture spoke to the horse in a language only he could understand. The timing and rhythm were so well choreographed that I heard drumbeats inside my head. Still, every muscle in my body tensed each time they reached a jump. I leaned forward to propel her over safely. Bobbed my chin to the beat of horse hooves. She sailed through without any faults or errors. Polite applause followed when her time was announced, and I wolf-whistled, causing heads to whip my direction. I lowered my head, mouthed "fuck off" to an arrogant-looking jackass who I caught sneering at me with disapproval. I tugged at my skullcap, angled my chin away from him.

Sky won, and I beamed, which was silly because I had nothing to do with it. Before the awards were given, the riders grouped together behind the stable. I lit another cigarette, fumbled with the lighter. I was getting up my nerve to go and congratulate her. I moved to the end of the bleachers, watching and waiting for the right opportunity.

I was about to make my way down the stands when a mother holding the hand of a small child looked at me, wide-eyed and fearful. She blanched, then jerked her son the opposite direction, all but shielding him with her body as they made their way to a group of spectators a few rows away. My knees locked, imagining what she saw when she looked at me. In between puffs of the cigarette, I covered the lower half of my face with the program. I was missing a tooth, I could smell my own sweat fermenting in the heat, and my shirt looked more like a wadded piece of trash than clothing. Still. I had come this far. I couldn't just leave.

I yanked at my shirt to pull out some of the wrinkles, adjusted my skullcap, dipped my chin to my armpit to determine on a scale of one to ten how bad I smelled, giving it a solid seven. Could I do this? I flicked an ember to the ground. Parents swarmed the area near the barns where the riders had congregated.

Mrs. Fielder strode across the paddock and patted Sky on the shoulder. Words were exchanged. I imagined Sky's mother was telling her she was proud of her. Sky faced her with tears in her eyes. In a flash, I saw the mother–daughter drives to horse lessons, the years of dedication, ribbons and trophies—the many falls and shared heartbreak that must have led to this moment.

The program hung from my hand like a flag at half mast. My face flushed. I didn't belong here. Sky didn't need me, and what's more, she wouldn't want to see me—not like this: fresh out of prison, dressed in donated clothes, having slept in a park the night before.

I started to turn, but as I did, Sky glanced my way. I ducked, but the man in front of me moved, and it was too late. I was in full view of her, and she was staring at me. I smiled, terrified but hopeful. She kept looking. My pulse beat in my temples. Her eyes scanned over me, past me, with zero recognition. My legs buckled and I steadied myself with a hand on the railing. She looked back toward the people congregated around her and accepted congratulations from the other riders. She no longer knew me. Either that, or she wanted nothing to do with me.

My mouth went dry, and the back of my throat itched.

I wasn't family anymore. I was a stranger.

I left the arena. I wandered out past the curb of the well-landscaped grounds, the banner at the entrance. I found my backpack behind the hedge where I'd stashed it. I folded the program and tucked it inside a pocket. I walked until I got back out to the main highway, stared through the waves of heat rising off the blacktop. Right or left? Did it matter? I had no plan. For the first time I could remember, I was completely and utterly lost.

♦ 30 ♦

2019

I TAKE MY TURN driving. We are getting close to Tucson. Close to my brother. I keep praying that he'll stay alive. I don't know if I'm still Catholic or not, but I say all the Our Fathers and Hail Marys I can. While I drive, Laura searches for information about the accident my brother was in—about the fall. She finds a link to an article in an Arizona newspaper, one that leaves me with more questions than answers.

An unidentified man believed to be in his mid-twenties was critically injured after a fall in the Peloncillo Mountains in Skeleton Canyon. Hikers discovered the unconscious man at the bottom of a ridge near the Devil's Kitchen trailhead. The man's belongings were found inside a pack in a Forest Service cabin at the top of the canyon. There were no signs of a struggle, and foul play is not suspected. Police presume the man to be a transient camping in the area, who got disoriented, perhaps in the middle of the night, and accidentally fell off the ledge. Drugs and alcohol are not suspected, and the investigation has been closed.

Eight lines. A transient. Skeleton Canyon. Case closed. Except that it isn't.

My mind scrambles to make sense of everything. He was found in Skeleton Canyon. Was he still on his way to Mexico? How did he fall? I have so many unanswered questions, but none of them matter more than being with my brother—and I feel time slipping away. It seems he had nothing and no one, and I want him to know that's not true. I remember thinking that love was irrelevant because it couldn't pay your bills or feed you. But perhaps I've been wrong.

At Banner University Medical Hospital, we are directed to the ICU waiting room, where I am given paperwork to fill out for Ben—on his behalf. There are so many blanks—things I don't know. Ben's medical history, address, phone, email, allergies, insurance, spouse, children. It goes on. When I hand the clipboard back, I apologize. "I haven't seen him since I was eight," I explain. I take a seat. Every sound makes me jump: the squeak of gurneys being wheeled down the hall. Beeping machines. Quick footsteps.

My brother is seriously hurt, and on top of that, he's spent his life in jail, only to end up homeless and alone. I put my forehead into my hands, folding in on myself. Laura wraps both arms around me and holds me close. "What can I do for you?" she asks.

I whisper—though I'm not sure she hears me, "Even if I push you away, don't let go."

After an hour or so, the receptionist leads me to a room. Only family members are allowed, so Laura stays in the waiting room. I feel her support, even though she's not physically present with me. I open the door. I see a man lying in a bed. His cracked lips hold the tube enabling him to breathe, and small hoses run along his arms into his veins, punctured with needles and stained with iodine. I approach him with hesitant steps. Two nurses are in the room. One tells me, "We'll just be a minute. Make yourself comfortable."

I sit in a chair near the bedside. I keep quiet as if I might wake him. I fight back a panicked sob, because I don't recognize him from this angle—my brother, not yet. What if there's been another mistake? What if this man is someone else after all?

I watch the nurses, the tender care they give their patient. One nurse leans the man forward so that another can run a sponge across his back and neck. The taller one dips the rag into a bin of water and wipes the patient's skin in gentle circles.

As they wash the man, I picture my brother riding bareback and shirtless across the fields near our trailer. I remember the smell of the sun on his skin, my arms wrapped as far as I could reach them around his stomach, and my chin nestled beneath the crook of his neck.

I watch the sponge move across the man's shoulder, the back of the gown untied and exposed. It feels as if I'm moving in slow motion, but I stand and walk over to the bed. Without saying anything to the nurse, I stop the motion of her sponge and lift it. I ignore the tattoos. Instead, I take my hand and place three fingers against my brother's skin, into the white birthmark, the one he hated. Much of his skin has been worn away from abrasions he suffered during the fall, but this part of him remains untouched, as identifiable to me as a fingerprint. I take his hand in mine, I lean and place my cheek against his.

After the nurses leave, I watch Ben's chest rise and fall, hooked up to machines, swaddled in blankets and gauze. Up close, I take him in—finding my brother inside the man. The scar along his hairline from broken glass, the crook in his arm where he broke it falling from the tree swing in Skeleton Canyon and it never got set right, the cowlick refusing to lie flat. So much lost time. Though his letter answered so many things, I still have too many unanswered questions. *Where have you been the last few years?* I go back and forth between anger and grief. And when those feelings haven't taken over every last part of me, I pray to God to let my brother live.

I sit for minutes, maybe hours. Shadows cross the wall. I study my brother's face, weathered and brown—but still, a softness there. I'm holding his hand when a woman, Dr. Nez, walks over to me and introduces herself. She's in her early sixties, perhaps, kind eyes beneath round, wire-rimmed glasses. She sandwiches my outstretched hand between her own like I am an old friend. This small act of compassion nearly breaks me. I have so many questions, but the biggest one is—now that I've found him—whether he will open his eyes again.

Dr. Nez motions to the chair again and pulls another alongside it. She sits next to me. I'm afraid of what she will tell me, of things that must be said, so I ask an easier question. "Can he hear me?"

Dr. Nez rounds her shoulders, smooths the papers attached to the clipboard in her lap. "I like to believe that he can," she says, her voice soft, as if this is a holy place. We both look at Ben lying motionless on his bed. "I wish this could wait, but I need to talk to you more about his condition if you're ready," she says. I nod. I'm not ready, but I will never be ready, so. "He's not breathing on his own, and the brain and spinal cord damage he suffered in the fall are substantial enough that even if he survives, he might never function independently."

I cling to the word *might* as if it's all she's said. Five letters. I can't lose him again, not now, not after coming this close. She places a hand on my knee and continues, "If he lives, he will likely remain in a vegetative state—bedridden. He might never regain the ability to speak or walk or feed himself. But he will feel pain. It's possible he will need to eat through a feeding tube, have special bedding to prevent pressure sores, require a catheter or diapers. We're talking round-the-clock care."

Likely. Possible. Might never. Her words are porous, and I hear only what I'm thirsty for. "I'll do it. I will."

"You have to think about him now, about what's best for him. Would he want to live that way?"

I swipe at my eyes. Her words echo inside my head because I received the exact same well-meaning guidance after I gave birth at St. Catherine's—just before giving my baby away. I also remember what my brother wrote in his journal. "If you love someone, you fight like hell for them." Dr. Nez takes my fists into her palms and holds them there.

I stare at her hands, which are crooked but strong, knotted like an old oak in a way that makes me trust them. She is a healer. So, heal him.

"No," I say. "Sorry. I can't accept that." Her brows arch, crinkling her forehead like lines on a map. She's at once taken aback and, I think, impressed too. It gives me courage. "There's got to be something else you can do for him. Something we can try. I'm not giving up on him."

She searches my face, settles on something—a decision flickering in her eyes. "Okay, well, right now, we've been relieving the pressure inside his brain, reducing the swelling. There's a spinal surgeon, Dr. Zahed Pujahma, from San Francisco. I can arrange for a consult."

I nod. "Okay, yes, I'd like to talk to him." The machine beeps and I hear nurses scurry down the hall. The wheels of a gurney squeaking past our door. Dr. Nez releases my hands and I rub my own shoulder, wrapping myself in an embrace, suddenly feeling cold and alone in the room. "Has anyone else come to see him?" I ask.

Dr. Nez shakes her head. "The police seemed to think he was homeless, living in the canyon. That he slipped and fell over the edge."

An ache pulses below my ribcage, keeping time with the sad whir of the machines breathing for my brother. She stands and heads toward the door. As she reaches for the handle, I say, "I think you mentioned you had his belongings. Can I see them?"

For a moment, I think she'll say no—as if there is a statute of limitations on claiming to be his sister—or that my delay in coming to the hospital, of denying him, should be punished. "I'll have the receptionist bring them to you. Where will you be staying tonight?"

Relief. I sigh and realize I've been holding my breath. "Here, can I stay here?"

Her eyes crease softly at the corners. "There's really no need. The machines are keeping him alive. He's not likely to wake. You can get some rest and visit in the morning." I have no intention of leaving my brother again. I don't have to respond. She gives me a sad smile. "I'll have them bring in a roll-away."

I update Laura, and she agrees to get a hotel in town. I walk her out to the parking lot, and she stops with her fingers on the car's door handle. "I'm not leaving you, Biscuit," she says. "You're stuck with me." And I believe her—not just because I want to, but because I can see that it's true. She lets go of the door and places both hands against my face, her eyes soft and kind and drinking me in. Then she kisses me. The press of her lips against mine says every word we've left unspoken between us. She does not pull away. I cradle her face in my hands and pull her into me. When we finally separate, we both have tears rolling down our cheeks. "I'm here, Sky. Go be with him." A breeze picks up, drying my face. Next to us, several birds flutter from the branches of a tree. I watch as one of them dips its wing, trusting the wind to carry it. And it dawns on me then that love is like that. This thing you can't see, that's there to catch you when you fall and lift you when you fly.

A half hour later, the receptionist wheels in a folded cot with a worn, tattered, army-green backpack riding on top of it. When the door closes behind her, I move the pack to the floor, open the cot, and sit and stare at the pack for a while, as if another person has joined me inside Ben's hospital room, and we are getting used to each other. What secrets does this bag hold? I pull air deep into my lungs and open the main compartment.

Inside, I find the photo of me and Ben, the original one he stole from our social services file. I examine the picture, including our scrawled names and dates on the back. I think about Ben's plan to take us to Mexico. It seems ridiculous to me now. I unearth a pocketknife, a jacket, a blue bandana, a couple of books, a greeting card with a charcoal cabin sketched on it. I take Ben's jacket into my lap, covering my legs with it. I lift the collar to smell it. Sawdust and sage. Soil and sweat. Next, I find an envelope. I shake the contents onto my cot, and newspaper clippings float across the sheets. I pick them up and turn them over, examining them one by one: me at a dressage event, my honor roll listings, a photo of my confirmation, my graduation from cotillion.

"You've been busy," I tell him. My hands move clumsily as I place the clippings back inside the envelope. It's a shock and a comfort, this knowledge that my brother has kept up with me over the years. I dig further into the bag and unfold the program from my Junior Championships two years ago. I open it to the page he has dog-eared, the listing of riders where my name appears. These items, all of them, were the last things my brother touched—the most important things to him. There are three journals, bound together, one of which I recognize from Laura's—the one we read and she finally sent back. Another is the deer-hide covered one I remember from our childhood. But the third one looks newer. It has a pattern on its cover—an orange graphic of a sun with a kind of Southwestern style to it. It starts where the others left off. I begin reading, hoping it will tell me how my brother ended up at the bottom of Skeleton Canyon.

♦ 31 ♦

2015

I RIFLED THROUGH A dumpster behind a McDonald's and found a few bites left of a Big Mac wrapped in paper. I ate them in a single swallow and kept rooting around for more. Street-corner panhandling was out of the question until I got farther away. Everywhere I went, I was looking over my shoulder for the ABT. I caught a ride with a trucker heading west, and I decided to spin the wheel, see where he let me off, as if it were fate—which was how I ended up in Arizona.

After I climbed out of the semi, I hiked up a bluff overlooking the barbed, dry plains. Wide open spaces, cactus, sand. Along the highway, a town, part of an Indian reservation maybe, laid out below the rise, buildings and cars strewn about and glaring in the sun like spent shotgun shells. Billboards offered help for domestic violence and addiction. Another advertised a casino. Trailer homes lined a couple of blocks. Basketball hoops were missing nets. A couple of kids jumped on a trampoline. They weren't smiling or laughing. Just bouncing up and down, like it was their job. One wore a Nike T-shirt, Just Do It. Inside the high weeds beneath the trampoline, a rat of a dog poked its head out. No collar. Tongue dipped against the ground. It looked like every other West Texas town I'd been in, which meant that it looked a lot like home.

I slid down scree, eating my own dust, wiping the paste of sweat from my eyes. I needed to clean up and cool off, so I headed for a shopping mall. Inside the building, I let the air conditioning bring me back to life. I hit the public restroom, pooling water in my hands and splashing it over my face, leaving a ring of dirt in the basin. Afterward, I strolled to the food court, where someone had left half of a drink from Orange Julius on a table. The plastic cup was still sweating from the ice inside. I gulped it down. Dear God, nothing tasted so good. The dude behind the counter watched me, so I decided to give him a closer look.

"Hope she didn't have herpes," he said. He scratched at the elastic where his hairnet met his forehead. He spoke slowly and with an impediment of some sort.

"Who?"

"Kiera," he said. "The girl who left that drink there." He looked at the counter when he spoke, while I looked him in the eye.

"That a possibility?"

"More like a given." He handed me a napkin. "I'd wipe that off. My name's Gabe."

I hesitated. I thought about the far-reaching arms of the ABT and my chance to reinvent myself. I said the first name that came to mind. "Zane."

"You aren't from around here."

"Passing through. What gave me away?"

It took him a while, but once he started speaking, he kept going. Still the words trickled out. Sometimes I'd think he was finished speaking, but then more would come. "If you lived here, I'd know you or your cousin or your grandmother or your sister. I'd be related to you in some way. I'd have talked you up in court or bailed you out of jail. I would have run to get the out-of-bounds balls for you while you played shirts and skins. You'd be wearing about twenty silly bands on your wrists, made by my cousins." He held out his arm and showed me a rainbow of strings tied to his arm. "I have five sisters." He shrugged. "You'd be listening to eighties music out of a Sony Walkman, because this place never changes—wearing MC Hammer baggy pants."

He took a deep breath and I waited for more. But he was done. He turned around and started wiping the counter. Clearly, Gabe had something wrong with him, but he seemed like a nice enough guy. Funny too and smart, qualities that people might overlook because his expression was so open, almost childlike, with sort of droopy, sluggish eyes, that were set too far apart. I instantly liked him.

When he turned back around, he offered me a hamburger and fries.

"I don't really have any extra money," I said. "So it's cool. No thanks." But I was salivating just smelling it. He pushed the tray toward me and went back to work. It was all I could do not to finish it in one bite. I tore it apart like a dog. When I was done, he still had his back to me, as if he'd been helping me preserve what was left of my dignity. "Thanks, Gabe," I said.

"You should stick around. Lots to do and see here. You'd like it." He went on to give me directions to where he lived, said they might be looking for some seasonal help on the rez, and that I should check it out.

* * *

I followed Gabe's directions, passed a deer crossing sign someone had used for target practice, and found a place to camp on an empty lot near the reservation. Smoke from burning trash filled my lungs, and I laid my sleeping bag out so that my head would end up beneath sweet-smelling sagebrush. Like a man who's being hunted, which I was, I watched my surroundings carefully, especially people.

Over the next week, I observed the bustle and hum of the rez. Like anywhere, people came and went, going about their business. But on the rez, I noticed that the men, women, children, and teens took the time to stop and talk to one another. So much so, that it became almost impossible for me to tell who lived where and with whom. There was an ease about the relationships—you could feel the sense of connection and security that ran through them like a current.

I went to the mall every day and watched Gabe work, and every day, the same pair of white kids came by and messed with him. Sometimes it was small stuff, like spilling drinks on purpose and knowing he'd have to clean it up. They were stupid and mean and Gabe took it all in stride, like he probably had his whole life. I couldn't help myself, though. It just ran all through me, how shitty they were being to him. So finally I lost it. One of the boys went to buy something and while the register was open, another grabbed Gabe's hairnet and ran off with it. Gabe left the register and ran after the kid with his hairnet, and the other swiped a few handfuls of bills while Gabe wasn't looking. That was it. I'd talked to Gabe enough to know how much he loved this job and what it meant to him to be given this opportunity. He'd been born with fetal alcohol syndrome and was likely autistic or something else. Mom died in a drunk driving accident. Papa nowhere he knew of. If his drawer came up short, they'd fire him.

As soon as the kid swiped the cash, his buddy stopped running and handed Gabe back the hairnet. Gabe was out of breath and still said thank you to that asshole. The two of them strolled out the double doors laughing their asses off. I let them get to the parking lot and waited until they were busy counting their money, leaning in together, to sneak up on them. Just like something out of the movies, I took both their heads and slammed them together. Their noses hit, their eyes watered, and they struggled to make sense of what was happening. Hands went to faces, money fluttered to the ground, and I kicked each of them in the balls, which sent them sprawling on the ground, face up, holding onto their junk and screaming.

I picked up the money—tried to make sure I had it all. And without saying a word, I walked back into the mall and handed Gabe the cash. He gave me a confused look, dipped his head into the neck of his shirt, and gnawed on the collar. He had no idea what had happened, that he'd been tricked. I tried to explain it to him without hurting him. He had this sad, disappointed expression on his face, and I just kept telling him, "It could've happened to anyone, Gabe. Anyone." At some point, he took the money and put each denomination carefully back in its slot and without looking at me said, "Okay."

Gabe lived in a ranch-level house with a couple of cousins. Word got around the rez that I'd stuck up for Gabe, and one of Gabe's uncles offered me work. So, pretty much every day, I hammered an unfinished addition to the barn, and when Gabe had a day off or got home and wasn't too tired, he helped me. Several of Gabe's cousins, sisters, and aunts lived on the rez—like one huge family. I needed the money, dreamed about finding a piece of land, buying it, and building a small cabin on it. In my mind, I'd save up money, get settled, have a couple of dogs, some chickens, running water, and electricity. I'd make a life—one I wasn't ashamed of.

Gabe's sisters reminded me of me and Sky, the way they played together. The youngest ones crawled all over me and begged for piggyback rides, and I never got tired of it. I tried not to think about Sky, but it happened all the time. I pictured her strolling onto the rez, waving at me—like no time had passed at all.

One of Gabe's cousins, a guy named Junior who lived with him, was a tattoo artist with a studio at a strip mall in Tucson. Junior, who looked more like a Sumo wrestler than a Native American, was unassuming and patient, and even though he had to be almost 400 pounds, his cleaver-like hands moved with surgical precision. The first day he worked with me, I sat in a swivel chair facing a wall displaying hundreds of designs from anime to death metal. Junior stood next to me. "You have something in mind? I can do anything, really."

I took off my shirt, embarrassed. "Can you make them into something else? Anything else? I don't care what." I bared my past, all those symbols of hate, and waited for judgment. He nodded, patted my shoulder with a thick, heavy hand. "No worries. Relax." He had me stand, circled me a few times, like he was deciding what to make of the canvas in front of him—the one that had already been scarred by poor decisions. I thought about Doc and what I had done to him, shearing off his tats. If Junior couldn't fix my ink, I'd have to get rid of my past some other way, and I wasn't beyond using a razor blade to do it.

I was sure Junior knew my tats were from a gang, likely knew they were ABT. I didn't have to tell him how ashamed I was of them. Over the next few weeks, I sat in his chair, and Junior worked on me. The transformation was slow, but by the time he finished, the tats were completely new. Stallions with flying manes and a wolf baying at the moon. On the last day, I took a long look in the mirror and hugged the man. He smiled, carefully tended the new tats by rubbing a jelly-like substance over them and covering them with clear plastic. Later, I took my time unwrapping them like a gift. For the first time in a long time, I was happy.

♦ 32 ♦

AFTER WORKING ON THE rez for a month or so, my whole world changed. After Gabe and I finished repairing the roof on a hay barn, one of Gabe's uncles sent us over to fix some fencing next to one of the horse corrals. Inside the round pen where we worked, a stallion kicked and stomped the dirt, nostrils flaring, eyes wide like he wanted to murder us. Since I'd gotten the tats altered, I'd started taking off my shirt while I worked. I was self-conscious at first, but no one said anything about my new ink or the white splotches of the birthmark I used to hide. I couldn't imagine wearing a shirt in this kind of heat. I was free in a way I hadn't been since I was a kid running around with Sky in Skeleton Canyon, and it felt like a relief—natural—easy.

I was hurling a post hole driver onto a metal stake of rebar while Gabe strung barbless wire through the ones I'd already set, when I got too close to the corral and the horse bit the back of my bare shoulder, hard enough to draw blood. "Christ!" I yelled. And Gabe shrugged. "He's one of the wild ones that wandered off the wild horse preserve onto our land. He's ours now."

"You might want to let him accidentally escape and wander right on back," I said. "You're not going to break that one."

Footsteps crunched behind me. "No, but we can gentle him." A woman with black shiny hair tied into a ponytail behind her hat led a spectacular horse, a well-muscled paint, chocolate brown patches on a coat of pure white with an asymmetrical blaze on her nose, behind her. The woman wore overlapping silver bracelets and a loose choker made of leather around her neck with a dangling pendant of a crescent moon inset into a turquoise stone. Beyond those delicate pieces of jewelry, she looked like a woman ready to work. Suede leather gloves, Carhartt pants, the smell of sunscreen and DEET.

She brushed past us, tied out her mare, and walked into a loafing shed that served as a tack room. She emerged with a lunge line and a blanket and entered the corral. Gabe and I both stopped working and watched. She entered the round pen without looking at the horse. It charged, stopping inches from her, a warning of dirt and grit hanging in the air. She set down the blanket and walked away. The horse keyed into her, flattened his ears, neck arched with every muscle pulsing with heat. She spoke, not directly to the horse, maybe a mantra, something quiet and gentle and soothing. She stood in the center of the ring, still not looking the horse in the eye, while he pranced around her, snorting and tossing his head, alternating from galloping in a fury to rearing in repetition and snapping at the air. His coat lathered and his mouth foamed.

When he stopped, it was almost as if he realized how silly he looked, making a fuss when absolutely nothing was happening, just a girl standing there. He seemed to be waiting for something. His ears pricked forward and rotated in different directions, like satellite dishes searching for a signal. The woman sat down. The horse bucked and ran off again. After about another fifteen minutes, the stallion calmed down and stood sideways about ten yards from her. She seemed to be waiting for something from him, and when he lifted his back hock the way horses do when they're just hanging out and resting, she stood, picked up the blanket, and left the corral.

What happened next stunned me. The horse followed her to the gate. Not to kick or kill or bite her. Because he was drawn to her, something I had to admit I understood.

I followed her too, getting up the courage to talk to her, which felt like the scariest thing I'd ever done. I helped her put up the tack, with Gabe grinning at me the entire time, like he knew I was in trouble. I ignored him.

"Gabe says this guy's a mustang?"

She kept working, hanging the halter. "Mmmhmm. There's a wild herd living near the rez. Hundreds of horses on BLM federal land, along with grazing cattle."

"So the government takes care of them?"

She untangled the reins. "That would be something," she said. "No, they leave them to fend for themselves until the herd gets too big. Then they round them up with helicopters, cull them."

"They kill them?" I imagined park rangers shooting at stampeding horses from the air.

"They used to—but they're a protected species now. So they keep them in holding areas, which is cruel, if you ask me. Wild horses function in family bands; they aren't meant to be separated."

I watched her hands, the sheen of perspiration along her wrist. I wanted to keep her talking. "What happens to the ones they capture?"

"They just keep them, indefinitely. Some of them get adopted out, but not enough. It's expensive to keep a horse that won't cut cattle." She hung the lunge line on a hook. "Most ranchers think mustangs are too stubborn, mean, and wild to be used on the ranch. They don't see their value."

"But you do," I said.

"Don't you?" We both looked out the door at the mustang. He was a little on the skinny side, ribs showing through a shiny charcoal-colored coat. Scars etched across his neck and flank where he'd been bitten in battles with other stallions. But when he arched his neck and pawed the ground and ran, his strength showed as a fierce thing of nature—muscles rolling like the waves of an ocean, glistening in the sun.

Every day, I went out to the corral to watch her work with the horse. I learned her name was Sara and that she was related to Gabe in some way or other. He called her a cousin, also said she was part Apache. On the second day, she sat in the usual spot with the blanket in the middle of the pen, and the horse came over and sniffed her and the blanket before jumping backward and pawing at the dirt. The third day, she rubbed his muzzle with her hand and then with the blanket. The fourth, she rubbed the blanket all over him. On the fifth day, she bent over and grabbed his front hoof, as gently as if she were cradling a sparrow, and pulled it forward, until he knelt. She used her other hand to press against the side of his neck, with no more pressure than one might use to nudge open a door. The horse lay down on his side in the dirt. She moved behind him and sat, running her hands over every part of him before resting her head against his mane and closing her eyes, as if she might fall asleep. A few moments later, she put one leg across the prone animal, and he rose to all fours. She adjusted to the motion as if she were one with him. With a fist of his mane in her hand and her hair flying out behind her, they loped in a circle. It was as much a thing of beauty as I'd ever seen.

Two days later, I was up on the roof of the tack shed fixing shingles when she appeared at the bottom of my ladder. She shielded her eyes from the sun and the light reflected off her hair like you could see the whole world in it if you looked hard enough. I almost rolled right off the pitch. I had been too shy, or maybe stunned is a better word, to say much to her when I saw her. What did I know about girls? Next to nothing. I'd been just a kid when I went to jail and turned into a man behind bars. I was sure I'd make a fool out of myself, and the last person I wanted to do that in front of was her.

"You want to ride him?" she asked and tilted her head toward the stallion. "I could use some help." I rubbed the top of my shoulder, remembering his bite, but the word "no" seemed to disappear when Sara was around. Yes, yes.

I helped her saddle him up and we led him into the round pen. She laid a rope on the ground, along with a plastic tarp and a pile of leaves and pine needles. "I've been doing a ton of ground work on him, lunging him, leading him through gates and over obstacles, but I need someone on him to take it to the next level."

I climbed atop the stallion. He flicked his tail and turned his head, giving me a wary eye. Most of the horses I'd ridden were old farm horses that were used to people and didn't spook easily. I remembered riding bareback in Skeleton Canyon with Sky, the freedom of it. I missed her always, but especially at times like this—wondered what she'd think if she knew I was here riding a mustang and blushing at a girl.

I wasn't afraid of the stallion, and it seemed important to be able to show Sara that I could handle the furious beast stomping the ground beneath me. Sara took the lead rope and I held the reins. "Give me his head," she said. "I'll lead him like I've been doing. Only difference is that now there's a rider on his back." She walked in front of us and took us through a wide circle before cutting through the middle of the ring toward the plastic tarp. The horse flattened his ears and jerked back with his head. Sara pulled gently and made a clicking sound. He took a tentative first step and then bolted across it. She held the end of the lead rope and I pulled back on the reins. The horse stopped; his breathing settled, and Sara ran her hands over his neck.

We did this several times until the horse walked over the tarp without showing fear or hesitation. Then we moved on to the rope, which was a stand-in for a snake on the trail. And finally, the pile of leaves. I loved watching Sara work, but felt sort of childish and a little impatient, like a kid at a carnival being led around on a pony ride.

So I was happy when Sara unhooked the lead halter and asked me to take the horse through the obstacles on my own. Of course I was an idiot—I wanted to show her I could make the mustang run the course, not just walk it, and be absolutely in command of the situation.

That was how I ended up in the dirt.

The horse balked at the tarp, which rustled and rose in the wind and sent him bucking and bolting the other direction. I yanked at the reins and kicked the shit out of him, and he strained at the bit, lathered and tossing his head, but not yielding it to me. He threw me off where I landed on my ass, rolling to a stop with my tennis shoe wedged in a pile of horse manure. Humiliated, I got up slowly. Wiped myself off. From beneath the brim of my hat, I peeked up at Sara.

I guess I expected her to be angry or to be laughing her head off—one or the other. Instead, she was looking at me with compassion, like she was sorry I'd been thrown, like she'd known it would happen and was regretting not having spared me the wounded look she saw on my face. She smiled and walked over to me. "Hey, cowboy," she said. "You okay?" I nodded because that was all I could muster with her standing so close to me, staring into my eyes. She took her bandana off, reached out and used it to wipe away the grit and sand beneath each of my eyes, before handing it to me. I wiped the back of my neck, my forehead and mouth, inhaling a scent of sage and warm leather from the fabric—imagining that was what her neck smelled like where that bandana had been tied and making myself dizzy. After I'd dusted myself off and picked up my pride, I watched Sara take the lead rope and halter, and I followed her over to the stallion.

"Show me," I said. "I'd like to learn." And I meant it.

"Seriously?"

I nodded, and her face lit up. "Okay," she said and then jumped right into it. "This is where I think girls have an advantage, because they already know they can't out-muscle a thousand-pound horse." She said it in a way that wasn't lecturing me or scolding—more like she was grateful to be able to talk about these things that she'd learned. "Horses know you better than you know yourself—they reflect your emotions back to you—your anger, excitement, fear. You want to fight, the horse will fight. Of course, I could make this horse do what I want because he's afraid of me, which was the old way they used to break horses. But it doesn't make a willing horse; it makes a scared one. And personally, I don't want to ride something this powerful that's afraid of a jackrabbit in the brush. So instead, I work with him and earn his respect. He does what I want because we're a team—it's a partnership. And what I ask of him, I will always ask with the least amount of pressure. So he trusts me."

"Least amount of pressure," I repeated. "I don't get it."

She took her palm and faced the horse. She pressed it against the bridge of his nose as if she were trying to make him back up. He resisted and she continued to push. They seemed to be in a standoff. The minute he shifted his weight in the direction she wanted—the slightest lean backwards—she took her palm away and rubbed the side of his neck. She came forward again with her palm, pressing it against his nose, and he stepped back more quickly than the first time, and she released and rubbed him. Then she came toward him with a fingertip and touched the soft muzzle of his nose, and he stepped back again. Finally, she held a finger up in the air and the horse took a step backward. It all happened within the span of fifteen minutes.

This tiny bit of a woman, little more than five feet tall and a hundred pounds, could move the stallion just by lifting her finger. She wasn't doing it to show off, either. She was doing it because I needed to see it—needed to learn there were other ways to deal with the world around me than I'd seen so far—that just maybe there was more power in kindness than there had ever been in a fist.

I got up on the horse again and we went through the course. This time, when he showed any fear of an obstacle, I didn't kick him to move through it. Instead, I backed off immediately and circled around to settle him before introducing it to him again. Eventually, he trusted me, and when I dismounted, I couldn't stop grinning. On the way to the barn, Sara walked close to me, brushing her shoulder against mine as we put away the tack. "Thank you," I told her, and she trailed a hand across my back as she left the room.

♦ 33 ♦

THAT NIGHT I COULDN'T sleep; I kept thinking about Sara. I'd been crashing on the couch at Gabe's place, bunking with two of his roommates, including Junior. I felt attached to Gabe and Junior, and that scared me. I read something once about kids who survived early traumatic events, that they couldn't turn off the fight or flight response. It felt like that—I stayed alert—ready for an attack. I didn't want to care about Gabe, Junior, or Sara enough for it to hurt when I inevitably lost them or couldn't protect them. But it became harder and harder to hold back a part of myself; they were all starting to feel like family.

Gabe and Junior wouldn't take any of the money I earned while working on the rez, but I wasn't a freeloader. I used some of the cash I made to buy groceries and cook, and I cleaned up the place so it didn't resemble a ramshackle bachelor's pad. I wasn't part of the tribe, and my people had done shitty things to Native Americans. What right did I have living there? When Gabe and Junior asked what I thought about tribal matters—casinos, tourism, oil leases—I told them that what I thought didn't matter because I wasn't part of the tribe.

One day, we sat playing GTA, sunk into the couch in the living room, and Junior said, "How do you know you don't have

Indian in you? From what you told me about your dad, he was born near Mexico and lived off the land. Mexico had Mescalero Apache blood, Aztecs too. Don't get me wrong, you're a mutt for sure, but you look Indian. That dark skin, hair and eyes—you could be my brother." He held out the beer, as if he were making a toast with: He pointed at me with the game controller. He continued, "Let me tell you a story. Americans say they got to America and made their way west and found 'no other people, only Indians.' When you look at Gabe, what do you see?"

Gabe smiled, wiggled his toes atop the coffee table in front of us, took a swig of his soda. "I see a person. I see my friend." I lowered my eyes to the ground. This simple man, my friend, humbled me. Junior, too, who likely had already figured me out and had forgiven me for where I'd been and what I'd done.

"When I look at you, that's what I see. After everything you've done here, it's not being white that makes you an outsider. Only you can do that," Junior said. He jabbed his index finger into the center of my chest. "Plus, I see the way Sara looks at you. You're welcome here."

⋆ ⋆ ⋆

A few days later, Sara mounted her mare, a horse named Sundance, and I saddled up the mustang, and we rode out through acres of pinyon and sage and tall grass. She led me across two trickling streams and into a canyon with walls of red clay with trees clinging to the edges.

My horse wouldn't let her ride ahead. He insisted on being even with her, head to head with the mare. "He won't let you out of his sight," I said. "He's determined to be next to you." I could feel myself blush and turned my head left to pretend I was looking at a cactus.

"He's majestic, isn't he? I hope he keeps a bit of wild in him. That spark in his eye. That bit of mischief."

"I think he would do anything you wanted." Again, I realized the words the minute they left my lips. I was being a complete and utter idiot. I still hadn't kissed her. I wanted to, but it never seemed to be the right time. I changed the subject and pointed toward the trees jutting out of the crumbling clay walls around us. "I've always wondered how trees survive like that. There's nothing for them to hold onto, especially with the kind of wind you get out here."

She looked up at the branches arching toward the sun. "I think it held on long enough to take root. This is where that tree belongs, so maybe it decided it would stay, and that's more than enough."

I liked listening to her—she was smart and beautiful and didn't seem to be tired of me yet. "So where are you taking me?" I asked.

"You'll see."

We rode together in silence, surrounded by mesas and buttes and canyons. A breeze sang through the trees, cooling us in the ragged heat. Even in the driest summer, the land pulsed with life. Blooming cactus, paintbrush, and lupine. Pronghorn bounding across the open plains. The perfume of desert willow in the air and the knocking of a woodpecker against the birch trees, bark etched like the lines of an old woman's face.

We rode until we reached an overlook and Sara pulled out a small pair of binoculars. "There," she said and pointed. She handed me the lenses and I glassed at the valley below. A herd of a dozen or so horses grazed among the sagebrush and junipers. There were two foals, several mares, a few stallions. Their manes hung in tangled dreadlocks and dirt caked along their spines.

"The wild horses," I said. I didn't see a water source or much grass. "How can they survive out here?"

"It's kind of amazing. The government had to put them somewhere, so they put them on the crappiest piece of land—out here, in the middle of nowhere. And yet here they are. Surviving." She pushed back a strand of hair from her eyes. "Sort of like us Indians."

The horses seemed to be grazing on something—finding sustenance in the dry, cracked ground.

"That's a family band," Sara said. "The lead mare, the bay, she tells them where to go and when, and they follow her. The stallion, the roan in the back, trails behind protecting them, watching for predators. The other males are young, too young to be a threat to the stallion yet. They'll be pushed out soon though. The other stallion over there"—she pointed—"is a satellite. He stays on the fringes of the herd, trying to seem useful to them by scaring off predators. Really, he's just waiting for a chance to steal away one of the mares. The stallion tolerates it, until he doesn't. Then he puts the guy in his place."

I watched, awestruck, at the relationships—the silent communication between each animal. In the family band, I saw every coat color in every shade: chestnut, dun, palomino, Appaloosa, dappled gray, buckskin, sorrel, pinto. Each one so unique, and not just in color, but personality too, and yet they traveled as one. "Do you think this stallion had a band?" I asked Sara, running my hand along my horse's neck.

"No, he was a bachelor stallion. If he was part of a band, he wouldn't have wandered over to us by himself."

I felt relief—we hadn't stolen him away. He'd come to us.

At some point, the satellite got too close to the herd, and the stallion took off after him. The satellite held his ground, and when they met, they rose up on hind legs, eyes wide, teeth on skin, hooves kicking, manes whipping in the air, in a violent, furious dance. The satellite gave up first, resumed his acceptable distance from the herd, and the stallion returned his post.

"Two boys fighting over a girl," Sara mused. "You'd think horses would be different, right?"

Heat rose to my cheeks again, and I turned my head so she couldn't see. I couldn't think of anything to say, and it seemed like everything that came out of my mouth ended up sounding stupid.

On the way back home, we paused at the top of the canyon and watched the sun set, our horses side by side. The sky exploded into pink, casting the surrounding mesas and outcroppings in a brilliant fire of red. A new moon already cresting the top of a butte took over where the sun left off, as if they'd exchanged shifts. Beneath the hooves of our horses, we watched the dead brush come to life with creamy white and yellow blooms. "Deer-horn cactus," Sara said. "It only blooms in the summer when the sun is going down. Most people never see it. When the sun rises, it's gone."

When I turned to look at Sara, she was staring at me.

"I've never seen anything quite like it before," I said. It was the truth, and I meant it, and this time I didn't blush.

That last bit of light bathed us both in gold, and I took her hand inside of mine. A serenade of crickets started up on cue and a coyote's howl echoed off the canyon rim. We might have stayed like that forever, but clouds were rolling in from the west and we needed the moonlight to pick our way down the terrain to home.

An hour later, when we reached the paddock, I tied out both horses, undid the front and back cinches on her mare, and slid off the saddle and pad. "I've got her," I said—and with the saddle and blanket cradled in my arms, I had a flash—really more like a vision. I wasn't holding a saddle. I was holding an infant, and I was putting her to bed. It was as real as if it had already happened—as if I'd shifted in time and space.

I regained my composure and unsaddled the stallion. But Sara stopped me. She took both my hands inside her own and kissed me.

34

IN THE MORNING, I found Sara already in the barn. Draped in a woven blanket, her hair loose around her shoulders, light cascading in through the loft window above, she stood silent with the beginning of a smile stretching across her lips. She took a few steps toward me and gold flecks of hay created a halo around her body, floating in the angles of light. I couldn't speak. Couldn't tear myself away. Couldn't stop staring at her. She let the blanket drop, and though some part of me already knew it, I quivered with surprise at her naked body in front of me. Even in this moment, I had so many questions. Why me? Was she sure?

And then, fear. I had no idea what to do. I had never been with a woman. I would embarrass myself or worse. I would lose her. She held out her hands to me. They were callused from work, and yet softer still than a puff of goose down. She guided me to the earth where she lay like an offering. I was sure if I touched her, I would ruin everything. She placed her hand around my neck and pulled me toward her. I leaned over her body and kissed her. She arched up to meet me and when the curve of her breast grazed my chest, I could no longer breathe. It was a slow fall from there until no space remained between the two of us—just the gentle rhythm of movement to a dance she was teaching me—step by step, breath by breath.

When we were done, she rested her head beneath my chin, and I covered us both with the blanket. It was then I let the tears come. I had never experienced the warmth of an embrace given out of love. Nothing soft had survived the life I'd lived so far. Sara wiped my tears with her fingertips, placed them to her lips, and ran her tongue over them. "I'm sorry," I said. I felt weak, a helpless newborn, stunned and terrified.

"There's no need for apologies," she said. We held on like that for a long time, just taking in each other's heartbeat, breath, skin. I thought that loving her would make me feel less afraid, but it didn't. I was terrified of losing her, of not being able to protect her, of being so much less than she imagined me to be.

♦ 35 ♦

THREE YEARS PASSED LIKE a river, sometimes sweeping away everything in its path, and other times flowing sweet and slow. I should have known it couldn't last. One day, Junior pulled me aside when I was working on repairing a fence line. He had never asked me questions about my tats, and I'd been grateful for it. Next to the pile of rebar, he shoved his hands deep into his pockets, shifted his substantial bulk from foot to foot like he was trying to dance away from the subject at hand.

"Couple of guys came to the studio yesterday. Ink like you had before." He pointed to his shoulder. "Asked me if I'd seen a white guy from Texas with the same tats—someone going by the name of Sweetwater or Ben."

I twisted the wire in my hands, strung it through the rebar. Despite the hundred-degree heat, I shivered.

"They're staying across the highway from the strip mall. Canyon Motel off Bowie." Junior yanked at his jeans to pull them up. It took some effort. "You need help?" He placed a hand on my back.

"Nah. I'm sure they're looking for someone else," I said. He didn't say so, but he could tell I was lying.

I looked different than I had in Danville—my hair was long instead of buzzed the way they had made us keep it there. My old tats were flawlessly camouflaged. My skin was dark from the sun. I had grown a beard and kept it, even though I hated it, and Sara admitted that she did too. "I want to see your handsome face again," she said. "Plus, it scratches me when we kiss." I continued to wear a bandana outside to block out the dust, as well as a shirt to hide my birthmark, and I went by the name of Zane. I was sure Sleet or whoever it was from the ABT didn't know I was living on the rez. Didn't know what these people meant to me. But it was only a matter of time.

So I kept my head down, working hard, ignoring the voice inside telling me to run. At night when I couldn't sleep, I counted backwards from a hundred, tried to convince myself that the terrain was vast, that a man could get lost out here. Many men had. The ABT would stick to the city, give up looking for me, and move on. But I couldn't help but feel like the longer I stayed, the more I was putting everybody in danger.

Sara and I spent almost every evening with the wild mustang herds, a ritual that ended with us in each other's arms. There was something so quiet and still and soft and strong in Sara that I was undone every time I got around her.

And yet, each night I kept watch. Every snap of dry grass was a footstep. Every shadow in the waning dark, a man. My stallion's ears pinned back, something worth fleeing from. Sara knew, but didn't know. She warned me not to be so guarded with her, but I protected her from my secrets. I was too afraid she wouldn't love me if she knew where I had been and the things that I had done. She had fallen for the man I was now, not the one I'd been. And I hoped that would be enough.

* * *

One afternoon, Junior, Gabe, and I worked on a new project on the rez: a community center we were building that we still lacked funding to complete. Junior and Gabe were raising the frame of one of the interior walls, and I was below them shooting a line to make sure we got it plumb. Bent over, I hadn't seen the men walk into the middle of the foundation we'd poured. Junior whistled, and I recognized it as a warning. Even before he sounded that alarm, I sensed the presence of people who didn't belong there. I knew it in my bones, the same way you knew an animal was hunting you. On all fours, I crept behind the generator, pulled my bandana up and my ball cap down low.

"Hey there, Chief," I heard one of them say, which made me grind my teeth. Junior and Gabe set down the frame, and Junior stood to his full height and girth. Gabe stayed put.

"What did you call me?" Junior said. Out of the corner of my eye, from my crouched position hidden by stacks of two-by-fours, I watched Junior muscle up to the man. Sleet. Older, but definitely him. I recognized the other man as Ajax. Sweat trickled down between my shoulder blades. My pulse rushed in my ears.

"Aw, don't get your feathers matted up, Chief. We're just looking for someone. Mind if we have a look around?"

"Yes, as a matter of fact, I do mind," Junior said. "You boys"—he looked down at Sleet when he said it—"need to leave. You're on rez property."

"We know exactly where we are. We heard there's a white guy that's been hanging around this area for a few years now. From Texas. Maybe goes by the nickname of Sweetwater, maybe Ben. Got tats like these." He pointed to his arm. Then recognition hit him. "I know you. The fat guy from the strip mall tat shop."

Junior didn't look at Sleet's arm. He stared in his eyes, boring into them. He didn't blink. Ajax released a burst of tinny, nervous laughter. It sounded like a dog yipping. Sleet was tough, but he was also smart. Over 400 pounds of angry Indian stood in front of him like a massive brick wall. Junior never wavered. His focus was laser sharp, slicing into Sleet without moving an inch. It was impressive.

Ajax scuffed the toe of his shoe against the ground. "Fuck it. You're not going to get anything out of this one." He looked around, spotted Gabe. "Hey you! You seen a white asshole with tats like mine?"

From my place behind the wood, I mumbled quietly, no, no, no, and watched as Gabe approached Ajax. "Goddamnit, Gabe," I whispered. Gabe stood in front of Ajax and looked at the ABT patches.

"That's it, kid; look real good." Ajax studied Gabe's face. "This kid will tell us the truth, won't you, right, buddy?" Ajax spoke to Gabe like he was a five-year-old.

I would have pulled out my own fingernails one by one to get Ajax to stop. I gripped the flesh on my thighs, creating a different kind of pain to hold me there. When Gabe took a single step closer to Ajax, I started to stand, and then wondered if they'd do what they were known for, kill me and everyone who had helped me. Gabe said, "Nobody with those tattoos here. Never seen any like them." He wasn't lying. He wasn't capable of it. Those early days, I'd never taken off my shirt. He'd never seen my original tats.

Junior nodded, put a straight arm between Gabe and Ajax, gently shifting Gabe a few steps back. Junior said, "We get a lot of white guys working on the rez. Usually from construction companies that do contract work for us. Their guys are always white. Almost all of them wear ink."

Sleet appeared satisfied. "Alright then. But I'll find out if you're lying. Where there's smoke, there's fire, right, Kemosabe?"

Sleet let the threat hang in the air between them, and when Junior took a step forward, Sleet wheeled around and left, shouting over his shoulder, "We're at the Canyon Motel a few more days in case you or your friend have something to tell us."

I rose from my hiding place, wandering over to Junior to thank him, tail between my legs like a puppy caught pissing on the carpet. Gabe seemed confused but let it pass.

After that, I threw myself into punishing, physical work, trying to rid my body of its rage and keep my mind from becoming utterly unhinged. But inside, I knew what I had to do. It was time.

I never expected to be this happy—and I surely never meant to bring harm to the rez. They didn't need my kind of trouble, and if the ABT found out that I loved these people, that they were my family, they would destroy them. I took care of my own, and there was no way for me to have both: I couldn't hold onto the people I loved and keep them safe. It was the legacy I created. Violence led to more violence. There was just no end to it. It was one thing for them to go after me, but I couldn't let them hurt Gabe or Sara—God no. Not now. Not ever. The only option I could see was to leave before Sleet or someone else saw me on the reservation—connected me to it. A rumor was one thing. I'd dodged a bullet, but the minute they had proof, it was all over. Maybe I'd been wrong about fighting for those you love. If I wanted to protect them, I had to let them go.

There was no room for indecision, no other answer. Telling Sara goodbye face to face would have been the brave thing to do, but I wasn't brave, and I also knew that if I looked at her, if she touched me, I would never go. It crushed me to know that she would never fully grasp why I'd left—that I would hurt her deeply.

How do you explain to someone that you are leaving because you love them?

That night, I sat on Gabe's front porch beneath a flickering light. I wrote several letters, getting a few lines into them before crumpling them in my fist. I listened to the sounds of the rez, rocking back and forth to the cadence of a frog croaking somewhere near the creek. I penned a note to Sara and one to Gabe and, finally, one to Junior to share with his uncle and the others. In order to protect them, I couldn't be specific about exactly why I was leaving or what my plans were. I asked them not to look for me and apologized for any harm or distress I might have brought to them. I thanked them for giving me a home and a family—something I thought I'd never find again.

I sobbed when I wrote the letters—and even more so when I kissed Sara's forehead while she slept. It was the best and the hardest thing I've ever had to do—to know that I was saving the people I cared about by walking away from them. It didn't make me noble. If I hadn't been such an idiot and made so many mistakes leading up to this, well, I wouldn't be where I was now. I also wasn't stupid. I knew how this ended—the only way that it could. I thought about the killdeer protecting its nest by drawing the predators away.

Junior was the only one to see me go, and I told him not to stop me. He handed me a folded piece of paper, wrapped me in a bear hug that lifted me off my feet, and sent me on my way. I grabbed my backpack and walked downtown. The clerk at the Canyon Motel confirmed that my "buddies" were staying at the hotel and agreed to deliver the envelope I left for them.

In the letter, I told the ABT that I'd gone to get a new tat the day before, and that the fat-as-fuck asshole who ran the place

ID'd me, said a couple of gang members had been looking for a guy matching my description, that I could turn myself in or he'd do it for me. I hated to insult Junior, but I needed it to sound like we were on different sides. I couldn't implicate him in any way.

"So, you want me," I wrote. "Come and get me." I scribbled a map and directions to where they could find me. "I'll be waiting."

♦ 36 ♦

I HITCHHIKED WHEN I could. When I walked, the hundred-degree heat left me dizzy. Windstorms blasted my skin with sand, shearing off exposed layers and leaving my eyes raw from grit. The farther I got from Tucson, the more the landscape changed.

Huge canyons appeared where the earth dropped away, and layers of rust and clay morphed into spires and towers. At one overlook, I climbed down out of the wind and sat beneath a formation that looked like the ears of a rabbit and crumbled beneath my fingertips. I rubbed sage into my hands and inhaled the scent of home—the smell of the rez—of Skeleton Canyon, running from here in Arizona all the way to the place in Texas where Sky and I played.

I faced the sandstone and granite cliffs, the creek below with its swaying cottonwoods and mesquites, the dry floodplain that could drown a man within minutes of a big rain, and the desert beyond that, which held more life than most people imagined or would ever see. I knew the howl of a coyote and the warning of the owl. I knew that survival was being one with the land, not fighting it or changing it. I walked along the bottom of a riverbed, looking up at the callused elbows and knees of the foothills around me, the stubble of brush growing from the jutting chin of an overhanging cliff. The sheer magnificence of it made me weep.

I hiked deep into Skeleton Canyon to the location I had drawn on the map for the ABT. I made camp on a slab of slickrock called Devil's Kitchen, next to an old Forest Service cabin. I prowled the cracked riverbeds. I scaled a tower of rock that jutted like a fist overlooking distant steppes. I dug through hot sand to reach the cool beneath it, pressing my palms against the earth. I leaped over rocks and bathed in a creek. As I made my way across that land, freedom came to me in the breeze that dried the salt on my skin, and sorrow crumbled beneath the soles of my feet. Inside my pocket, I had Junior's note, and I sat with my face to the sun reading it. He'd written words from an old Apache prayer, one I'd seen tacked to the wall in Gabe's bedroom: Looking behind, I am filled with gratitude. Looking forward, I am filled with vision. Looking upwards, I am filled with strength. Looking within, I discover peace.

The next morning, the sun came up, as it always did, and the saguaro cactus silhouettes morphed into the arms of men, reaching for the sky. I didn't plan on fighting Sleet when he came for me, and it was okay. Really. I wasn't afraid to die. The closer my enemy came, the less I felt like running. I found more love and warmth and happiness than I even knew existed or was possible for someone like me—and I knew that my death meant that those things would survive. Perhaps that had been my purpose all along.

I could go now. I could finally surrender.

♦ 37 ♦

2019

Over the next several hours, I don't sleep or eat. I devour every sentence, every drawing, sketches of birds and trees, every note scribbled in the margins. Nurses come and go, checking Ben's vitals, jotting them onto his chart. They are quiet, reverent, though there's no one in the room who they could waken. By the time I get to the last page, it's after two AM. I sit in stunned silence absorbing the details about Ben's life on the rez, about Sara, Gabe, and Junior—this whole other life he created—about changing his name to Zane. I reframe his story, placing a woman and two men into the vacancy I imagined in his life. Ben wasn't alone. There are people who love him—people he loves.

I use the phone in Ben's room to call Laura. I don't want to wake her, but I need her to help me get in touch with Sara as soon as day breaks. I plan on leaving her a message, but she answers on the first ring. I tell her everything, and she agrees to go to the rez, to wake them and tell them that

Ben, who they know as Zane, has had an accident but is still alive.

The next time the nurse comes in, I ask for some soap and a bowl of water, some scissors, and a razor. In Ben's journals, he wrote about how much he hated his beard, that he didn't recognize himself anymore, that it only reminded him that he was in hiding. I need a task to settle my thoughts. It is something I'm capable of, something I can do.

I snip small swatches, dropping the hair into the bedpan I've laid on his chest. I lather his sharp cheekbones, the indent beneath his nose, the rounded upper lip, and his jawline, which is no longer tensed and pulsing.

My brother was always in motion, the wind I tried to catch in my hands.

I have never shaved another person; I worry I will cut him. There are scars I don't recognize—a fine white line like a road stretches across his lip. Square, discolored swirls and pit marks beneath his left eye, etched like petroglyphs into his cheek. I trace the curves of his face with small and careful strokes. I work with precision. Even so, I cut his chin and a line of blood emerges. I panic and dab at it with the edge of his sheet. "I'm sorry. So sorry," I say. But he doesn't move or flinch or cry out.

I place two fingers over the wound and hold them there. When I pull them away, he is no longer bleeding, and a daub of red remains on both of us.

I cup his clean-shaven face into my hands. His skin is rough and weathered, but beneath all that coarseness, the boy I knew emerges. The sun has lined his eyes, creased the edges of his mouth, but there is still a youthfulness about him, despite everything he's been through.

When Laura calls, she tells me that she's found Sara, Gabe, and Junior, and that they are on their way. After I hang up, I hold my brother's hand, lean to his face.

"They'll come. These people you love," I tell Ben. I pull the chair to sit next to him. His eyes flutter, and even though it could just be a reflex, I like to think it's because he hears me.

EPILOGUE

Present Day

I DRIVE THE DIRT roads across West Texas trying my best to access memory by the smell of sagebrush and cotton. Ben sits beside me, trying to grip the armrest. He still has trouble speaking, but one look tells me what he thinks about my driving. I'm showing off, and he knows it. I stare out the window.

Fifteen years ago, Ben and I ran barefoot through this world, one we made our own—out of survival or maybe desperation or both. I pass the church and jail—Jesus Saves on a sign—with a scripture verse missing a few letters. So little has changed, and yet it's all different. I expect to see our house when I turn past the No Trespassing sign. The tall grass waves, beckons me. I round the corner, slow up the hill, follow the rise until my path is blocked by a herd of cattle, tagged and branded, grazing on the land where our trailer once stood, which is now a pile of rubble.

I cut the engine, enveloped in a soft wind and the bucolic quiet of this part of the country. Ben looks at me as the motor ticks down in the heat.

"What're you waiting for?" Ben asks.

"I'm not sure," I tell him. I help him get out of the car and into his wheelchair, the fancy fat-tire one the cousins made for him—an all-terrain beast designed just for him. We move down the path through the weeds, inside the maze of prairie sunflower, coneflowers, and firewheel.

I suggested this field trip, a way to come full circle—to connect the past and present. Ben had rolled his eyes, but he quickly agreed—the draw to Skeleton Canyon innate—as natural to him as seasons. The arroyo is running—carving its message into the earth.

Ben does a wheelie down the path—this jackass I love with all my heart. I think about Ben at the hospital, how five of us stood by his bedside when the doctors unhooked the machines that were keeping him alive. Sara, Gabe, Laura, Junior, and me. All of us prayed for him to stay with us. We held him, embraced him with love, each of us touching a part of his body and each other. We waited for his last breath.

Whether a miracle or from the energy poured into him from all of us who refused to let him go, Ben survived. And though each day since has been a struggle for his recovery, he makes progress. His speech remains slurred, but we understand him. Most days he uses a walker, except on rough terrain, where the wheelchair works best. At first Ben was terrified that the ABT would find out that he'd survived and come to hurt all of us. Junior just laughed, because once Sara realized she was pregnant, there was no stopping the cousins—that barricade of impenetrable love.

My daughter, Hope, who is never far from my thoughts, is seven now and living in Houston. Laura used some of her old contacts at DHHS and helped me contact Hope's adopted family, and so far they've allowed me to send and receive photos and messages—with a plan for me to see her one day, when they feel that she is ready. The first thing that I did was send her Bunny, with a note letting her know that Bunny was very special, just like her. A photo her parents sent to me shows her walking with Bunny tucked under her chin; both appear well-loved, comforted, cherished.

Laura and I make our home near the rez—and no one seems to care that we are together—though it wouldn't change things if they did. My old picture frames are filled with photos of our families, both sides, mine and Laura's, with room for new memories to make. I spend my days helping Sara take care of Ben and enjoying time with Eva, my niece, who at two years old, reminds me of Ben, a firecracker lit from within. Laura runs an art studio two doors down from Junior's tattoo shop. The space is filled with crafts, paintings, weavings, sculptures, and other works from Native artisans in the community, along with a few of her photos honoring the people and landscape.

Her latest show features the wild horse herds in Arizona, with proceeds donated toward the nonprofit sanctuaries that take care of them when they are culled and captured.

Ben, who always wanted to be a writer, is working on a book, a memoir about foster care and the system that failed us. Even though I agree with him that the system is broken, I also know that if one second of our lives had been different, we might have become someone else. And I finally like who I am and who I've become.

My mother comes to visit occasionally. She still hasn't quite adjusted to my relationship with Laura, but she's making progress. Laura has convinced me that I bear some responsibility for running away from people and then blaming them for abandoning me, and I know that she's right.

However, in a surprise turn of events, my mother *did* leave my father and is trying to have their marriage annulled. It goes beyond my father's lies about Ben, which should've been enough. It seems that in his quest to keep my mother wealthy and committed to him, my father had engaged in fraudulent business practices and lost most of his investors' money.

In the end, Mom turned him in to the FBI, along with the investment records she found inside his safe. She could have kept quiet, but she didn't—and I'm proud of her for that. She lost her friends, her reputation, her money, and yet she seems happier and freer than she's ever been. There's a lightness in her eyes, and she smiles—often. As for our relationship, my mother is doing the best she can. I haven't changed who I am, and she hasn't asked me to. I've come to realize that none of us are who we seem to be on our best or worst days, and that family is as big as I make it. Love doesn't run out after all.

⋆ ⋆ ⋆

A herd of cattle parts for me as Ben and I wind our way toward a pile of wood and plastic, at what has to be the remains of our trailer. I pick my way through, lifting planks, examining them for traces of our life. Wildflowers rise through the rubble, yucca plants and twisting vines reclaim our home and bring it back into the earth. The thick, musty smell of rotted wood yields fertile soil beneath my weight atop the cracking timber.

A board strewn sideways, apart from the pile, looks familiar and I grab it. Notches up the side mark the plank, and initials are etched above the hashmarks, along with dates. Mama recorded our heights every year on our birthdays. I stand the board vertically next to me and look at where the markings cease, where the world stopped. I am five. Ben is eleven. Ben stares ahead, and without a word between us I help him to his feet. I measure him against the board, this survivor of our childhood, and use my keys to mark the top of the crown of his head. With a bit of effort, he does the same for me. I scratch our initials into the wood.

We explore the canyon for a bit, looking for treasure, for gold that doesn't seem to matter now that we have found everything we really need. After we are done, we load the plank with our heights notched in it into my car.

On the drive out, Ben tells me "The Legend of Skeleton Canyon," but with a different ending this time, one I like. When he is finished, I roll down my window and let my hand ride the wind, and Ben does the same. We move forward against a Texas sky with a piece of the past we can carry.

ACKNOWLEDGMENTS

SO MANY PEOPLE WERE involved in bringing this book to life. In particular, I'd like to thank my agent, Michael Signorelli, who believed in me and Sky and Ben from the very first draft. My editor at Alcove Press, Tara Gavin, saw an important story and committed to it without reservation. The Bunny Bitches: Hannah Nordhaus, Buzzy Jackson, Rachel Walker, Radha Marcum, and Haven Iverson . . . the most talented, loyal, and patient friends and writing group members on earth—your feedback and optimism kept me going, stomped on my doubts, and inspired me to do my best. The amazing staff at Crooked Lane Books and Alcove Press worked tirelessly to edit, proof, design, and market the novel, including Madeline Rathle, Dulce Botello, Hannah Pierdolla, and Rebecca Nelson. Sarah Brody created the beautiful cover. In portraying life on a fictional Native American reservation, the author relied upon fictional and autobiographical depictions from notable Indigenous writers including Tommy Orange and David Treuer, with special thanks to staff at the Wind River Wild Horse Sanctuary on the Wind River Indian Reservation in Lander, Wyoming. For my sissy-in-law and digital webmaster extraordinaire, Susan Hayse, I don't understand what you do, but I'm so grateful you do it. Ever-steadfast early readers, friends, and family: Corrynn Cochran, Lynda Gregory, Sheridan Samano, Chuck Bass, Cheryl Wolfe, Tracy Ross, Lisa Jones, Gail Giles, Carol Kauder, Gina Wagner, Kay Christmas, Tracy Stockton, Sylvia Theall, Lynn Erickson, Helen Crews, Michael Salamon, Jane Gibbs, Susan Sommer, Deborah Fryer, Sharon Vary, and Angela McCormick. My wife, Amy Thompson, allowed me the space, freedom, and support to be creative without ever having to suffer for my art. And finally, to my son, Logan: You are the heart of these pages. I'm so glad you are ours.

AUTHOR NOTE

THIS BOOK HAPPENED BECAUSE my wife and I know the foster care system well. We adopted our son from the system. He was one of more than 100,000 children waiting for a family to bring him home. At any given time, almost half a million kids are removed from their houses, through no fault of their own, and placed into foster care. Race and poverty remain disproportionate factors—with the need for social justice to remedy the chain reaction of broken families. Child Protective Services requires a complete overhaul, but until that happens, it's the children who suffer most—and with them, a society left lamenting the growing rates of homelessness, addiction, and untreated mental illness in their communities. The systemic disfunction of foster care and child welfare stands as one of the greatest moral failings in America. While this novel is fictional, it's also horrifically accurate—from the lack of communication between counties and states, lost files, separated siblings, inadequate group homes, juvenile incarceration, underpaid and overloaded caseworkers, underserved at-risk families, and the alarming scarcity of approved placements for kids in immediate need of love, consistency, shelter, food, and safety. There are big and small ways to help—donating kids' clothes and toys, offering transportation or respite, mentoring, fostering, and adopting. Start with your local community or go to: https://www.acf.hhs.gov/cb/focus-areas/foster-care.